# SECRET AGENT

SECRET AGENT

# Praise for Michelle Larkin

### *Sylver and Gold*

"I loved Larkin's first two books, *Mercy* and *Unexpected Partners*. *Mercy* was a paranormal thriller and *Unexpected Partners* was more of a police procedural thriller with two women on the run from a psychopath. *Sylver and Gold* is a police procedural with a paranormal twist, and it's a lot of fun trying to solve the crime along with the detectives and Sylver's trusty sidekick Mugshot the dog. My overall take from this book? Fun, romantic, crime without too much violence for squeamish romance readers, paranormal lite for those of us who get annoyed with the woowoo. A pleasure to read."
—*Late Night Lesbian Reads*

"*Sylver and Gold* is a paranormal crime / mystery that kept me on the edge throughout the entire reading. It is intense with great leading characters...If you're looking for a riveting suspense, this is your choice."—*Hsinju's Lit Log*

### *Endangered*

"What a unique and interesting story. Good for fans of urban fantasy and shapeshifters. This was fun, and funny, with a great cast of characters. Plenty of action and great chemistry between the main characters. Loved the world building and can't wait to read more."—*Kat Adams, Bookseller (QBD Books, Australia)*

"When X-Men meets Twilight, the outcome is this wholly enjoyable paranormal fantasy. Grab this book, suspend disbelief and cosy in for feel-good impossibilities."—*reviewer@large*

"This was a very impressive novel. It was a skillfully crafted story, and one does not have to look too far to see parallels in today's America."—*Kitty Kat's Book Review Blog*

"*Endangered* by Michelle Larkin is a delightful novel with some heavy moments but enough lightheartedness to keep you thoroughly entertained."—*Romantic Reader Blog*

"What I liked most about this novel was its tone, mostly linked to Aspen's sense of humor and the banter between the characters in times of danger…[T]he rhythm, the humor, the interesting and endearing characters were enough to keep me hooked…"
—*Jude in the Stars*

### *Unexpected Partners*

"There is a lot of action in this story that will keep you interested and sometimes on the edge of your seat as you read…I liked the main characters and could see the chemistry between the two, and enjoyed the way the romance was treated throughout the story. The secondary characters were also well-developed and made the tale better."—*Rainbow Reflections*

"I loved the fast pace and nonstop action in this crime thriller/romantic intrigue novel…*Unexpected Partners* finds a nice balance between action and the reality of two strong women facing down their enemy."—*Late Night Lesbian Reads*

# By the Author

Mercy

Unexpected Partners

Endangered

Sylver and Gold

Secret Agent

Visit us at www.boldstrokesbooks.com

# SECRET AGENT

*by*

## Michelle Larkin

2022

This Trade Paperback Original Is Published By
Bold Strokes Books, Inc.
P.O. Box 249
Valley Falls, NY 12185

First Edition: April 2022

**CREDITS**
EDITOR: RUTH STERNGLANTZ
PRODUCTION DESIGN: STACIA SEAMAN
COVER DESIGN BY TAMMY SEIDICK

# Acknowledgments

Endless thanks to my editor, Ruth Sternglantz, for her guidance, support, and keen eye to detail.

A standing ovation to Tammy Seidick for designing another beautiful book cover.

Heartfelt gratitude to my BFF, Deb Roberts-Arthur, for joining me on this adventure...and for giving me the gift of her love and support.

A nod of appreciation to Della for being a fast reader, a wonderful friend, and a kindred spirit.

And a sincere thank you to Mandi, the love of my life, for reading this story numerous times and adding the term "love cave" to Zoey's vocabulary.

I'm also deeply appreciative of my sons, Levi and Jett, for teaching me more about life and love than I ever could have learned on my own.

Acknowledgments

This book is dedicated to Sterling…

I never had the chance to meet you, dear one, though I think of you often. I trust, by now, you know how much you're loved. Hope you're enjoying those Angel wings.

# CHAPTER ONE

Agent Zoey Blackwood shifted uncomfortably in her wooden chair—no armrests and not much of a cushion to sink into, not even for a reasonably small ass like hers. After all these years, she'd thought the good doctor would've taken pity on her patients and sprung for a more comfortable chair. She eyed the blue velvet sofa across the room but resisted the urge to nap through the rest of her psych eval. "That's right," she said, returning her gaze to the sexy, fiftysomething psychologist sitting cross-legged in front of her.

"Really? Still no memory of your life before you met Sterling." Dr. Pokale looked up from her notes, frowning at Zoey over the rims of her Cartier eyeglasses. "Correct me if I'm wrong, but you were twelve when he took you in."

Zoey nodded. There was an awkward silence. She checked her watch.

Dr. Pokale set her notebook on the small table beside her chair, slid her glasses off, and folded them neatly in her lap. "Zoey, we've done the same song and dance every year for the last twelve years." She sighed. "Isn't this getting kind of old?"

"Then stop asking about the first eleven years of my life." The fortress Zoey had built around her past was impenetrable. It was high time this doctor accepted that.

Dr. Pokale remained quiet and studied her with a scrutinizing gaze. The doctor was a striking woman with stone-gray eyes, high cheekbones, and short gray hair who seemed totally at ease within the confines of her aging body. She, and she alone, administered the annual psych eval to every CIA agent. Known around the local field office as *Dr. Poke*, she'd ruthlessly poke and prod until you revealed your deepest, darkest secrets. She was the only thing standing between Zoey and the rest of her career.

Dr. P uncrossed her long legs and leaned forward. "When will you let me see you?"

"Naked?"

"Not where my mind was headed, no." Dr. P leaned back in her chair, gracefully recrossed her legs, and resumed her scrutinizing stare-down.

"But now you're thinking of me naked. Am I right?"

"Naked or not, you still need to answer my question. You're safe in here, Zoey. Whatever you share will stay between us." She let a beat or two of silence hang in the air. "When will you let me in?"

"You make it sound like I'm a big steel safe that you don't have the combination to, but you have me all wrong. I'm more along the lines of a cozy little beach house that nobody bothers to lock because the neighborhood's so safe. You don't need a combination to get inside." Zoey stood and turned in a full circle. "What you see is what you get."

"You used the word *safe* twice in that little spiel."

"So?"

"That's your subconscious saying you don't feel safe enough here to talk about your past."

"Nothing to talk about."

"Which is it? You don't remember anything, or there's nothing to talk about?"

Zoey sank back down to her chair, squeezed her eyes shut, and brought her fingers to her temples. For the life of her, she couldn't figure out why the CIA wasn't making better use of this doctor's interrogation skills. The Anti-Terrorism Task Force could really use her right about now. "Either give me your stamp of approval, and let me get back to the field, or—"

"Or what?" Dr. P prodded.

"Or don't." Zoey shrugged. "Your call."

"What happens if I don't sign off this time, Zoey?"

"The Earth will be knocked from its orbit, and life as we know it will cease to exist."

The doctor nodded. "Knowing what's at stake is a good first step. Do you have a plan B?"

"For what?"

"Your career."

Zoey cringed at the thought of being ousted from the CIA. She was made for this job. And she was damn good at it. She'd pretty much shot out from the birth canal with a *reserved for the CIA* Post-it on her forehead. "Are you serious?"

"Very."

She sighed. "When will you realize you're better off just skipping this eval and letting me get back to catching the bad guys?"

"We both know what you do as an undercover field agent isn't that cut-and-dried. If it was, you wouldn't be here."

Zoey recognized the truth when she heard it. She'd definitely witnessed more atrocities while working oversees than she cared to admit. "It's just you and me in here. One of us has to cave." She crossed her arms. "Your tedious collection of notes from our sessions over the years should've already told you it's not going to be me."

"I'll ask one more time." Dr. P centered her gray gaze on Zoey. "When are you going to let me in?"

"Fine. You win." Zoey reached inside her coat pocket, withdrew her iPhone, and started scrolling through the calendar. "How's November 9 at two o'clock?"

"Three days from now?" Dr. P asked, clearly surprised as she stood and reached for the day planner on her desk.

"In the year 2085." Zoey grinned as she watched Dr. P's shoulders drop in defeat. "It's a Friday, just in case you were wondering."

"Since it's doubtful I'll live to see my hundred and tenth birthday," Dr. P replied, "that won't work for me."

"Sorry, but I'm booked solid until then. Can't say I didn't try." Zoey pocketed her cell. "Not my fault if your lack of availability prohibits the completion of my psych eval."

Dr. P returned to her chair. "Last chance, Zoey. It's now or never. If you leave this office today without revealing something—any-thing—about your past, your security clearance will be revoked in-definitely."

"Why're you being so pushy today? Our annual chats are usually way nicer than this."

"The difference is Sterling."

"Sterling?" Zoey leaned back in her hard-as-a-rock chair. "Has he been paying you off for the last eleven years to pass me?"

"He was your handler, Zoey, and therefore able to vouch for your psychological fitness. As you know, he's since retired."

"Then just go ask my current handler."

"Which one? You've had *five* in the last eight months."

Zoey thought for a moment. "Peyton…something or other."

"I've already spoken with her. Agent North finds herself in the same predicament as me."

"Adrift in a sea of despair because I haven't given either of you the hug you deserve?" Zoey stood and opened her arms. "Come on. Bring it in."

Stoic as ever, Dr. P remained seated. "Despite her numerous and well-documented attempts to work with you, you've shunned Agent North at every turn."

*Well-documented?* Henceforth, her handler's new name would be Agent Tattleface. Hug-less, Zoey sat back down, her thoughts on Peyton North. How could anyone expect her to work under a recently promoted handler who'd been in the field less than she had?

"Your connection with Sterling was genuine," Dr. P went on. "But there's no one to vouch for you this year."

Zoey slipped her phone out once again and started dialing. She put it on speaker.

"Hey, Zo. What's up?" Sterling answered in the calm, soothing tone that Zoey was accustomed to hearing.

She cut to the chase. "Any concerns about my psychological fitness?"

"Annual PEs," he said with a sigh. "That time of year already?"

"Better than Christmas," she replied, rolling her eyes for the doctor's benefit.

"One of the many perks of retirement is not having to be in the middle of you two anymore. Best of luck, Zo. See you for dinner at seven." There was an awkward silence as Sterling ended the call.

She stared at her cell phone's dark screen.

Dr. P raised an eyebrow.

"There." Zoey stood, reached for her trench coat, and draped it over one arm. "If Sterling had any concerns, I'm sure he would've voiced them. We good?"

"Far from. Sit down, Agent Blackwood."

She did. Being addressed so formally was a step in the wrong direction.

"What are you thinking right now?"

"You want an honest answer?"

Dr. P crossed her legs. "Is your first inclination to lie?"

"I'm thinking about your legs," Zoey admitted.

"What about them?"

"They're long…and kind of sexy."

"What else?"

"Now I'm thinking about pizza. And beer." She rapped her knuckles softly against the side of her head. "Sorry to disappoint you, but that's all that's in here. Sexy legs, beer, and pizza."

Dr. P stood and walked to her desk. She opened a drawer, withdrew a thick file, and returned to the diamond-tufted armchair across from Zoey.

"Is that my file?"

Without a word, Dr. P reached for her glasses, slid them on, and riffled through several dozen pages until she found what she was looking for. "Your test scores are off the charts. It's noted here that your IQ was the third highest of anyone the CIA has tested in the last twenty years."

*Third* highest? She was tempted to ask who had landed the top two slots but held her tongue. "I'm a good guesser."

Dr. P removed her glasses and pierced Zoey with a forthright gaze. "They tested you twice to be sure the score was accurate. In fact, the results from your second test were tied with number two."

"What's your point?" she asked impatiently.

"My point"—Dr. P closed the file and set it aside—"is that I know there's more going on inside that head of yours than just pizza and beer."

"And legs." Zoey tilted her head to get a better view and raised an eyebrow. "You forgot the legs."

Dr. P said nothing, her expression deadpan.

"Fine. You caught me." Zoey threw her hands up in surrender. "Blueberry pie."

"Pardon me?"

"I'm craving a slice of your homemade blueberry pie right now. With hard sauce," she added in the resultant quiet.

Dr. P cast a cursory glance around her office. "What blueberry pie?"

Zoey pointed to the minifridge in the corner.

"What makes you think there's pie in there?"

"I watched you carry it in from your car this morning."

Dr. P checked her watch. "That was six hours ago, Zoey."

She shrugged. "I like to be early for my appointments." She could see the doctor's wheels turning.

Dr. P stepped to the minifridge, pulled it open, and withdrew a round green container. "This?"

Zoey nodded.

"How do you know there's blueberry pie inside?"

"Just a hunch."

Dr. P lifted the lid, withdrew a silver pie server from a basket atop the fridge, and set two slices on harvest-themed paper plates with matching napkins. She scooped a generous helping of hard sauce onto their plates. "I baked it yesterday and put it in this container last night before bed." She stepped over to Zoey, handing her a plate, fork, and napkin. "But you already knew that."

"Are you accusing me of being psychic?"

"I'm accusing you of being clever." Instead of resuming her post in the armchair, Dr. P sat in the twin wooden chair beside Zoey. "You knew about today's appointment."

"Obviously," she replied around a mouthful of pie. "I'm here, aren't I?"

"You also knew I'd be pushing you for more because Sterling can't vouch for you this year."

Chewing, Zoey said nothing.

"So," Dr. P went on, "instead of participating in this mandatory evaluation with any degree of authenticity, you chose to stalk me—"

"Surveil," Zoey interjected, her mouth still full. "Not stalk."

"You chose to *stalk* me in an attempt to dig up some dirt, something you could use to strong-arm me into signing off on your evaluation."

Fork halfway to her mouth, Zoey simply returned the doctor's gaze, neither confirming nor denying. But, yeah, that about summed things up.

"Do tell." Dr. P trimmed off a bite-size portion of the pie with her fork. "How'd that go?"

Zoey casually took another bite, chewed, swallowed. "Not well," she confessed.

Dr. P nodded thoughtfully.

"To be perfectly honest, I couldn't find a single sketchy thing about you. Have you really led such a squeaky-clean life? Or are you just as skilled at covering your tracks as you are at baking?" She turned in her chair to meet the doctor's gaze. "Because this is really, *really* good."

"Thank you." Dr. P sipped her water. "So, what now?" she asked, scooping in another dainty mouthful.

It suddenly occurred to Zoey that bringing an entire pie to the office was, perhaps, a tad peculiar. No parties or office get-togethers today. The goody-two-shoes doctor had spin class after work and would head home after that for dinner with her husband and teenage kids. "Who's this pie for, anyway?"

"That's a very good question," Dr. P answered in a patronizing tone.

She stopped chewing, gazed at what remained of her pie, and regarded Dr. P suspiciously. Perhaps it was no mere coincidence that blueberry pie with hard sauce was her all-time favorite dessert. The only soul on earth who knew that was Sterling. "Have you seen Sterling lately?"

"Funny you should ask. We caught up over coffee just last week."

She nodded, slowly coming to terms with what had happened. "So this was a setup."

"Looks that way."

"Sterling figured I'd come snooping around and told you to bake me a pie?"

"After Sterling's retirement, *I* figured you'd come snooping around. I contacted him because I wanted to know your favorite dessert."

"Why?"

"You tell me."

Zoey set her fork down on the empty plate and thought for a moment. She had to give credit where credit was due. Not only had Dr. P anticipated Zoey's surveillance, but she'd baked a pie and brought it to the office in an effort to bait her, knowing all the while that she was being watched. Dr. P had undoubtedly chosen blueberry pie because she was trying to make Zoey feel comfortable, comfortable enough to share the secrets of her past. This was the doctor's way of showing she cared.

The pieces came together in slow motion. Zoey realized, too late, that she was in over her head. "I know you can't talk about the other two smarty-pants in the CIA, but I'm assuming the person in first place is a—"

"Psychologist?" Dr. P finished for her. "You *are* a good guesser."

Zoey winced. Figured. She had only two plans left up her sleeve, both of which had a slim-to-none chance of working. Dr. P was just too smart. Not to mention ethical.

"And in case you're considering a last-ditch attempt to pay me off or, worse, seduce me—"

"Why would seducing you be worse than paying you off?" she asked, insulted as she watched her last two ideas spontaneously combust.

"You should know I'm financially stable and happily married. I'm impervious to your wit, charm, and beauty, so don't waste your time." Dr. P set her empty plate down and glanced at her watch. "You have exactly fifteen minutes to spill your guts. Convince me you're mentally equipped to continue your work in the field after what happened in Niger."

## CHAPTER TWO

Peyton North tiptoed up the brick steps of her Beacon Street brownstone in Boston, Massachusetts. She quietly unlocked the door and slipped inside before Horace could poke his head out and offer his condolences...again. Living next door to a man with a traumatic brain injury was taxing, especially when he kept telling her how sorry he was to hear about her husband's death. As luck would have it, his brain's ability to retain information had frozen in time to the day her husband died. Like Bill Murray in the movie *Groundhog Day*, she was being forced to relive the moment over and over.

She rested her back against the door and gazed around the open living room and kitchen. Lilies, orchids, roses, and irises—all of them, white—occupied every available table, corner, and shelf. Similar sympathy bouquets also dotted all fourteen steps leading up to the second floor before spilling into the bedrooms, study, and workout room upstairs. She was actually starting to wonder if the flowers were grown with a fountain of youth elixir. They lasted an unseasonably long time.

Changing the water in the vases was an all-day affair and took up the majority of her one day off each week. Part of her longed to shed the immense responsibility of their care and just let them go, but she couldn't bring herself to do it. Horace had gifted them to her. She would continue to honor both Horace and her late husband by taking care of them. There was simply no other acceptable course of action to take.

A knock at the door jolted her from her thoughts. Right on cue. She didn't bother peering out the peephole. She knew Horace would be standing there with another bouquet. Her stealthy-as-a-ninja entrance made no difference at all. She was half-convinced he spent all day, every day, watching the video feed from his security camera, like a faithful dog waiting for his master to return.

Peyton took several deep breaths. She actually welcomed his visits. She just needed a few moments to collect herself and mentally prepare.

More than once, she'd considered leaving the doorbell unanswered, only on especially hard days when the grief felt much too heavy. Today was one of those days. But she'd be damned if she was going to keep an old man waiting on her stoop in the cold.

Peyton opened the door and welcomed Horace inside, ready for another rerun of The Handyman Horace Show.

He handed her the bouquet—more white lilies—and leaned in for a hug. "I'm so sorry about Ben," he whispered.

"Thank you," she said, accepting the hug and flowers with a smile.

Horace was wearing the clothes she'd set out for him last night: dark-blue Levi's, a long-sleeved forest-green shirt, and an insulated red-and-black lumberjack button-down in case he went outside and forgot his coat again. "My goodness!" His eyes grew wide as he gazed around the room. "I see I'm not your first visitor. Ben must've had a lot of fans."

She nodded. One flower-loving fan in particular.

"Anything I can help out with while I'm here?" he asked, a hopeful tone keeping the usual gruffness of his voice at bay.

Peyton pretended to give his question serious thought. She had run out of projects for him months ago. If she didn't give him a project, he wouldn't accept dinner. He was old-school, through and through. "I hate to impose on you," she said, biting her lip in feigned uncertainty.

"No imposition," he shot back. "Just give me a list. I'll take care of it." He followed her gaze to the gaping hole in the bathroom door.

She'd become proficient at removing doorknobs around the house each morning before work. It gave Horace something to do while she cooked. "I bought new doorknobs," she said, careful not to lie. She had, in fact, purchased all the doorknobs in the house four years ago when she and Ben had finished renovations. "There are three more holey doors upstairs. Do you mind?"

"Not at all." He plucked the doorknob off a nearby bookshelf and knelt on the folded towel she'd already set on the floor for him. "I'll have these on in a jiff."

"I really appreciate it, Horace. Thank you."

"Don't mention it," he said proudly.

"Will you stay for dinner?" she asked, sticking to the usual script.

He slipped the metal hardware in place. "As long as I can earn my keep," he replied on cue without looking up.

She set a hand on his shoulder and squeezed, grateful for the distraction that his daily companionship offered. She knew he wouldn't remember any of this tomorrow. Horace would probably never regain his short-term recall. But she was okay with this new routine.

He didn't have any family left. His sweetheart of a wife had died eleven years ago, and their only daughter had perished before that, after a lifelong battle with cystic fibrosis. Peyton and Ben were the only people Horace had come to trust over the years. She wasn't about to betray that trust by putting him in a long-term care facility when he was perfectly capable of day-to-day functioning. The routine they'd established gave him the independence she knew he would have wanted.

She glanced at her watch: 7:01 p.m. Right on schedule. Horace was always in bed by nine and asleep by nine fifteen. She unlocked his door at nine thirty on the nose every night to check mail, pay bills, add some groceries to the fridge, and set out his clothes for the next day. Without the ability to recall the previous day's events, he had no way of remembering which clothes were clean. He had the same annoying habit as her late husband: he'd undress at the end of the day and toss his clothes over the nearest piece of furniture. More than once, he'd mistakenly dressed himself in his clothes from the previous day. Since Horace was a heavy sleeper, sneaking into his room each night to gather his laundry carried minimal risk.

Peyton readied the sauce for fettuccini Alfredo. She'd stop by the flower shop on her way to work tomorrow and reload the balance on her gift card. At her request, the florist had stopped accepting payment from Horace weeks ago, only pretending to run Horace's credit card each time he dropped in to buy more flowers.

She decided she'd also drop by the senior center and donate his most recent bouquet. Real estate was at a premium, and there simply wasn't enough space in her home for the newcomer.

"Alexa, play *Bing Crosby's Christmas Classics*," she announced to the Echo Dot beside her. Thanksgiving was still weeks away, but she decided to kick off the holiday season early. Ben had always been a sucker for Bing.

Ben would have been pleased with her decision to transition from agent to handler. Less risk in the field. Less traveling. The only wrench in the mix so far was Zoey Blackwood—a headstrong agent whose list of successful missions abroad was longer than a supermarket receipt for a family of ten. For reasons beyond her comprehension, the CIA's pairing algorithm had matched them, having ranked the union as *Successful to a high degree of certainty*. The algorithm failed to tell her, however, exactly how she was supposed to connect with Zoey and break through the smart-ass attitude that teetered on insubordination.

"All set," Horace said, joining her at the sink to wash his hands. "Do I smell garlic bread?"

She nodded, setting thoughts of Zoey aside for the moment.

"Smells delicious."

She stirred the sauce and handed the dish towel to Horace. "Salad, garlic bread, and my grandfather's famous fettuccini Alfredo."

He grinned as he dried his hands. "I should install your doorknobs more often."

❖

Niger. Zoey took a shallow breath, willing her voice to remain even. "Nothing to talk about. It was a successful mission."

"Why was the mission successful?" Dr. P asked. "Was there one defining moment, in particular?"

No way. Dr. P *knew*? Had Agent Tattleface seriously included that in her report? Zoey shrugged as nonchalantly as possible. "I completed the mission objective. End of story."

"And the mission objective was…"

"Shared on a need-to-know basis." She crossed her arms. "And since you weren't part of the mission, you don't need to know."

"You're already aware that my security clearance supersedes yours, which means you're free to discuss the details of your missions here."

"As far as I know, I'm only authorized to discuss them with my handler."

"Would you prefer, then, to talk about this with Agent North?" Dr. P stood and reached for the phone on her desk, her movements confident and graceful.

Zoey caught a whiff of her signature perfume, a subtle fragrance with traces of sandalwood and vanilla. "You mean Agent Tattleface?"

"Agent North is on standby. I can ask her to swing by and lend the two of you my office for an hour." Dr. P held the phone's receiver to her ear, finger poised and ready to dial. "Your choice."

Zoey sighed defeatedly. "I'd rather stick needles in my eyes."

"Good." Dr. P returned the phone to its cradle and sat on one corner of the desk. "Whether you like it or not, we need to discuss what happened in Niger."

She felt her fight-or-flight instinct kick in as the snare around her cinched tighter. "To make sure it doesn't happen again?"

Dr. P eased her chastising tone. "That's up to you, Zoey. The CIA allows you to use whatever tools are available to you during a mission."

Zoey rolled her eyes at *tools*. She still couldn't believe Agent Tattleface had the audacity to, well, tattle. Sterling never would have included such sensitive information in his report. Hell, he would've run interference by crashing the party himself with guns blazing, so it never would have happened in the first place. She realized then how angry she was with Peyton. Her handler had let her down.

Dr. P collected their empty paper plates and tossed them in a nearby trash can. She returned to the armchair and crossed her long legs, her charcoal-gray Karen Klein skirt suit crisp and wrinkle free. "Let's start by acknowledging the elephant in the room."

Zoey stood, stepped behind her chair, and set her hands over the chair's wooden slats, aware that she was placing a symbolic barrier between them. "I did my job. Why can't we just leave it at that?"

"Because you identify as a lesbian."

She cringed. She had always hated that phrase. Why couldn't she just *be* a lesbian? Like a physical characteristic, it was just…part of her. She didn't identify with having brown eyes. They were brown. Simple as that. "Would you be bringing this up if I'd had sex with a woman on the mission?"

Dr. P paused for a moment, her gray gaze unwavering. "No," she said finally. "But you didn't have sex with a woman. You had sex with a man."

"As a last resort."

"I know. I read the report. Your reasons for doing so were sound."

"Then why're we talking about this?"

"You tell me."

Zoey already knew where this was going. Could see it a mile away. "You think I'm gay because there's some trauma in my past that was perpetrated by a man. You're worried having sex with a man during my mission opened old wounds."

Dr. P studied her. "The thought has crossed my mind."

"Then let me put your mind at ease." She let a brief silence punctuate the moment. "I've never been assaulted or abused by a man."

"I believe you."

"Great. Then we can move on."

"Were you ever abused by a woman?" Dr. P asked.

The question knocked her off balance. She reached for a clever comeback but came up empty-handed.

"Tell me about it."

"You're mistaken," she countered, a beat too late. "Never happened."

"You're lying. Try again."

She wasn't lying. Exactly. But her subconscious probably thought she was lying. The good doctor had obviously cued in on a tell that Zoey wasn't aware she had. She made a mental note to pinpoint the subtle action that had betrayed her, so this would never happen again.

Zoey thought back to her childhood, loath to return to the place where she'd learned her hardest lessons in life. She paced the office a few times before retracing her steps to sit in the world's most uncomfortable chair.

## CHAPTER THREE

Zoey met the doctor's gray-eyed gaze. "From the time my dad split, my mom was addicted to heroin. There wasn't much I admired—or even liked—about my mother. But there was one thing."

"What's that?" Dr. P asked.

"Her all-or-nothing attitude. When she did something, she gave it every ounce of energy she had. Like, full-on commitment."

"Can you give me an example?"

"Two, actually," Zoey said, looking away as she fought the urge to get up and move around. "My mother set her sights on two goals in life—doing heroin as often as possible and having sex with as many men as possible to obtain said heroin." She shook her head, still in awe of her mother's fervor for self-destruction. "Her dedication to the cause was seriously mind-blowing. Safe to say, she had sex with every interested man in the tristate area."

Dr. P nodded, a knowing look in her eyes.

"No one ever touched me," Zoey went on, "but I saw enough to know sex with a man wasn't for me."

"Do you think seeing that as a child—"

"Do *not* ask if that's what made me gay." Something deep inside told her the circumstances in which she was raised had nothing to do with her sexual orientation. She simply was who she was. She had no animosity toward men. She'd just never been interested in them. Period.

"Do you think seeing that as a child made having sex with your target more difficult?" Dr. P finished.

A question that cut right to the heart of things. Dr. P was on her game today. "Yes," she said honestly, aware now that her tell would probably give her away if she tried to lie again. There was no going back now. Better to just plow through these questions, give the doctor what she wanted, and get this over with as quickly as possible—kind of like having sex with her target. "I've asked myself why it was so hard for me to have sex with a man, and I keep circling back to the same answer."

"Which is?"

"You'll just have to go with me on this one because I know it's a stretch. Could it be because I'm, oh, I don't know"—Zoey leaned forward and sighed—"gay?"

"Had you ever been intimate with a man before?" Dr. P pressed.

Convinced the doctor had no funny bone at all, she leaned back in her chair. "No."

"Agent North reported that what she heard through your earpiece sounded consensual. Was that, in fact, the case?"

"I made the choice to seduce the target, yes."

"In an effort to stop him from engaging in sexual relations with a minor."

She nodded. Such behavior was commonplace in that region of Niger. Her target had planned to sample the goods three days before his scheduled marriage to the nine-year-old girl in question. "It was either seduce the target or put a bullet in his head." Which she'd seriously considered.

"And had you gone through the proper channels to request the latter, that request, more than likely, would have been denied."

"Which is why I seduced him."

"Do you regret your choice?"

That was a complicated question. Part of her did—and always would—regret sleeping with a man. An even deeper part of her knew she never would have been able to live with herself if things had gone the other way. "It was the right thing to do."

"That's not what I asked." Dr. P leaned forward. "Do you regret your choice, Zoey?"

"Yes and no," she said finally. "If I had to go back and do it over, I'd make exactly the same choice."

"And how do you feel, knowing your target is now dead?"

"Do you expect me to say I feel sad about it?"

"I expect you to give me an honest answer."

If Sterling hadn't retired, none of this would be happening right now. This was all his fault. Damn him for wanting to travel, relax, and enjoy life. "As soon as my target gave me the name of the man responsible for transporting arms into Chad, he was no longer my focus. If he'd died *before* I got that name, and you asked me how I felt about it, I'd say, well…slightly pissed off."

"I'm asking you now. How do you feel, knowing your target is dead?"

"If I had to pick one feeling out of a lineup, I guess it would be *indifferent*." The truth was, she felt indifferent about it now. At the time, however, she'd found the news of his death immensely gratifying.

"Any ideas on the person responsible for his murder?"

Photos of Zoey's one-night affair with the target had mysteriously appeared on the family's doorstep. She'd worn a disguise and made the two-hour trek on foot under the cover of darkness to deliver those photos herself. Polygamy was an accepted practice in Niger, but the target's choice to sleep with an outsider would've been viewed as a betrayal. "My money's on the nine-year-old girl's father. She also had four older brothers." Zoey shrugged. "In all fairness, I guess it could've been one of them."

Dr. P gave her a once-over, frowned in silent accusation, and glanced down at her notes. "And how do you feel about Agent North as your handler?"

"Fine."

"Another lie. Should I start calling you Agent Pinocchio?"

This was getting annoying. How had she lived for thirty-five years without knowing what her tell was? Sterling had to have figured it out by now. He'd obviously been keeping it in his back pocket this whole time.

"Let me break it down a little more for you." Dr. P slipped her glasses off and set her notebook aside. "How do you feel about having a woman as your handler?"

"Let me get this straight. No pun intended," she added. "You're asking *me* how I feel about having a female handler who's drop-dead gorgeous?"

Dr. P raised an eyebrow. "So you've noticed."

"Who wouldn't? You'd have to be dead not to."

"Do you think that's how people see you?"

"Dead?" She laughed. Where was Dr. P going with this?

"I'm sure it doesn't come as a surprise when I say you're quite beautiful. As you noted with regard to Agent North, it's impossible not to notice."

She was sure Dr. P wasn't flirting with her, but she couldn't resist the opening. "It's never too late to switch teams, you know."

"You've used your beauty to your advantage in the field for years," Dr. P stated matter-of-factly.

"It's a tool that comes in handy when I need it," she admitted.

"Has that tool been compromised?"

Zoey leaned back in her chair and shook her head. Everything made sense now. "I'm nothing more than an asset to the CIA. You're here to determine if this particular asset has been damaged. Since we've already established that it was, your next order of business is deciding if said asset should be salvaged or sent to the scrap heap. Right?"

Dr. P looked genuinely offended as she uncrossed her legs and got to her feet. "Stand up, Zoey."

"Are you going to hit me?"

"Of course not."

Zoey narrowed her eyes. "Kiss me?"

"Good God, no."

"Fine. Everything else I can handle." She stood, meeting Dr. P eye to eye.

"May I?" Dr. P opened her arms.

"Why do you get to decide when it's time to hug?"

"It's my office."

Fair point. Zoey stepped forward but halted halfway through and drew back. "Hold up. Why are you bestowing me with the honor of this hug?"

"Because you're more than just an asset," Dr. P said, leaning in to finish the job with a warmth and sincerity that took Zoey by surprise.

There was a soft knock at the door. Dr. P released her and checked her watch. "I also thought a hug might soften the blow."

She should've known better. A hug was never just a hug. "Who's at the door?" she asked suspiciously.

"Agent North."

"You invited Tattleface to my psych eval?"

"We've concluded your PE." Dr. P walked to the door and set her hand over the handle. "I'm approving your return to the field."

Best news ever. Zoey reached for her coat.

"Pending a sit-down with Agent North." Dr. P opened the door and waved Peyton inside.

❖

Zoey willed herself to stay calm and keep her anger in check. Peyton was now sitting in the identical twin of the world's most uncomfortable chair, her posture as ramrod-straight as the chair's wooden slats. Dr. P had repositioned both chairs so they were facing each other. Agent and handler were knee to knee, mere inches apart. With Zoey's career in the balance, Dr. P encouraged them to look at one another and speak openly about what had happened in Niger.

Zoey watched as Peyton crossed her legs and laced her fingers together in her lap. Peyton was feminine and strong all in one breath. The dark auburn hair that she sometimes wore in a thick ponytail fanned out in wavy locks over a sage-colored blazer. Her eyes were green today, but their mysterious hues could change at a moment's notice to match Peyton's mood or chosen attire. Save for an occasional layer of rose-tinted lip balm, Peyton never wore makeup. Her natural beauty was riveting. She shared a body type similar to Zoey's: lean, athletic, and curvy in all the places that mattered. Peyton was always impeccably dressed, her nails short and well-manicured. But the biggest draw of all was how she smelled. She smelled *amazing*—a tantalizing blend of shampoo, body cream, and fragrant oils. Zoey was convinced her handler had a part-time gig as a walking ad for Bath & Body Works.

They'd already rehashed the events in Niger, everything leading up to her decision to seduce the target. Peyton studied her. "From what I heard, it sounded like you were enjoying yourself."

"I wasn't," Zoey shot back.

"Then you're really good at—"

"Faking an orgasm?"

Peyton stared at her, expressionless.

"I'm gay," Zoey blurted.

Peyton narrowed her eyes. "That's not listed anywhere in your file."

"Well, I am. Happy to prove it to you." She raised an eyebrow, giving Peyton a once-over. "If you're game."

Peyton broke the staring contest to glance at Dr. P. "Is that true?"

"You're asking *her* when I'm sitting right here in front of you?" Zoey said, incredulous.

"I'm asking her to corroborate the information," Peyton replied calmly, her gaze focused on Zoey once again.

"I'm gay. Trust me."

"Like I trusted you when you told me where to buy the best baked goods in Niger?"

Zoey shrugged. "That was my way of congratulating you on your promotion."

"By sending me out to unknowingly purchase marijuana chocolate chip cookies?"

She rolled her eyes. "They're called *cannabis* cookies. And you needed to loosen up." Peyton was as high as a kite by the time she returned to the hotel where they'd shared adjoining rooms. Zoey had watched in amazement as her handler downed a party-size bag of chips in record time. Finished, Peyton had gazed into the empty bag for long minutes. When Zoey sat beside her and asked if everything was okay, Peyton had burst into tears, convinced the chips had families—mom and dad chips, little baby chips, grandma and grandpa chips—and she'd just killed them all. She was inconsolable. Zoey finally left to buy more chips, intent on returning to eat them and show Peyton that they really were just food. But Peyton confiscated the bag and threatened to call the police if she heard any telltale crunching during the night. Chip by chip, Peyton lined them up on the bed, placed cotton balls under their heads as pillows, and covered each one with a square of toilet paper as a blanket. Then she tucked them in for the night and sat in a bedside vigil until morning.

Even in all Dr. P's stoic wonder, Zoey could see she was finding it difficult not to laugh.

"I'd never been high before," Peyton said in her own defense. "And I'll never look at a potato chip the same way."

"Then I guess we're even. Because I've never slept with a man before."

Peyton looked up. "Never?"

"Never."

"You believe I should've run interference." It was more an accusation than an admission of guilt.

Zoey nodded. "Would've been the considerate thing to do."

"How was I supposed to know that?"

"You're my handler. Omniscience is in your job description."

Peyton uncrossed her legs and leaned forward. "If you had talked to me and opened up a little, the mission could have gone differently, Zoey."

"Goes both ways. You're not exactly an open book yourself."

Peyton sat back, quiet, as she searched Zoey's face. "Listen, I know you and Sterling were together for a long time. Having a new handler is a big adjustment. Just ask for help the next time you need it. I'll be there."

"When was the last time *you* asked for help?"

"I'm here to provide guidance and support when you need it." Peyton frowned. "Not the other way around."

"That's where you're wrong. The whole reason Sterling and I worked so well together is because we supported each other. Give and take. Trust and be trusted."

Peyton studied her. "What do you want from me, Zoey?"

"I want you to loosen up, for one. Learn how to take a joke."

"Fine. I'll try. What else?"

"Don't ever let what happened in Niger happen again. If I'm getting naked for a man—any man—that means I'm backed into a corner and need a way out."

"Understood."

There was an awkward silence as they regarded one another, knee to knee.

Zoey's next question was make or break. "Will my sexuality be an issue in the field?"

Peyton was visibly taken aback. "Are you asking if I'm homophobic?"

"Are you?"

Peyton glanced down at the floor and hesitated before meeting Zoey's gaze. "No," she answered firmly.

Another awkward silence. Peyton shifted in her chair, visibly unsettled.

"You must realize that I'm waiting for you to elaborate," Zoey prompted. "We can't move forward until you do."

Peyton took a breath and folded her hands together neatly in her lap. "I'm bisexual."

Now they were getting somewhere. "That's not listed anywhere in your file."

Peyton's mouth dropped open. "You read my file?"

"Of course I read your file."

"That's off-limits and against protocol, Zoey. I'm your handler."

"You're married," Zoey went on, ignoring her, "to a man."

"I was. Yes."

"Was, as in...past tense?"

Peyton nodded. "Ben worked Secret Service. He was killed overseas."

"I hadn't heard. I'm sorry."

"That's because I prefer to keep my personal life private."

Zoey's recent search of Peyton's home had revealed her marriage to Benjamin North—a tall man with kind eyes and a boyish smile. "That explains all the flowers."

Peyton's mouth dropped open once again. "You've been inside my house?"

Zoey shrugged, perilously close to feeling guilty. "You seriously never smoked a joint before?" she asked, trying to change the subject.

"No."

"Not even as a rebellious teenager?"

Peyton shook her head. "Until you, I was a cannabis virgin."

Zoey blinked once...twice...never taking her gaze from Peyton's. "Did you just make a joke about me losing my virginity?" She watched, amused, as Peyton's cheeks turned a deep shade of crimson.

"Too soon?" Peyton asked, still holding her gaze.

"A little," she admitted with a wink. "But the effort was solid."

## CHAPTER FOUR

Secretary of Defense Griffin Bick strode through the Pentagon's corridors with purpose, mentally reviewing his list of checkpoints for his phone briefing with the president. It was only mid-November, and 73.6 percent of Americans had already received a flu shot. Prior to President Cooper taking office three years ago, that vax rate was simply unheard of. The president's behind-the-scenes campaign to encourage employers to make the flu shot mandatory had been largely successful. Griffin shook his head, marveling at the president's brilliance. He'd had doubts, just as anyone in his position would, but he should've known better. President Cooper's resolve to make this happen was unparalleled.

He stepped inside his office, shut the door, and sat in the leather chair behind his desk. He set out his notes from his phone call with the director of the CDC and stared at the number in amazement: *73.6.*

He had no doubt that number would be closer to 100 percent if the American people knew what he knew.

Peyton lifted the binoculars and zoomed in on Zoey from behind the wheel of Ben's black Volvo XC90. She'd parked on the far side of the lot to avoid being spotted as Zoey circled the track. Zoey's long raven hair was pulled back in a thick ponytail, which dipped and swayed as she ran. Her running form was flawless, relaxed, and natural, like an Arabian horse that was bred to race.

Zoey's body seemed to adopt the characteristics required for any situation. She could be strong, athletic, and unyielding one minute, and then sexy, voluptuous, and alluring the next. With long black eyelashes and eyes as dark as her inky-black hair, she'd held Peyton captive in her gaze more than once.

Peyton lowered the binoculars and checked her watch as Zoey finished her final lap. She added another line in the notebook on the seat beside her, totaling twenty-eight lines. Zoey had just completed seven miles in under an hour. Not bad.

She'd been tailing Zoey on and off for the better part of a week, something handlers were required to do every few months to ensure the integrity of their operatives. Blending into the background and surveilling a target without being noticed fell well within her skill set. Years of training and hard-won experience in the field meant her chances of being spotted were negligible.

She hadn't made any headway with Zoey since their meeting with Dr. Pokale last week. Maybe it was time to ask Zoey to join her on a trail run. Could handlers run with their agents? She wasn't aware of any rules prohibiting the practice. She knew just the place, too. Ben had been the one to introduce her to her all-time favorite run, an arduous nine-mile trail that snaked through state conservation land. She ran it every weekend all year long, even in winter. Looked like they ran about the same pace, so Zoey shouldn't have any trouble keeping up.

Peyton made up her mind to extend the invitation first thing tomorrow. She slid the key in the ignition, switched the heater on high, and glanced at the time on the dash: 4:17 p.m. The daylight was drawing to a close. She'd head back to the office and kill some time while Zoey returned home to shower and change. Today was Sunday, which meant Zoey would be heading to Sterling's for football and pizza. That gave her all the time she needed to comb through Zoey's belongings at her apartment—a task she despised. But she knew it had to be done.

❖

Zoey finished her run on the track, grabbed her thermos off the bleachers, and squirted some water in her mouth as she walked a final lap to cool down. The track lights switched on as daylight faded.

Bostonians often complained about these shortened days, but she'd always loved this time of year. Colder, shorter days made most people feel lazy, longing to curl up with warm blankets and hot chocolate. But it did just the opposite for her. The colder it got, the more she felt like everything was coming alive. She grew energized as crisp, clean edges sprang up all around her. After being cloaked in burdensome attire, nature finally shed its clothing to reveal the more startling beauty of bare, jagged branches.

Darkness ruled this time of year with an iron fist, unforgiving, cold, and sometimes calculating. But to Zoey, darkness symbolized freedom. The freedom to do and be whatever the hell she wanted. Cast in shadows, the world became secretive. This was the world to which she belonged—a world of dark beauty and secrets.

Aware of her handler's binoculared gaze, she pulled her sweat-soaked tank top over her head and slipped into the Burberry sweatshirt that had once belonged to Sterling. She'd won it in a bet they made when she was twelve. He'd been trying to win it back ever since.

Zoey paused her workout music and, still wearing her wireless earbuds, called Peyton's cell from her Apple Watch.

Peyton answered on the first ring. "Agent North."

She skipped the usual niceties and cut straight to the dig on Peyton's last name. "Who has the most sculpted body in the North Pole?"

Peyton sighed. "Fine. Who?"

"The Abdominal Snowman," she said, grinning at her own joke.

There was a prolonged silence. "What do you call a blackwood tree that practices espionage?" Peyton finally asked.

Zoey shook her head, amused as Peyton gave her a dose of her own medicine. "What?"

"A leaves-dropper."

Peyton was learning how to take jokes *and* dish them out—a sign that her handler was starting to loosen up. "Not bad."

"Thanks."

Zoey set her hands on her hips. "But no points will be awarded to you at this time."

"I don't care about points."

"Whatever. I'm up by one." Zoey waited, confident she'd tapped into Peyton's need to be the best at everything when she'd hinted at a friendly competition several days earlier. Peyton, of course, hadn't fallen for it then. Zoey knew she'd eventually come around.

"But if I did care about points—which I seriously don't—why wouldn't I get any for that joke? It was better than yours."

"Because you looked it up on your phone after I told mine. That's cheating." The prolonged silence during Peyton's online search for a joke had given her away.

"And you didn't look yours up before you called me?"

"Nope," she said proudly.

"You just happened to have a joke with my last name in your back pocket."

"Sure did." Zoey slipped behind a tree, unzipped her duffel bag, and withdrew her binoculars. Under the cover of darkness, she lowered her body to the ground and zoomed in on Peyton's car.

"I don't believe you."

Fortunately, just as she'd hoped, Peyton had exchanged the binoculars for a cell phone. She watched as Peyton rolled her eyes, unaware that the tables had turned. "I've memorized every book of jokes ever published since nineteen sixty-eight."

Peyton's bewilderment was palpable on the other end of the line when she asked, "Why?"

Zoey had timed her run perfectly and now used the darkness to her advantage. "Why not?" she asked as she hurried along the tree line toward Peyton's car.

Peyton sighed. "Is there a reason you're calling me on a Sunday?"

"I'm inviting you to Sterling's to watch the game." She kept her breathing in check so as not to give away the fact that she was on the move.

"Pats against Ravens?" Peyton asked.

"Against a background of obnoxiously loud cheers and delightful commentary from yours truly. But I must warn you: potato chips *will* be present"—she sidestepped a gnarled tree root—"which will likely result in a lot of crunching."

"Thanks, but I can't. Prior commitment."

"Suit yourself." Zoey circled Peyton's car and approached from the rear. "By the way, your hair looks lovely today. I've never seen it in a braid."

Peyton looked over as Zoey knocked on the passenger's window. Frowning, she disconnected the call and unlocked the door.

Zoey slipped inside with a grin.

"I...I came here to go for a run," Peyton stammered. "I saw you and decided to wait until you were finished."

She took immense pleasure in letting Peyton squirm in the resultant quiet. "Thought you preferred trail running," she said finally.

"I do, but..." Peyton narrowed her eyes. "Wait a minute. Have *you* been following *me*?"

Zoey pointed to the binoculars around Peyton's neck. "This is like one of those Lifetime movies where the wife finds her husband in bed with another woman and accuses *her* of cheating."

Peyton said nothing and continued to glare at her from the driver's seat.

"Here." She held out a Mr. Potato Head keychain.

Peyton made no motion to accept it. "What's that?"

"A key," she said. "To my apartment."

"Why would I want a key to your apartment?"

"So we can start our illicit affair. Why else?"

Peyton rolled her eyes. "How long have you known?"

"About your attraction to me?" she asked, half joking. She watched as Peyton blushed. A palpable tension had existed between them from day one, but she'd never been sure if that tension was sexual in nature. Until now. She raised an eyebrow, gave Peyton a once-over, and decided to show her some mercy. "Are you asking how long I've known that handlers tail their agents, break into their homes, and rifle through their personal belongings, emails, and bank accounts to see if they've been compromised by a foreign entity?"

"Yes." Peyton sighed, visibly relieved. "That."

"Figured it out my first year on the job." She studied Peyton. "You didn't?" There had to be others within the agency who'd uncovered the same truth over the years, but such secrets never sprang a leak and trickled through the ranks. Field operatives were inherently tightlipped. In the CIA, it was every spook for themselves.

Peyton looked away but didn't answer. Her competitive ego had just taken a hit.

"In case you were wondering, you suck at surveillance," she went on in an effort to really drive it home. "You're even worse than Sterling, and Sterling was *awful*—"

"Fine. I get it," Peyton said impatiently. "You've made your point."

Zoey winked. "I'm kidding. Sterling's way worse. You're actually pretty good. If I hadn't been anticipating it, I probably never would've spotted you."

"And you're giving me a key to your apartment because…"

"It'll make snooping a lot easier. No need to pick a lock or risk being spotted by one of my neighbors."

Peyton studied her. "What's the catch?"

"No catch."

"I don't believe you."

"Sterling and I had the same arrangement. He had a key, too."

Peyton glanced at the keyring. "On a Mr. Potato Head keychain?"

"My way of paying tribute to your fallen comrades." Zoey watched as Peyton's wheels started turning.

Peyton shifted in her seat, her gaze accusatory, her tone indignant. "You only invited me to watch the game today because you knew I wouldn't come."

"I can't help it if you made other plans." She thought for a moment. "Did you *want* to come to Sterling's to watch the game?"

"No, not really."

"I see. You're upset because you wanted the chance to turn down a genuine invitation as opposed to a fake one."

"I am *not* upset."

"Right. That steam coming out of your nose is just, what, a result of smoking too much reefer?"

"Just give me the key." Peyton plucked the key ring from her grasp. "If there's a booby trap waiting for me inside your apartment, it's going in your file, Agent Blackwood."

"*That's* the worst you could come up with?" She grimaced, feeling disappointed in Peyton's lack of creativity and offended at being addressed so formally. "It's going in my file?"

"Are you saying you've booby-trapped your apartment?"

"I'm neither confirming nor denying the existence of a booby trap."

"Let me put it this way." Peyton paused for a moment before looking up. "If you've rigged some kind of booby trap, I'll make it my life's mission to stand on your last nerve. Every. Single. Day." She fixed a fierce hazel gaze on Zoey. "Like you're standing on mine right now."

She couldn't take her eyes off Peyton. Anger only accentuated her beauty.

"Well?" Peyton stared back at her in evident frustration. "Aren't you going to say something?"

"I like hearing you say the word *booby*." She shrugged. "I was just sitting here quietly, hoping you'd say it again."

"You can leave." Peyton leaned across the seat, careful not to touch her as she opened the passenger's door.

Zoey inhaled deeply, reaping the benefits of Peyton's talent for mixing such intoxicating aromas. "I'll make you a deal," she said, not budging.

"Not interested. Get out."

"Are you good at guessing passwords? Because mine are totally unguessable. You'll still be there when I get home from Sterling's, trying to puzzle them out. Neither of us wants that, right?" She glanced at the duffel bag on the back seat. "Unless you have Feejays packed in there."

"What are Feejays?"

"Have you been living under a rock? They're sweatpants with feet. Best invention since the wheel."

Peyton rubbed her temples. "What do Feejays have to do with your passwords?"

"Nothing, really. Since you don't want my list of passwords, I'll swing by the store on my way home and pick up some ice cream for our slumber party. I have an extra pair of Feejays you can borrow." She held up the red paper that she'd folded into a pair of origami lips. To keep Peyton on her toes, she'd written in the tiniest print possible, a skill she'd perfected as a note-passing student in her youth. Once Peyton unfolded the lips, she'd need a magnifying glass to read the passwords inside.

"You're offering to give me your passwords in exchange for something."

Zoey nodded. "Unless you have your heart set on Feejays and ice cream."

"Hard pass on the slumber party." Peyton frowned, looking back and forth between Zoey and the origami lips. "What do you want?"

"A secret," she replied without hesitation.

"You can't be serious."

"And it can't be something trivial or made-up."

Peyton rolled her eyes and sighed, quiet for a long moment. "I've wanted to get my nose pierced since I was fifteen." She glanced at Zoey. "Not a hoop or anything gaudy. Just a small stud."

"Why haven't you?" she asked, her instincts insisting that Peyton was telling the truth.

"Because I'm not ready for the way people might see me."

"As a rebel?"

Peyton nodded.

"Are you saying there's a part of you that longs to be rebellious?"

"Maybe." Peyton shrugged. "A little."

"Wow. That's deep." This cast a whole new light on the straitlaced rule follower beside her. Maybe she'd been too quick to stuff Peyton inside a box. "But a desire to put a hole through your nose doesn't begin to match the magnitude of listening to me having sex with my target."

"So *that's* what we're doing here." Peyton said, shaking her head. "You're trying to put us on even ground."

"You're my handler. As far as I can tell, you're not going anywhere. I can already see you're too stubborn for that. Fact is, you heard me having sex with a man for the first—and, hopefully, *only*—time in my life. I feel exposed. We'll never get past it unless you give me something of equal or greater value."

"You're making *your* choice *my* problem?"

"You're the other half of this relationship, so…yes. Unless you want a divorce like the other four handlers before you."

Peyton pursed her lips determinedly. "I was raised Catholic."

"Then give me something juicy to balance the scales."

"Watching me mourn the loss of my potato family in Niger was compensation enough."

"I disagree."

Peyton turned away, switched on the headlights, and stared out across the parking lot in silence. "I'm pregnant," she said finally.

Zoey sat back in her seat and stared at Peyton's gold wedding band. She had no idea when Peyton's husband had died. She threw a glance at Peyton's stomach. She wasn't showing at all. "How far along are you?" she asked, treading carefully in case the baby wasn't her husband's.

"Sixteen weeks."

"And...the father?"

"My husband, of course. I'm not confessing some illicit affair." Peyton shrugged. "I just haven't told anyone yet."

That meant Peyton was pregnant during their trip to Niger. It took Zoey a moment to grasp what she'd done. "I corrupted your baby with drugs?"

"And managed to slaughter generations of innocent potato chips in the process." Peyton narrowed her eyes. "You should feel proud of yourself."

"What if the marijuana hurt—"

"It didn't," Peyton said, cutting her off. "I saw my obstetrician. The baby's fine."

## CHAPTER FIVE

Zoey studied Peyton's profile in the resultant quiet. *Pregnant.* Wow. "When did Ben pass?"

"Three and a half months ago."

Zoey thought back to her search of Peyton's home and frowned in confusion. "But all those flower arrangements looked...fresh."

"Courtesy of my flower-loving neighbor." Peyton sighed. "Long story."

Zoey put two and two together. Now it all made sense. Peyton's neighbor had a brain injury. He couldn't remember one day from the next. "Ah." She nodded. "Horace keeps buying you sympathy bouquets."

"My God, Zoey." Peyton shook her head. "Do you even know what the word *privacy* means?"

She met Peyton's gaze, undaunted. "Don't get me wrong—I admire what you're doing for Horace. But how long can you keep looking after him?"

"I have the situation under control." Peyton crossed her arms. "And that's really none of your business."

"You already have your hands full with your career, this recent promotion, and with me," she admitted. "We both know I can be a handful."

"*That's* the understatement of the century. Five Horaces would be easier than supervising you."

Five? No. Three, maybe. "And now, with a baby on the way..." She glanced at Peyton's washboard stomach. "All I'm saying is, sometimes you have to prioritize."

Peyton frowned. "How'd this trade deal turn into a lecture from my agent on prioritizing?"

"You're the one who decided to drop the mother of all secrets."

"Like I had a choice?"

"You could've picked something else." Zoey inhaled deeply, feeling the weight of this secret squarely on her shoulders. "*Anything* else."

Peyton stared at her blankly. "But I don't have any other secrets."

"You're kidding. Just the nose ring and the pregnancy?"

Peyton nodded. "What did you expect?"

"Something juicy. Like you slept with your college roommates."

"Roommates," Peyton repeated with a frown. "Plural?"

She shrugged. "Maybe you had a threesome once when you were drunk."

Peyton stared at her. "Have you met me?"

"Or maybe you masturbate to 'Push It' by Salt-N-Pepa."

"First—not that it's any of your business—I don't masturbate. Second—"

"Ever?"

"Never."

She stared at Peyton, dumbfounded.

"Second," Peyton went on, "why do all your imagined secrets for me have to do with sex?"

"Need I remind you why we're here in the first place? You listened to me having sex with a man hairier than Bigfoot." Her target easily could've endured subzero temperatures without clothes. "I was hoping for something equally compromising."

"Well"—Peyton glanced down at her stomach—"I had sex to get this baby. Doesn't that count?"

"With your *husband*. That's a far cry from listening to me fake an orgasm with Sasquatch." She looked away from Peyton's gaze, feeling somewhat disgusted with herself as her thoughts drifted to Peyton's boss. "Have you told Alvarez?"

"It was in my report."

Zoey frowned, confused. "You put your pregnancy in a report?"

"No." Peyton looked over. "Sorry. I thought we were still talking about...the other thing."

"Have you told Alvarez about the pregnancy?"

Peyton looked away. "Not yet."

"He'll sideline you until you have the baby."

"I know. And that's why it's called a secret. By definition, a secret is designed to elude discovery."

"Until when?" Zoey pressed.

"Until I decide it's not a secret anymore."

"Hate to break it to you, but babies have this habit of growing. All soon-to-be mothers inevitably look like they've swallowed a basketball."

"Not there yet."

"You will be." Zoey reached down for the overflowing trash can at her feet and held it aloft. "And very soon, from the looks of it." Discarded food wrappers succumbed to the pressure of tight quarters and burst forth. Snack-sized potato-chip bags—too many to count—sailed through the air, spilling countless crumbs as they landed on the front seat. "Oh. My. God. Tell me these aren't yours."

"They're not mine," Peyton blurted.

"Must be—what—twenty…thirty bags here?" She sifted through the carnage and looked up. "You *ate* your new family?"

"Hormones make you do terrible things."

"How can you eat like this and still look like that?" Zoey pointed to all of Peyton.

"I run, and in case you've forgotten, I'm eating for two now."

Zoey tried to stuff the empty bags back inside the small trash can, to no avail. "But how much can a tiny human actually consume?" she asked, finally giving up and letting the bags scatter.

Peyton lifted her shirt to reveal a flat, well-toned stomach. "She's three inches long and weighs an ounce."

"She?" Zoey asked, her eyes on Peyton's stomach as she tried to imagine a tiny replica of her handler floating around inside.

"I had a blood test." Peyton lowered her shirt. "It's a girl."

Peyton hadn't smiled once since sharing the news of her pregnancy. Understandable, Zoey acknowledged, considering the circumstances. "You know," she said, softening her tone, "it's okay if you have mixed feelings about this baby. It's a lot to take in."

Peyton was quiet for long minutes as she gazed out the window. "Ben and I never planned on having kids," she said finally. "The CIA scouted me when I was still in high school. Once they got their hooks in me, I never looked back. Never wanted anything as much as I wanted a career in the CIA." She set a hand over her stomach. "And now…"

Was Peyton saying what Zoey thought she was saying? "If you're not ready…"

"I'm definitely not ready." Peyton met her gaze with a tenderness that surprised her. "But I've never wanted anything more than this baby."

Peyton's pregnancy would be a liability on their missions. If her handler intended to keep this from Alvarez, maintaining a united front was critical. "Have you told anyone else?"

"No. And I only told you because you threatened me with Feejays."

They held one another's gaze in silence. Zoey was acutely aware that something had just changed between them. Peyton had shared a secret. Revealed a vulnerability. Doing so had forged the beginnings of a bond. "Fine. I'll keep your secret." She pried her gaze from Peyton's and studied the dashboard clock. 4:59 p.m. Kickoff was at six. "On one condition."

Peyton rolled her eyes. "God. What now?"

"If things get hairy during a mission—no pun intended—you'll accept my help and let me have your back. No arguments. No pushback." Without a doubt, this would be the most challenging part for a proud new handler who believed help should be given, not received.

Peyton narrowed her eyes. "Define *hairy*."

"Anything that puts you or the baby at risk."

"I know how to handle myself in the field, Zoey."

"No doubt about it. You're a badass," she said with a wink. "I'll keep your secret. But I'll put in for a new handler if you don't agree to my terms." She was offering Peyton a way out of their partnership. The ball was in her court now.

Peyton took a long moment before turning to meet Zoey's gaze. "I'll agree to your terms but only on the condition that—"

"Stop." Zoey put her hand up. "You can't put terms on my terms."

"Technically, I was placing a *condition* on your terms."

"Whatever. Your condition isn't getting anywhere near my terms."

"To be fair, you didn't specify no conditions as part of your terms."

"Didn't know I had to," Zoey said. "Besides, that's not a recognized loophole."

"It most certainly is."

"Is not."

Silence reigned as they locked one another in a staredown. They were at an impasse.

"Fine." Zoey crossed her arms. "Then I'm making an addendum to my terms that no conditions are allowed."

"You can't make an addendum to your terms *after* you've proposed them." Peyton frowned. "Besides, I was only going to suggest that we draft a list of preapproved scenarios."

"Preapproved scenarios," Zoey repeated. "For what?"

"Plausible situations in the field that would require intervention on my behalf because of a legitimate safety concern."

"Let me get this straight," she said, shaking her head. "You want to list every possible scenario where I might have to step in and save not only your ass, but the still-developing ass of your baby?"

"I just think it could be helpful to draft specific parameters that must be met to set your terms in motion."

Zoey sat in silence, pretending to give the suggestion some thought. "My answer," she said finally, "starts with an *n* and rhymes with *glow*, which you're not doing much of, by the way. Your stubborn handler persona is disrupting the whole pregnancy glow thing."

"That's not a thing. Women do not glow when they're pregnant."

"Glowing is a useful tool that I think you should seriously reconsider. It could distract the casual observer—for example, our boss—from the steadily increasing size of your stomach. It would be in both our best interests if you started glowing, like, yesterday."

Peyton stared at her like she'd just proposed marriage. "I can't *make* myself glow."

"You can try. Just think happy thoughts. Puppies, kittens, rainbows, shit like that."

Peyton shook her head and sighed angrily. "You're being unreasonable by denying my request."

"And you're being unreasonable by denying mine," Zoey shot back.

"To start glowing?"

"That's right."

Peyton set both hands on the steering wheel and gripped it hard, as if to keep herself from strangling Zoey. "All I'm saying is, optimal results are achieved when the expectations are clearly understood by all parties involved. Which is what we would accomplish by drafting parameters for your terms," she insisted.

"How the hell did you survive in the field as an undercover agent?" Zoey asked.

"By utilizing a very specific formula: *R-P-C.*"

"Ooh, I'm good at acronyms. Let me guess..." She grabbed an empty bag of Lays off the seat and held it up. "Regurgitate potato chips. Am I right? Because what you ate here could feed a small village. All that grease is bound to come back up." She searched the floor and then turned to scan the back seat. "Where's your barf bucket?"

"Research. Plan. Communicate," Peyton went on, ignoring her. "A tried-and-true formula under which my handler and I consistently operated. It might interest you to know that our mission success rate was six percent higher than average."

Zoey reached over and pinched Peyton's arm. Hard.

"Ouch!" Peyton swatted her hand away.

"Just testing to see if you're human."

"What's that supposed to mean?"

Zoey sat upright, stiffening her body, arms, and neck. Jerky, robotic movements accompanied her monotone voice. "My name is Pey-ton. Fun is not a-llowed."

"Just because I take my job seriously doesn't mean I don't have fun."

"Taking this job seriously and having fun are synonymous," she explained, baffled by Peyton's insistence on coloring inside the lines. Where was the fun in that? "The best part of this job is making decisions on the fly. Each mission is like a mystery vacation. Sure, we know what the ultimate objective is, but how we achieve it is entirely up to us. We read our targets, engage, improvise, and adjust accordingly. A mistake in the field can cost us our lives—*that's* the part I take seriously, in case you were wondering. The rest is, like you said, *R-P-C.*" She grinned. "Relax. Party. Celebrate."

"Successful to a high degree of certainty," Peyton muttered under her breath.

"What is?"

"After reviewing our files, that was the conclusion reached by the CIA's pairing algorithm."

"We have a pairing algorithm?"

"Yes. Designed and implemented four years ago to ensure the successful assembly of all agent-handler teams." Peyton stared at her. "Don't you read the internal memos?"

"Not if I can help it."

Peyton shook her head. "Honestly, I have no idea why we were paired."

"Couldn't be more obvious. Al saw how tightly you were wound and knew you needed me to help you loosen up."

"Who's Al?"

"The algorithm."

"No one refers to the pairing algorithm as Al," Peyton said matter-of-factly. "It's known as CHUK, and it stands for—"

"Looks like *Al* hooked me up with an intelligent, no-nonsense, take-charge handler with a keen mind for detail."

The compliment stopped Peyton in her tracks. "Thank you," she offered, looking somewhat perplexed.

"But even the tug-of-war world champions couldn't pull *that* needle out of your ass."

"I am *not* uptight. Disciplined, yes. Which you could use a hefty dose of, by the way." Peyton pressed a button on the center console. A cover slid aside near Zoey's knee, revealing a hidden compartment. Peyton withdrew a miniature handheld vacuum and sucked up the potato-chip crumbs from the front seat before they even knew what hit them. "There. That's better. Now I can think," she said, slipping the tiny vacuum back in place.

"Missed one." Zoey pointed to a partially concealed crumb near Peyton's thigh.

Once again, Peyton deftly withdrew the tiny vac, showed no mercy, and sucked up the last brave soldier.

Zoey raised an eyebrow. "I'm seriously starting to wonder if you're beyond my help."

# CHAPTER SIX

There was a knock at Griffin's office door. "Mr. Secretary?" Robin, his sexy new intern, stepped inside his office with long, stockinged legs that he regularly envisioned wrapped around him in the throes of an orgasm. She'd been there less than a month, but he could tell she already had a crush on him. "The director of the CDC is on line one, sir. He says it's urgent."

"I'll take it. Close the door, please," he said with a dismissive wave. "Oh, and Miss Rossi?" Addressing her so formally made it look like he respected her, a card he'd played countless times in this very office. "You're a great fit here," he said with a wink. "I appreciate all you're doing to make my job easier." If he intended to have a secret affair with his intern, keeping up the appearance of professionalism was critical. Best to get that drilled into this new piece of ass from the start.

He lifted the phone from its cradle as Robin backed out of the room and shut the door with a bashful smile. Putty in his hands. She'd be writhing beneath him in ecstasy by the end of next week. Or, better yet, on her knees underneath his desk as he unveiled his gift and slid it inside that bashful mouth. "Arnold," he said, louder than was necessary. "Only have a minute. What's up?"

"Adverse effects of the vaccine are being reported."

Griffin leaned back in his chair and sipped his sparkling water. The ice cubes clinked against the glass as he drained it, his thoughts still on Robin.

"Told you we moved too fast," Arnie went on. "We should've

sought FDA approval and gone through the proper channels. Now we're facing an inevitable shitstorm."

"Cool your jets, Arnie. Shitstorms are my specialty. What are we talking here? Headache, fever, chills?"

Arnie sighed. "Along with a higher-than-average occurrence of Guillain-Barré syndrome."

"How much higher?"

"One or two cases per million is expected. We're currently at 2.3 cases per million and counting. The reports are still coming in, so it's too early to give an accurate projection of what that final number will be."

"Most vaccines carry a negligible risk. You, of all people, should know that." He propped his feet on the ottoman nearby, the one his wife had lovingly reupholstered by hand to match the navy-and-gold-striped curtains in his office. "So, what's the problem?"

"I'm quashing these reports for now, but it's only a matter of time before an ambitious reporter puts two and two together."

Arnie was clearly making a mountain out of a molehill. Nothing he'd said so far set off any alarm bells. "*If* that happens—and that's a big if—then we'll just chalk it up to a new ingredient in the vaccine. Shitstorm averted. Trust me, no one'll have time to worry about side effects from the new-and-improved flu vaccine—not once Bird of Prey is wreaking havoc on the population. That nasty little bugger will soon be making headlines around the world. *Then* we can tell the American people the truth about what they were inoculated against. When all of this comes to light, our people will understand why we needed to expedite the immunization process." Griffin refilled his glass from the pitcher of water on his desk and watched the ice cubes bounce and sway, his thoughts on his leggy intern once again. "We're the heroes in this story, Arnie. Not the villains."

❖

Peyton parked the Volvo in Zoey's parking space at Mattapan Heights and cut the engine as her Apple Watch vibrated. She flicked her wrist and read the text from Zoey. One simple word: *feejays*.

Feejays? Was Zoey reminding her about the threat of a slumber party if she failed in her search of the apartment? Or maybe Zoey was a big believer in the product and wanted her to get a pair. Either way, she decided it didn't matter. There was no way she'd be caught dead in a pair of Feejays. Sweatpants with feet. Ridiculous. She slept only in silk.

She reflected on their earlier chat in the car. She'd just about lost her lunch when Zoey demanded a secret and proposed the possibility of an affair with a college roommate. She hadn't thought about Callie in years. Part of her wondered if Zoey had fished around in her past and found out about Callie. To her knowledge, there wasn't a soul alive who knew about Cal. She shook her head. No, that was just a lucky guess.

Peyton set foot on the cracked, uneven pavement and activated the car alarm, but she doubted the alarm would do any good. She needed more visible protection. A SWAT team in full riot gear might help. This was Mattapan—one of the most dangerous neighborhoods in all of Boston. She wasn't especially keen on leaving Ben's Volvo here. She glanced back nervously at Ben's car. *Her* car now. She hadn't driven her Subaru since she'd received word of his death. Driving the car he'd loved made her feel like he was close. It still smelled like him.

She withdrew a flashlight from her coat pocket, switched it on, and trekked across the dark parking lot. Every single bulb in the surrounding streetlamps had been shattered by bullets or rocks. Of all the neighborhoods she could've chosen in the entire state of Massachusetts, this one would rank very last on Peyton's list. Why in the world would Zoey pick a place like this to live? According to Zoey's file, she'd been living in the same apartment for twelve years. Her salary was more than sufficient to cover living expenses in a much safer neighborhood, but she owned no property, drove a beat-up Toyota, and lived *here*. Peyton was anxious to review Zoey's finances and find out exactly how she was spending her income.

A gangly, preadolescent boy stepped out from the shadows as she approached the front of the apartment building. "Yo, mamacita."

She ignored him, kept walking, and reached for the door.

Two more boys—older and larger than the first—stepped boldly in front of her, barring her entry into the building.

She held up her badge. "Move aside, please."

The boys exchanged a glance before turning their attention back to her. "Password," they said in stereo.

"This isn't a joke, boys. Get out of my way."

Both boys lifted their hoodies to reveal the 38 Specials tucked inside the waistbands of their jeans. "Password," they repeated, unfazed.

She frowned. Those revolvers were probably unregistered. But handcuffing both boys and placing them under arrest here, by herself, was just too risky. Calling the Boston PD for backup wasn't an option, either. She'd be forced to explain why she was here. All CIA business, whether inside or outside US boundaries, had to be conducted with the utmost discretion. She was on her own but hadn't planned for this contingency.

Zoey's voice echoed in her mind. *The best part of this job is making decisions on the fly. We read our targets, engage, improvise, and adjust accordingly.*

It was time to think on her feet. Problem was, she wasn't very good at it. She'd been a planner ever since she could remember. Perhaps this was her moment to shine, to prove to herself just how versatile she could be.

"The password is Benjamin." Peyton reached into her coat pocket, withdrew her wallet, and held out two hundred-dollar bills.

To her surprise, neither boy budged. Whoever had given them guard duty was obviously paying them well. "Tell you what," she said. "I'll throw in another hundred for each of you if you step aside right now."

They stared at her, unblinking.

"That's two hundred apiece," she said, waving the money in the air. "Four hundred buckaroos."

Her audience was unmoved.

"Okay. Five hundred apiece," she said, emptying her wallet. "I have one thousand dollars in my hand. Final offer."

Nothing. Neither of the boys seemed even remotely tempted. Had Zoey put them up to this? Was this how Zoey was spending her money—by paying these guys to keep her out of the building? She felt her competitive nature ratchet up a notch.

"Ooh, what do we have here?" She made a point of peering into her wallet. "A credit card?" She slipped out her American Express and held it up. "Ten-thousand-dollar limit with a zero balance."

Still no reaction.

She refused to admit defeat and give Zoey the satisfaction of winning. "There's a Subaru Forester parked in front of my house. Only twelve thousand miles on the engine. It's yours, free and clear, but only if you step aside right now."

Both boys' feet remained firmly planted on the cracked pavement.

"Leather seats, alloy wheels, sunroof," she went on. Not even a flicker of interest. Impossible. No inner-city adolescent boy in the history of humans had ever passed up a free car. "You boys drive a hard bargain," she said, setting her hands on her hips with a sigh. "Has either of you ever heard of a 401(k)?"

The boy on the right finally took pity on her and broke ranks. "Lady, we're not lettin' you in without a password."

Zoey's text flashed through her mind. No. Couldn't be that easy. "Feejays?" she asked uncertainly.

Both boys instantly turned, reached for the lobby doors, and held them open for her.

She shook her head. "If you two ever apply for guard duty at Buckingham Palace, feel free to use me as a reference."

"No thanks," the taller of the two boys replied. "I'm studying physics at Northeastern."

Peyton hesitated in the doorway, unsure if he was pulling her leg. "How old are you?"

"Seventeen next month." He shrugged. "Graduated high school early."

She turned to the boy on her right. "Are you studying physics at Northeastern, too?"

"Nah," he replied, shaking his head and puffing out his chest like she'd just insulted him. "I'm a chem major at MIT with a minor in polymers and soft matter."

She stood at the door's threshold, looking back and forth between the two boys, trying to decipher if they were telling the truth. No telltale signs of deception in their expressions or body language.

Had she just entered an alternate universe? Mattapan was one of the roughest neighborhoods in Boston. Poverty and crime rates were at an all-time high. Try as she might, she couldn't wrap her brain around what was happening. There was no doubt in her mind that Zoey was behind this.

The taller boy nodded toward the lobby. "Shadow will take it from here."

"Shadow?" she asked, confused.

"Yo." A young woman stood from a worn leather armchair in the corner. Her no-nonsense military-style buzz cut revealed a startling beauty: warm terra-cotta skin, high cheekbones, emerald eyes, full lips, and a slender, delicate nose. Clad in a gray Harvard sweatshirt and jeans, she dog-eared the page of the book she was reading and set it down.

Curious, Peyton stepped over and stole a glance at the cover—*Surveillance Tradecraft: The Professional's Guide to Covert Surveillance Training.*

"Zoey's apartment is on the fifth floor," the young woman said, following her gaze. "I'll take you there."

"What makes you think I'm here to see Zoey?" Peyton asked, taken aback.

"CIA is stamped on your forehead."

Peyton studied the young woman. Gorgeous, bold, confident, and a little cocky. A young Zoey in the making. Zoey's *shadow*. "What's your real name?"

She narrowed her eyes and studied Peyton with equal scrutiny. "Sterling hasn't been around in a while," she said, ignoring the question. "My guess is, you took his place as Zoey's handler. You're here to search her apartment and make sure she's still loyal to the cause."

Peyton knew a future agent when she saw one. "Has anyone recruited you yet?"

"They tried. I'll finish my undergrad at Harvard first and explore my options after that."

Peyton nodded, impressed. She was tempted to talk up the CIA, but this young woman was smart. She'd figure out where she belonged.

Shadow slid a bright orange visitor sticker out of her book and handed it to Peyton.

"What's this for?"

"Just put it on."

"Not unless you tell me why."

"Put it on, or your ass will be capped. How's that for incentive?" The young woman grabbed the sticker from her hands, peeled off the backing, and slapped it over the arm of Peyton's coat.

"Did you just threaten to shoot me?"

"Of course not." Shadow rolled her eyes. "Armed sentries are posted on every floor to discourage uninvited guests."

"And they'll shoot whoever doesn't have a sticker?"

"Pretty much."

"Then I want more."

"More what?"

Peyton grabbed the sheet of visitor stickers from between the pages of Shadow's book and promptly began peeling and sticking them all over the front of her coat. She reached around behind herself and stuck four more on her back. "There." She handed the empty sheet to Shadow.

Shadow shook her head. "Feel better?"

"Much."

Frowning, Shadow turned. "Follow me."

"Where?"

"Zoey's."

"I don't need an escort. Now that I have...these"—she gestured to the stickers all over her body—"I can find my way just fine."

"All visitors must be accompanied by a resident."

"Who makes these rules?" Peyton asked. This was looking more and more like one of the many gang-run buildings in the projects. This gang just happened to be made up of...ridiculously smart college students? None of this was making much sense. One thing was certain, though—whatever was going on in this building had Zoey's fingerprints all over it.

"That's how we do things around here. Keeps the thugs out."

"Do I look like a thug to you?"

"You look like a crazy-ass white woman who got shitfaced at a visitors' convention." Shadow looked her up and down. "But seriously, you wouldn't be the first corrupt cop I ever met."

"I'm not a cop."

"Right. My bad. I didn't realize CIA agents were impervious to corruption." Shadow crossed her arms. "So, you're *not* here to search Zoey's apartment and make sure she's still working for our side?"

Peyton sighed. Shadow reminded her so much of Zoey that she momentarily wondered if Zoey was telling her what to say through an earpiece. "Fine. Escort accepted. Lead the way." She was determined to find out more about how this place was run.

They rode the elevator to the fifth floor in silence. The building was old, run-down, and in need of some fresh paint, but its overall condition exceeded her expectations. The elevator worked, the cement floors were clear of debris with no evidence of rodent droppings or cockroaches, the hallway lights worked, and the place smelled of old books. Not entirely unpleasant. She'd always liked that smell.

The elevator doors parted, and Shadow led the way to Zoey's apartment. "She's watching the game at Sterling's. You have a key?"

Peyton held up her Mr. Potato Head keychain.

Shadow raised an eyebrow. "Weird but…whatever. I'll be here when you're done." She settled in a chair a short distance down the hall, opened her book, and resumed her studies.

With a growing curiosity, Peyton unlocked Zoey's apartment and stepped inside.

# CHAPTER SEVEN

Zoey sipped her beer as Sterling set a big red bowl of potato chips on the coffee table. She balanced the beer bottle on her thigh with one hand and grabbed for some chips with the other. "Kickoff in five… four…three…two…"

Sterling lifted the remote and shut off the TV.

She stared at him, chip halfway to her mouth. She knew that face— his some-really-bad-shit-was-about-to-go-down face. She hurriedly stuffed her mouth and thought of Peyton. Her handler was pregnant. Now this. "How bad?" she asked, chewing as she braced herself for impact.

"Worse than *Contagion*," he answered, "but not as bad as *World War Z*."

She and Sterling had watched every end-of-world movie ever made. As the credits rolled, they'd dissect each movie down to the tiniest detail. They'd talk for hours about what went wrong, where it went wrong, and how better choices could've yielded a different outcome and spared the human population. End-of-world scenarios and human extinction had been their shared obsessions since she was twelve. "So we're talking about a deadly pathogen, but not one that reengineers the human genome into that of a crazed killer zombie?"

He nodded.

She glanced at the dark TV screen. If zombies weren't involved, was it really worth missing the game? "How deadly?"

"One hundred percent lethality."

"And the intel…is it credible?"

"Very."

"Stakes?"

"Billions of lives."

Damn. That was a pretty good reason to skip the game. "Fine. I'm in."

Sterling slapped his leg. "Hot diggity."

"On one condition," she added, thinking back to her session with Dr. P.

He raised one graying eyebrow, a stark contrast to his dark-as-night skin.

On more than one occasion, she'd seen Sterling virtually disappear from sight and blend seamlessly into the nighttime shadows. That level of camouflage wouldn't be possible now. The moment he'd retired, he let his hair, eyebrows, and impeccably trimmed beard assume their natural hues—an artist's blend of ash gray, silver, and stark white. The array of color added to the handsomeness of his open, round face, making him appear even more refined and gentlemanly.

"What's my tell?" she asked. "I need to know."

"Figured you'd come to me sooner or later about that." He pointed to her face. "It's your orbicularis oculi."

"My eye muscle?"

"The left side tenses for just a second," he went on. "That's the only tell I let you keep."

"*Let* me keep?" Sterling had spent years coaching her on how to overcome her tells whenever she was lying—an invaluable tool in her arsenal as a covert agent. She'd worked undercover for years, believing she was tell-free. "That tell could've cost me my life."

"Don't blow a gasket. It's infinitesimally small. The chances of anyone else picking up on it are negligible. They'd have to be professionally trained, know you for years, and—"

"Be super-duper smart?" she finished. "Yeah, I know. Somebody found it."

He frowned, quiet for a moment. "Ah," he said finally. "Meredith."

"You're now on a first name basis with Dr. Poke?"

"Another perk of retirement, I'm afraid."

If Dr. Poke wasn't so ethical, she'd wonder if they were having an affair. "I trusted you."

He shook his head, clearly annoyed. "What's the first thing I taught you when you came to live with me?"

"Trust no one."

"Precisely."

"But you insisted you were the exception to that rule. You always said you're the only one I *could* trust."

"I lied. For Christ's sake, Zo, pay attention to what I teach you." He studied her and narrowed his eyes disapprovingly. "Anyway, it serves you right for holding out for so long."

"Holding out? On what?"

"Discussing your past with Meredith."

Her back bristled. "Why the hell would I want to talk to her about that?"

"Because you've never talked about it with anyone. Not even me." The hurt was clear in his voice.

"You never asked," she said, caught off guard and feeling a little defensive.

He shrugged. "Didn't think you wanted to talk about it."

"How would you know if you never asked?"

Sterling leaned forward, set his elbows on his knees, and searched her face with genuine concern. "I'm asking you now, Zo. Do you want to talk about it? Here? Now? With me?"

"Of course not," she said, scooting to the other side of the sofa to put some distance between them. "Yuck. Retirement's making you soft."

He stood with a sigh, slid his hands in the pockets of his trousers, and started pacing the length of the living room. "Do you remember the hostage crisis in Iran?"

"November 4, 1979," Zoey said, nodding. "A revolutionary group stormed the American Embassy in Tehran and took fifty-two American diplomats hostage."

He held up a finger in correction. "Sixty-six Americans were there at the embassy that day. Fourteen were released, but the remaining fifty-two were American diplomats who were held hostage for—"

"Four hundred and forty-four days," Zoey finished, stringing the pieces together. The CIA was active in Iran at that time, keeping a watchful eye on a possible uprising. Sterling would've been about thirty in '79, already an undercover operative and making a name for himself. She felt her eyes grow wide. "You were a hostage?"

He sighed and shook his head, clearly disappointed in her summation. "After all the years you've known me, one would think you'd give me more credit than that."

"Oh my God." She felt her eyes grow wider. "You were the hostage-*taker*?"

He nodded. "I'd successfully infiltrated the revolutionary group, Muslim Student Followers of the Imam's Line. When the opportunity presented itself to be part of the embassy takeover, I volunteered."

Zoey mentally reviewed what she remembered from her International Negotiations class about the hostage crisis with Iran. The US military had attempted a rescue mission on April 24, 1980— Operation Eagle Claw—but the mission was quickly aborted after eight members of the rescue team were killed. "What about Eagle Claw?" she asked, finding it impossible to imagine that Sterling would've condoned those killings, even while undercover.

He hung his head. "An entirely avoidable tragedy. With the CIA refusing to share their intel, and the US military refusing to stand down, an already volatile situation exploded. I stopped it as soon as I could." He met her gaze, his sadness palpable. "But not soon enough."

"The Algiers Accords," she whispered, thinking aloud. The treaty that led to the eventual release of all fifty-two American diplomats. "That was your idea, wasn't it?"

He nodded and laughed dryly. "Had a hell of a time smuggling my notes out of Iran and getting them into the proper hands. Those notes turned out to be the basis for the treaty. That's why the hostages were held for so damn long. If I'd managed to get my notes to the US negotiating team sooner, Operation Eagle Claw never would've happened."

Zoey strained to see the bigger picture. Warren Christopher had been the deputy secretary of state and the head of the US negotiating team at that time. He signed the Algiers Accords on January 19, 1981. The hostages were released the next day. "What does any of this have to do with the pathogen?"

"When I joined Muslim Student Followers of the Imam's Line, I befriended another revolutionary in the group. Ardashir and I have kept in touch over the years. He came to me recently and shared some disturbing news." Sterling paused and met her gaze. "You're familiar with Executive Order 12170?"

She nodded. "We froze billions in Iranian assets after they seized the American Embassy and took those hostages."

"Fast-forward thirty-five years to 2015. We finally reached a deal with Iran to limit their nuclear capabilities. In exchange, we agreed to release those frozen assets—over one hundred billion dollars' worth."

"Let me guess." It didn't take a rocket scientist to figure out where this was going. "They suspended their nuclear program and invested their recovered assets in biosynthetic warfare."

Sterling nodded. "They built a state-of-the art biosafety level four laboratory, sought out the most talented synthetic biologists, and began modifying the DNA of pathogens with alarming speed. They paid particular attention to the H5N1 virus."

"The bird flu," Zoey said, on the edge of her seat now.

"They engineered it to be more deadly and more transmissible."

"How much more?" she asked, bracing herself for the answer.

"It's airborne, highly infectious, and one hundred percent lethal. Code-named by our government, Bird of Prey."

"Have they made a vaccine?" The logical next step in biosynthetic warfare. If they were going to take the time to engineer a deadly virus into something even more potent, she hoped they'd put forth at least a little effort into finding a vaccine.

He shook his head. "Not yet. But they're very close. Once that vaccine is finished, they have plans to begin an accelerated immunization program for their people."

The Iranian government would most likely release the virus in multiple super-spreader events around the world to guarantee global infection. Zoey knew their endgame could go one of two ways: sell the vaccine to the highest bidder as the world's population lay dying, or let the rest of the world die out to become the sole survivors of the entire human race. It boiled down to what was more important to them—money or supreme power. Well, that was a no-brainer. "Crap," she said, feeling suddenly sick to her stomach. "Is it too late to become an Iranian citizen?"

"Initially, when Ardashir came to me with this, I wasn't concerned. I knew the CIA had already planted a virologist in their lab. We were keeping close tabs on their progress with this particular virus. But then

I did a little digging. What I found within the confines of our own government was even more disturbing."

Zoey squeezed her eyes shut. "Please don't tell me we beat them to the punch."

"That's exactly what we did. For the first time in history, the CIA is working in tandem with a whole alphabet soup of agencies. We've already begun aggressively immunizing the American population under the guise of a flu shot." He paused, studying her. "Have you had yours?"

She nodded, feeling simultaneously relieved and guilty for being spared the fate that billions of innocent people might be forced to face.

"Our government's keeping news of the virus and the vaccine under wraps."

"Until when?" she asked.

"Until every country around the world experiences the virus's catastrophic effects."

She knew the US government was greedy, but she never would've guessed in a million years that they were capable of wiping out every other person on the planet. "They're keeping it a secret until..." She stared at him, momentarily transfixed. "Until everyone else is dead?"

"Not everyone," Sterling replied. "But close to."

Turned out our core motivations weren't so different from Iran's, after all. "Our government intends to sell the vaccine when countries are at their most desperate."

He nodded. "Money is power. China has had a firm foothold in the global economy for quite some time. Their rising status threatens ours. The House, the Senate, and the Administration unanimously agree on one thing: the US must strive to be the wealthiest, most powerful nation in the world, both financially and militarily. Anything less puts our country and its citizens in peril." Sterling paused, studied the floor, and paced some more as Zoey looked on.

"Given that China and Russia have been nipping at our heels for years," he went on, "we're looking more and more like an injured alpha wolf. Rival wolves will soon begin to see that as an opportunity to challenge the alpha and assume leadership of the pack. Take our current president, for instance." He looked up and met her gaze. "Cooper's convinced someone will view our perceived weakness—"

"As an invitation for warfare," she finished. Just like Iran had done. "Why not take advantage of the situation and do what we do best—let greed and a thirst for power be our guiding principles. Let's hoard the only known vaccine to a virus that threatens mass human extinction, and then sell it as the rest of the world is dying. Sounds like the perfect time to reclaim our alpha status in the global economy." She could feel her face reddening with anger. Best to get it all out now. After today, she couldn't run the risk of letting her emotions cloud her judgment. She'd have to keep them tightly contained until all of this was over.

❖

Peyton shut Zoey's apartment door, gazed around the living room, and set her hands on her hips. She opened the door and poked her head out. "Excuse me?"

Shadow set her book aside, stood, and walked over. She crossed her arms and leaned against the wall on the opposite side of the hallway. "You're wondering if you're in the right apartment."

Peyton nodded, at a loss for words.

"You are," she confirmed.

"I need to make sure we're talking about the same Zoey."

"Blackwood," Shadow said, nodding. "She's kind of a movie buff."

Obsessed fan who bordered on a disturbing break from reality was more like it. How was this information *not* in Zoey's file?

"Everyone here knows about Z's fondness for—"

"Grotesque decor?"

"Zombie movies," Shadow finished. "Makes her easy to shop for at Christmas."

Peyton knew from her research that there were two hundred and sixteen apartments at Mattapan Heights. "Are you saying everyone here gives her a Christmas gift?"

"Not everyone." She shrugged. "But a lot of us do."

"Why?" Peyton asked, more than a little curious.

"It's our way of saying thanks."

"For what?"

Shadow narrowed her eyes. "I thought CIA stood for Central Intelligence Agency."

"It does."

"Then go figure it out yourself." Shadow shook her head and returned to her chair with a sigh. "FBI's looking better and better," she muttered under her breath.

"I heard that." Peyton ducked back inside Zoey's apartment and shut the door once again.

Mystified and more than a little repulsed, she gazed around the living room. It was like a house of horrors. Framed movie posters from every zombie movie ever made adorned the walls. Lifelike arms with decomposing flesh protruded from the ceiling, making it appear as though rotting corpses were reaching down from the apartment above. Movement sensors brought robotic zombies to life. They jerked stiffly from side to side, uttering prerecorded threats to feast on her brain as she walked past. Like a moth to an incandescent bulb, she was drawn to the artificial Christmas tree in one corner of the living room.

With Christmas later this month, the holiday season was now in full swing. A lump of sorrow in Peyton's throat made it difficult to swallow. This would be her first Christmas without Ben. In her haste to keep the grief at bay, she'd decided not to put up a tree this year.

Contrary to their tree, which they painstakingly decorated each year with miniature versions of Yoda, Chewbacca, Luke Skywalker, Princess Leia, R2-D2, C-3PO, and all things *Star Wars*, Zoey's tree was decorated with decapitated heads, bloodied limbs, brains on pitchforks, and an arsenal of formidable-looking miniature weapons—serrated knives, brass knuckles, spears, machetes, tomahawks, axes, and crossbows. Peyton gazed up and shook her head in disbelief. Like the cherry on a hot fudge sundae, the tree had been topped with a skeleton zombie angel with protruding organs.

How in God's name had Zoey passed her psych eval for entry into the CIA? This apartment was beyond repulsive and suggestive of a mentally unbalanced mind. Moreover, it was a desperate cry for help. She'd call Dr. Pokale first thing tomorrow and request a more in-depth psychological evaluation of this operative.

Peyton tore her eyes from the zombie angel and took a deep breath. It was time to get down to business and search the rest of Zoey's living quarters.

She followed a trail of bloody handprints and footprints down a long hallway to a closed door. A large yellow sign read *Zombie Zone: You're entering an infected area. Turn back now!*

Every instinct in Peyton's body told her to heed the warning, which was silly because all of this was fake—no different than being inside a haunted house. She just happened to be touring the apartment of a brilliant and obviously deranged CIA operative.

Half convinced she'd find a sex dungeon with wax zombies handcuffed to metal hooks in the ceiling, she hesitated at the threshold of what she assumed would be Zoey's bedroom. The sense of dread Peyton was feeling now was new to her. She wasn't usually one to scare so easily. It had to be the pregnancy hormones. She took a deep breath and turned the doorknob, preparing herself in case Zoey had rigged something to jump out at her.

## CHAPTER EIGHT

Sterling set a reassuring hand on Zoey's shoulder. "Believe it or not, our government's decision to sell the vaccine was the lesser of two evils. The other scenario I'm told our president was seriously considering is too ghastly to fathom."

"America would achieve supreme power if we simply usurped the Iranian government's plan and let the virus run its course." Zoey inwardly cringed. "Let everyone else die out."

He stuffed his hands in the pockets of his trousers and shrugged. "There's bound to be a handful of people around the globe with natural immunity to the virus, but yes, I'm told it was something along those lines."

"Who talked our tenderhearted president off *that* cliff?" She needed to know. In case the shit hit the fan later—which, in all likelihood, it would—it'd be nice to have a contact in the president's circle who could be reasoned with and render help. Even if that help was under the radar.

"Who do you think?"

Shit. "Bellingham?"

He nodded.

Secretary of State Vivian Bellingham, a devout Conservative. She was on the president's short list of trusted confidants. Rumor had it she was also the president's conscience. Her powers of persuasion were a force to be reckoned with. Zoey should know. She was invited into Vivian's web for a fleeting affair that had ended rather abruptly.

"You still have her number?" Sterling asked with a knowing expression.

"Fuck," she muttered under her breath. She shot up and started pacing as Sterling claimed her spot on the arm of the sofa, watching.

"If I were you," he went on, "I'd consider calling her now to apologize for whatever it is you did."

"It's not that simple," she said in her own defense.

"Never is. But now's the time to make it simple. Set it up, Zo." He reached over, lifted her phone from the coffee table, and handed it to her. "Set it up so she's there if you need her."

She dialed Viv's personal cell and kept it short and sweet. They agreed to meet the following day at their favorite spot along the wharf. She hung up and tossed her cell on the sofa, resigned to do whatever it took to get Viv back in her corner. "Done. Now what?"

"Now you plan your mission accordingly."

"*Our* mission," she corrected him. "Now *we* plan *our* mission."

"I must admit, it is tempting." Sterling nodded slowly. "And I have been considering it."

They traded places once again as Sterling resumed pacing. Zoey kicked off her shoes, grabbed a handful of chips, and propped herself on the arm of the sofa. "Really?" she asked as she munched away contentedly, feeling optimistic for the first time in months. If an opportunity came along to ditch her pregnant handler and partner up with Sterling again, she'd jump at it.

"No." He halted, met her gaze, and looked at her like she was a five-headed alien life-form. "*Nothing* could make me consider coming out of retirement. Not even a world-obliterating virus. I'm too old to save the world."

"But this is what we've spent the last two decades training for," she insisted. "It's why we watched all those movies."

"This is what I've spent twenty-four years training *you* for— preparing you in case something like this ever came along. It was only a matter of time. I'm just surprised it didn't happen sooner." He placed a flash drive in her palm, closed her fingers around it, and held his hand over hers. "You'll be on your own with this one, kid."

They regarded one another in silence. The credits were now rolling for the greatest man she'd ever known—a legendary CIA operative whose covert missions had helped shape history. She knew, firsthand, that he was also a wise handler with the utmost integrity who would lay his life down for the greater good without a moment's hesitation. Sterling was making it clear that he was passing the baton to her.

A profound sadness welled up from the depths of her soul. Tears blurred her vision, but she didn't try to hide them. Sterling needed to know the truth of how she felt about him. The grief she'd felt so long ago over losing her own mother to drugs paled in comparison to this moment.

"Should you accept this mission," he went on, "you'll be required to make sacrifices of unimaginable magnitude."

Missing the Pats play Baltimore was one of them. She gazed longingly at the dark TV screen. "A small price to pay when the entire human race hangs in the balance."

"That's the spirit," he said with a wink, withdrawing a blue silk handkerchief from his pocket. He was never without one. Sterling wiped at her tears with a tenderness that just made them fall faster. He gave up with a sigh, stuffed the wet handkerchief back inside his pocket, and cradled her face in his hands. "Let me make this clear. Your failure would spell death for billions of people around the world. But more to the point and perhaps equally devastating"—he gazed into her eyes—"it would mean I've just wasted twenty-four years of my life training you when I could've been fishing."

Zoey couldn't help but smile through the tears. She'd traveled a long road with this man as her mentor. Their journey together was coming to an end. "I was hoping for a virus that turned people into zombies."

"Me, too," he said, his disappointment palpable.

"Any chance that'll happen with Bird of Prey?"

He shook his head. "Probably not."

"Maybe it'll mutate," she said, refusing to relinquish all hope.

"One can always dream."

They bumped fists and made sounds of an explosion in unison. The deal was sealed.

Sterling's expression suddenly softened, another look with which she was well-acquainted. His Hallmark-moment face. "Don't you dare hug me." She was finally getting the waterworks under control. A hug from Sterling would just break the dam wide open.

"Come on. Just a little one," he said, undaunted.

"Wait." She pointed. "Is that a new shirt?"

He nodded.

"Potato chip grease." She held up her hands. "My hands are covered in it. Hug me, and I'll wipe it all over your back." It was the only thing she could think of to keep him at bay. Sterling was a stickler for impeccable attire.

"A small price to pay when the life of my protégé, who's as close to a daughter as I've ever known, hangs in the balance." He leaned in for a long embrace and held her as she cried.

True to her word, Zoey ran her greasy hands up and down his back before grabbing hold of him in the fiercest hug she'd ever given another human being.

This, she knew, was their good-bye.

Peyton nudged the bedroom door open and did a double take. She glanced back over her shoulder to make sure she was still in the same apartment. A zombie with an open skull and one eye stared back at her. The maggot-riddled head and rotting torso were staged to look like it was crawling through the hallway wall. She stepped inside Zoey's bedroom, promptly shut the door, and fumbled with the lock on the knob. Having a locked door between her and that thing in the hallway made her feel safer.

She let out a long breath and gazed around the room. It was a perfectly ordinary space that doubled as Zoey's bedroom and office. Simple, uncluttered, organized, and tastefully furnished. No signs of an obsession with corpses. The zombie reprieve felt refreshing. It even smelled nice, a combination of Zoey's sultry perfume and the relaxing scent of lavender.

She stepped over to the white U-shaped desk in the corner—an unusually large desk for one person. Laptop, printer, desk lamp. A handful of books were stacked on the lower shelves. Curious, she knelt to read their spines: *Fiske Guide to Colleges*, *The Best 385 Colleges*, *The Complete Book of Colleges*, *The Financial Aid Handbook*, and *The Ultimate Scholarship Book*.

She thought back to Zoey's file. Zoey already had two college degrees, one in international affairs and another in foreign studies. She'd earned her dual bachelor's in less than two years, which was noteworthy because Peyton had never heard of anyone accomplishing such a feat in that amount of time.

Her thoughts returned to Shadow and the two guards at the front entrance of Zoey's building. Different races—Black, white, Latinx—but all three were young, living in one of the roughest neighborhoods of Boston, and attending three of the best colleges in the country: MIT, Northeastern, and Harvard. College tuition wasn't cheap. The odds that all three had received full-ride scholarships were low, which begged the question: How were they paying for college?

Peyton glanced at the college admissions books on Zoey's shelf and thought back to her conversation with Shadow. When she'd asked why the residents gave Zoey Christmas gifts each year, Shadow had said it was their way of saying thank you. Was that where Zoey's money was going? Was she paying for their college tuition?

She sat in Zoey's swivel chair, switched on the laptop, and, remembering the list of passwords, reached into her coat pocket to remove the red origami lips. She unfolded them to find the tiniest print she'd ever seen in her life. How on earth had Zoey managed to write this small? She *knew* the passwords were too good to be true, had sensed it the moment Zoey made the offer to trade. But Peyton had been so distracted by the need to reveal a secret that she didn't think to actually open the origami lips while Zoey was still in the car. Dammit. She glanced at her watch: 6:34 p.m. The game had started at six, so she still had plenty of time. She just needed to make sure she was gone by the time Zoey returned from Sterling's. Feejays or no Feejays, there'd be no sleepovers with Zoey. Not in this lifetime.

She studied her surroundings, her mind still chewing on a solution for how to read the world's tiniest print. The colors in Zoey's bedroom were rich, bold, and more masculine than she would've imagined: navy blue, orange, light gray, and stark white. A tall dark-blue wooden headboard loomed over a perfectly made king-size bed. The blue, orange, and white-striped comforter was pillowy and inviting, the matching shams starched and wrinkle-free. An assortment of throw pillows in complementing colors rested on the bed, adding a warmth and coziness that made her further contemplate the psychological complexities of her operative.

Orange represented enthusiasm, strength, endurance, and determination while blue symbolized power, intelligence, loyalty, and confidence. Gray, on the other hand, was often associated with loss. White, with purity and innocence. Peyton's intuition told her that every facet of Zoey's life was driven with intention. Zoey had received all the same training that she had and was no doubt aware of the psychology behind colors. She'd decorated this room in an effort to reveal herself in her truest form. The rest of her zombie-filled apartment was simply there for…entertainment? Distraction? Perhaps not. Peyton thought for a moment. The trail of death, destruction, and despair on the way to Zoey's bedroom was representative of how she'd become the woman she was today.

As Zoey's handler, Peyton was privy to the results of the psychological assessments administered over the years by Dr. Pokale. As she'd reviewed Zoey's file to familiarize herself with her new operative, one thing had stood out: Zoey consistently refused to discuss her childhood or anything whatsoever that had transpired prior to Sterling's adoption of her at age twelve. If the trail of zombies was any indication of how bad Zoey's childhood was, then Peyton could only begin to imagine the suffering she'd endured.

The truth of it all crashed into her. Hard. She suddenly found herself in awe of Zoey's courage and unabashed honesty. In that moment, Peyton knew she would never look at her operative the same way again.

❖

Zoey climbed behind the steering wheel of her beat-up Toyota Tercel. She pumped the gas pedal six times, thumped on the stick shift twice with her fist, and jiggled the key in the ignition—a series of steps that her ancient car insisted she follow to start the engine. Every now and then, she'd throw in an extra thump or two just to see what happened. After all, what car could count, right? Weirdly enough, her car. It always caught on and simply sat idle, refusing to start. With so much personality, she should've given it a name. But she'd always just thought of it as The Car. No further identification was needed. Her car was just as stubborn as she was.

Zoey backed out of Sterling's driveway and swung right onto Hartford Street, mentally reviewing the intel Sterling had provided. She popped her Bluetooth in and switched it on.

Shadow answered with her usual level of cool-cat confidence. "What's up, Z?"

"Did North make it inside okay?"

"She did, but I haven't seen her in a minute. I've been sitting here wondering if one of the zombies ate her. Been a while since we fed them."

If only it was that easy. "She's still there?"

"Yep. Been so long that I finished my book. Now I'm passing the time devising ways to take over the world."

A dangerous pastime and one well within Shadow's purview. Zoey was quiet for a beat as she thought. Last-minute change of plans. When an opportunity presented itself, a good agent could switch gears on a dime and run with it. She'd make the best possible use of this time while Peyton was inside her apartment.

"You want me to check and make sure she's still alive?" Shadow asked.

"Negative. But if North tries to leave, stall her until I get there."

"Copy. Everything okay with you and Sterling?"

"Fine. Why?"

"Second quarter. Baltimore's up by three." There was a brief, accusatory silence. "You left before the game ended."

Zoey fast-forwarded through a list of possible explanations. Since Shadow was like a human lie detector, she opted for the truth. "Something came up."

"Had to be really bad—like, world-ending—for you to miss a game."

"It is," she admitted.

Another brief silence. She could hear Shadow's wheels turning at warp speed. At the tender age of twenty, Shadow possessed a deadly skill set for anyone just starting out in life. Not only was she gorgeous, street-smart, resourceful, discerning, and amazingly intuitive, but she had one of the most brilliant and complex minds of anyone Zoey had ever met.

"If shit's about to go down, no matter what it is, I'm here if you need me," was all Shadow said.

The perfect response. Shadow was pledging her loyalty without asking questions or pressuring her for information. Trust was a two-way street, and they were in sync. Had been from the moment they'd met.

Zoey told her about Bird of Prey. In spite of Sterling's insistence that she should never trust a single human being on the planet, she trusted Shadow. The only way she'd been able to earn Shadow's trust in the first place was by extending her the same courtesy. Sterling's lessons had actually achieved just the opposite of what he'd intended. They made Zoey more determined than ever to find the people she *could* trust. And Shadow was one of them.

"No chance of zombies, huh?"

Zoey sighed. "None."

"That must've been tough for you to hear."

"It was," she admitted.

"It's okay. I'm sure there's an evil, supersmart freak out there somewhere who's cooking up a zombie virus as we speak. We'll be running for our lives from those rotting, foul-smelling, brain-eating cannibals before you know it."

Zoey frowned. "Running from?"

"Like I said, we'll be kicking zombie ass from here to kingdom come before you know it. And we'll do it using all those fake weapons in your apartment. Except our weapons will be real because we can't do much ass-kicking with plastic." Shadow took a breath. "Now that I'm thinking about it, we should probably start building an arsenal now, while we still have the chance."

"Already did. I have a storage locker. Remind me to give you a key." Zoey couldn't help but smile. Shadow's response to every bleak situation was humor. Zoey'd had a little sister at one point in time. If her sister had survived, she liked to imagine that she would've turned out like Shadow. She cleared her throat. "I need a favor. But it's asking a lot."

"A favor means you'll owe me. I don't roll like that with family."

She had mixed feelings about bringing Shadow into this. If anything happened to her, she'd never forgive herself. "This is high stakes," she admitted. "If you're caught—"

"I won't be. Just get on with it. Whatever it is, I'm in."

## CHAPTER NINE

Zoey turned up the volume on her Bluetooth. She had half a mind to read Shadow the riot act for agreeing to something she knew nothing about. "Your blind faith in me is heartwarming, but there are about a thousand different ways my plan could go sideways. The least you could do is hear me out before you agree."

"You're wasting your time. I already know the risks."

"How?" Zoey frowned. "You don't even know what I'm about to propose."

"Unless it's marriage, I have a pretty good idea."

No way. Shadow couldn't have figured out her plan so quickly. "Prove it."

"You're about to ask if I'll run point from here while you travel the world, spreading the vaccine's formula to the people who'll need it. It's not like you can send an email to every foreign government in one fell swoop. Nobody would believe you because you have no proof of an imminent pandemic. Like you said, all Sterling gave you was a copy of the vaccine's formula, graciously given to him by his contact in Iran. By the way, Ardashir's my new favorite person. We should really consider sending him a fruit basket when all of this is over.

"Anyway," Shadow went on, "if Sterling had tried to gather intel on Bird of Prey from the CIA database, not only would it have compromised the lives of his informants, but it also would've alerted the CIA to a security breach and given them time to run interference on your plan. So you'll need to do this the old-fashioned way and deliver the formula to country leaders in person. That's where I come in. I'll keep tabs on your whereabouts from here and provide you with the necessary intel on your next point of contact. If our government catches wind of our plan to distribute the vaccine's formula and give the rest of the world a fighting chance, they'll try to stamp me out first because I'll be the one running point. And if they capture me, I'll likely face torture, death, or prison, or—if I'm really lucky—all three. At this point in the game, there's nothing our government won't do to get what they want." Shadow finally paused in her monologue and took a breath. "Did I leave anything out?"

"Show-off." Zoey braked at a traffic light. Either she was becoming way too predictable, or Shadow was too smart for her own good.

"The real question is, where are we going to live when all of this is over?"

Zoey frowned. "Come again?"

"Assuming we succeed—which, of course, we will, because it's *us*—we'll need to find another country to call home because everyone on the planet will despise the US when they realize how greedy our government was. There are bound to be consequences for our country as a whole. I don't know about you, but I'd rather not stick around to see how *that* plays out."

Zoey hadn't thought that far ahead. It was a valid point.

"Well, we don't have to decide right now," Shadow went on, seemingly happy to fill the silence. "I'm sure we'll have pick of the litter when word gets out that we saved the planet's collective ass."

She smiled to herself, grateful for Shadow's ability to see the silver lining in an otherwise bleak situation. "We're only doing this together if you promise me one thing."

"What's that?" Shadow asked.

"If the CIA discovers you're helping me, you'll give me a heads-up so I can come back and retrieve you."

"Right. Like I'd agree to that." Zoey could almost hear Shadow rolling her eyes over the phone. "I know you, Z. You'd toss the entire human race aside to save me. As much as I appreciate that, you can't seriously expect me to be okay with it."

If push came to shove, Zoey knew she'd never be able to sacrifice Shadow. She hesitated, weighing her chances of mission success without Shadow's help against the possibility of losing her.

"You took me in six years ago because you saw something in me, and you've been training me ever since." Shadow pleaded her case. "I'm ready for this. I'm willing to face the consequences if I get caught." She sighed. "Besides, we both know you can't do this without me. Sterling's retired. You can't risk trusting anyone else. I'm the perfect candidate to run point. I'm a nobody—"

"You're *not* a nobody." Zoey's back went up. "Don't ever say that again."

"You know what I mean, Z. Chances are, no one'll give me a second glance. A young Brown woman from the projects. No family. I'm perfect for this. Besides, I'll be the youngest handler in CIA history. Let me help you."

Zoey took a deep breath and prayed she wouldn't look back on this moment with regret. "Daily check-ins are mandatory. If you miss one—and I mean *one*—I swear I'll pilot the plane to retrieve you and then torture you myself."

"Copy." Shadow laughed. "The family business continues."

"Family business?" Zoey repeated, barely paying attention. She was already wondering if she should renege on their agreement.

"Sterling trained you. You trained me. Now I get to carry the torch and pass it on to someone just as unlucky."

The truth of Shadow's words was like a punch to the gut. Did Sterling feel this way when he'd sent her out on her first mission? Not only had he taken her in, raised her like his daughter, and trained her—he'd also convinced the higher-ups at the CIA to let him be her handler. For the first time in her life, she realized how much strength it had taken for him to do that and knew immediately why he had. It was the lesser of two evils. He could either supervise her, collaborate with her, and keep track of her during dangerous missions or choose the way of ignorance and let someone else do the job. Since Sterling trusted no one, his choice was obvious.

The mere thought of involving Shadow in something so dangerous made Zoey's heart pick up speed. Seeing Shadow's potential and training her to be a covert operative was one thing. Including her on a mission that pitted them against the entire US government was another. The thought of losing Shadow terrified her. Despite the sixteen-year age gap between them, this young woman had become her best friend.

More than her best friend. She was family. Losing another little sister would break her. Shadow was her kryptonite. She just hoped no one ever figured that out.

Zoey took a long breath to steady her nerves. "We have a date with Vivian Bellingham tomorrow."

"You mean *you* have a date. She was your girlfriend, not mine."

"Consider this your first job as my handler. You'll be hacking into her cell phone and feeding me intel through my earpiece."

"Cool. I'm in. But if you two start getting all hot and heavy, I'm out."

"That's not the plan. And she wasn't my girlfriend." The sex was great, but when they'd made the mistake of talking, it quickly became apparent that they were like two Siamese fighting fish in the same tank.

"What's up with North's Potato Head keychain?" Shadow asked.

"Long story. I'll be there soon. If North tries to leave before I get there—"

"Stall her. I know."

Zoey checked her watch: 7:38 p.m. Peyton had probably headed straight to her apartment after their meeting at the track. If she was right, her handler had skipped dinner and should be approaching starvation status right about now. "If she tries to go anywhere, just toss her a bag of potato chips and start talking about *Star Wars*."

Griffin leaned back in his leather chair, propped his elbows on the armrests, and steepled his fingers together in thought.

"Sir?" Robin looked on from his office doorway. "Would you like me to tell Dr. Langston you're unavailable?"

Arnie had made the nine-hour trek by car from the CDC to the Pentagon. Griffin had installed a tracking app on Arnie's cell phone and had been following his movement all day. He'd also planted a bug in Arnie's car and was now privy to the panicked rantings of a man on the verge of a nervous breakdown. There was no way around it. The director of the CDC was officially a thorn in his side. He shook his head, sighed, and finally met Robin's gaze. "I'll make time for him."

As Robin ducked out to retrieve his visitor, Griffin withdrew an unregistered cell phone from a locked desk drawer and texted Vice President Grady to update him on this latest development. He suspected the White House would be Arnie's next stop.

Robin escorted Arnie inside Griffin's office a few minutes later. She poured each of them a glass of water and promptly shut the door.

"I know you're busy, but this couldn't wait." Arnie slid the tablet out from under his arm and set it on the desk.

Griffin decided to play along. He studied the graph on the screen. "What am I looking at?"

"Reports are coming in from pharmacies, physicians, emergency rooms, and urgent care centers all over the country. The incidence of adverse reactions to the vaccine is growing."

"You already told me that on the phone," he said, doing his best to hide his annoyance from the plump man taking up space in his office. He'd had the vaccine. Nothing bad had happened to him. Adverse reactions were inevitable for the unfortunate few. "What's changed?"

"Guillain-Barré syndrome, sir."

"What about it?" Griffin asked.

"It's a rare disorder that can be triggered by a vaccine. The body's own immune system begins attacking the nerves, resulting in varying degrees of paralysis." Arnie nodded at the tablet in Griffin's hand. "That's a graph of confirmed cases. Preliminary data puts it at 2.4, though I expect that number to increase as more data comes in."

"You said it was 2.3 when we spoke on the phone."

"My point exactly." Arnie crossed his arms. "It's going up."

Griffin stood from his chair, perched on the corner of his desk, and calmly laced his fingers together in his lap. The time had come to handle Arnie with kid gloves. "That's only a *fraction* of a percent, Arnie. We both know it could be a lot worse. The increase in cases is an unfortunate side effect of being dragged into a bio-synthetic war." The fact that Arnie was now having second thoughts came as no surprise. Griffin and the president had only been able to pull this off because they had a trusted circle of high-ranking officials who held firm to the president's agenda. Arnie, they'd already predicted, would be their weakest link, which was why they'd chosen to withhold much of the truth from him.

"But it's a war that hasn't even started yet," Arnie pleaded. "Maybe, if we're lucky, it never will." He brought a hand to his widow's peak, trying in vain to pat down the unruly stragglers standing at full attention.

At fifty-four years young, Griffin still had the full, thick hair that the Bick men were known for. His interns loved running their fingers through it.

Arnie set his hands on his hips and began pacing. "It's only a matter of time before an ambitious reporter connects the dots and realizes what we've done." Sweat beaded on his forehead and upper lip as he met Griffin's gaze with a look of panic. "We could be subjecting Americans to the unwanted effects of an *irrelevant* vaccine."

"Irrelevant?" Jolted from thoughts of his soon-to-be conquest with the bashful smile, Griffin rose to his full height. At six two, he loomed over Arnie and got an unobstructed view of the shiny, balding scalp below. "Has it slipped your mind that Bird of Prey is ten times more contagious than the common cold and twenty times more lethal than Ebola?"

"But what if the Iranian government came to their senses? What if they changed their minds and decided not to release the virus?"

"Come on, Arnie. You can't be that naive. You saw the same intel I did. We're doing the American people a favor by getting a jump on this thing. A tenth of a percent increase in the occurrence of a rare disorder is a lot better than a fatality rate of one hundred percent, which is what would happen if we didn't start the immunization process now." Arnie had no idea that the intel to which Griffin was referring had been doctored. He and the president's inner circle had gone to great lengths to make it appear as though Iran's execution of the pandemic was imminent. In reality, Iran wouldn't be ready to launch for at least another twelve months. Only Griffin, the president, and their trusted inner circle knew the truth.

Arnie reached for the tablet on the desk and held it up. "I can't ignore this graph. The American people have a right to know the risks and decide for themselves if that risk is worth taking. What if the intel you received was fabricated somehow? Then what? I can't, in all good conscience, be complicit in this any longer. The American people have a right to know the truth."

"Listen to yourself, Arnie. What you're proposing is ludicrous. If we gave anyone a heads-up on this thing—forget the vaccine—there'd be mass hysteria around the *world*. And when the rest of the world found out we have the vaccine to the deadliest pathogen in human history, we'd be the target of every weapons system on the planet."

"Plans for mass production and distribution of the vaccine are already underway. Why would anyone target us?" Arnie scratched his head in confusion. "That makes no sense."

"Because plans for doing something of that magnitude take time. We need to inoculate *our* people, make sure they're safe from this thing, before we worry about the rest of the world. We have a responsibility to protect the citizens of *this* country first. We'll tend to the rest of the world's population later, when we're better prepared for the Pandora's box this is bound to open. You and I both know there's still a lot of work to be done."

"I don't understand why we can't share the vaccine's formula. Let other countries get a jump start and make it themselves."

*Because that would negate our plans to sell it when we have the world in the palm of our hand.* "We already went over this, Arnie. We can't trust anyone to keep this under the radar. News of the virus would leak, and then—"

"Mass hysteria." Arnie shook his head, seemingly unconvinced.

"And what about the countries who don't possess the ability to replicate the vaccine or simply can't foot the bill to manufacture enough of it to inoculate their people?" *They'll be shit out of luck because we're not giving anything away for free.* "They're going to come to *us* for help. And when they do, we'll be there because we're the good guys—the United States of America. But we need to be ready. You can't expect those countries to wait patiently in line as their people are dying. They're liable to take drastic measures to ensure their own survival. We, as a nation, can't afford to take that risk."

Arnie stuffed his hands in the pockets of his wrinkled trousers. "So we're damned if we do and damned if we don't."

Griffin nodded solemnly and set a reassuring hand on Arnie's shoulder. "There's no easy answer here, Doc. Our best bet is to stay the course."

# CHAPTER TEN

Peyton stared at the red origami lips and tried her hardest to read the microscopic print inside. She spent several minutes squinting and turning the paper to make out the passwords Zoey had written. Impossible with the naked eye.

Desperate, she yanked Zoey's desk drawers open in search of a magnifying glass. Nothing. She eyed the locked bedroom door with a growing sense of dread. No way around it. She'd have to dig deep and find the courage to trek through zombie land once again.

"You're being ridiculous," she muttered. Everything out there was fake, for God's sake.

She walked confidently across the bedroom, opened the door, and came face-to-face with the lifelike zombie dangling from the wall, dead ahead. She reached out and tentatively brushed her fingertips across the bridge of its maggot-riddled nose. This zombie's true-to-life appearance was convincing enough, but it was made from nothing more than silicone.

A well-stocked arsenal of weapons adorned the wall on the opposite side, all of them plastic. Everything from pitchforks and axes to machetes and crossbows hung from carefully mounted brackets. She studied the impressive display. After careful consideration, she chose a black bat with spiked ridges and made her way to the kitchen. The bat felt reassuring in her hands.

One by one, she yanked the kitchen drawers open in search of a magnifying glass. No luck. She'd have to make one from scratch.

Peyton withdrew a pair of scissors from a porcelain zombie-head mug, found duct tape in the junk drawer, and opened Zoey's retro, baby-blue 1950s refrigerator. An unopened two-liter bottle of Pepsi rested on the top shelf. She poured out the Pepsi in the kitchen sink and used the scissors to cut two identical three-inch circles from the curved top of the plastic bottle. Curved sides out, she pressed the round pieces together, duct taped along their edges, and left a small opening. She found a bowl in the cabinet—blood-red, of course, to complement the overall decor—filled it with water, and submerged the soon-to-be lens. She squeezed the curved sides together and then released them. The small opening along the edge allowed the lens to fill with water. Once filled, she taped the area to seal it and dried the lens with a dish towel that was designed to look like a blood-soaked rag. She held the lens up for inspection and grinned. Presto—a DIY magnifying glass.

Peyton withdrew the origami lips and set the lens over the microscopic scribble. The once-illegible print suddenly enlarged to size twenty font. She reviewed the long list of passwords, committing them to memory as she read.

*PotatoChipsAreMyFriends*

*IamHungry*

*RunForYourLivesHelplessChips*

*PotatoChipMassacre*

*CrunchyAndSoSatisfying*

Magnifying lens in hand, Peyton looked up as the door to Zoey's apartment swung open.

"Good. You're still here." Zoey stepped over to join her at the counter. Her eyes grew wide when she spotted the empty Pepsi bottle. "You drank my Pepsi?"

"You left me no choice," Peyton shot back, holding up the red origami lips. "Why would you do this?"

"To annoy you. Did it work?"

Peyton leaned back against the counter, crossed her arms, and gave Zoey a stern look.

"Nice magnifier. I see my Pepsi went to a good cause." Zoey reached for the spiked bat on the counter. "What's this doing here?"

"Fell off the wall," Peyton lied.

Zoey's eyes narrowed as she gazed back and forth between her and the bat.

Peyton cleared her throat and glanced at her Apple Watch. The game should just be approaching halftime. "What are you doing back so early?"

"Have you searched the cabinets yet?" Zoey asked.

She pointed. "Just that one."

"Good. Close your eyes."

"Why would I do that?"

"Just…trust me."

"I *can't* trust you." She held up the list of microscopic passwords. "Case in point."

"Fine. Here." Zoey handed her the spiked bat, reached for the kitchen cabinet, and swung it open.

A zombie head with glowing red eyes popped up and screamed, "Brains! Give me brains!" His demonic voice was chilling.

Peyton nearly went into cardiac arrest right there in Zoey's kitchen. Before she knew it, the bat was on the floor, and her service weapon was in her hands, cocked, aimed at the zombie's decaying forehead, and ready for the kill shot.

"Those are the reflexes of a solid agent," Zoey said as soon as the creature's thunderous mantra came to an end.

She lowered and holstered her weapon, seething. "How *dare* you?"

"Hey"—Zoey threw her hands up in a gesture of surrender—"I tried to warn you."

"Your warning was like telling someone to bring an umbrella to a tsunami. I'm *pregnant* for God's sake."

Zoey rolled her eyes. "You're pulling the baby card?"

"It's not a card. What you did just now was—"

"Funny?" Zoey finished.

"Try reckless, unprofessional, and potentially disastrous."

"Relax. I did this to Sterling all the time. You'll get used to it." Zoey leaned down, retrieved the bat from the floor, and handed it to her. "And, for the record, I staged this prop *before* I knew you were pregnant."

Peyton stared at the bat in her hands and fought the urge to beat Zoey over the head with it. "You came back early to warn me." Now she understood why Zoey had ducked out of the second half of the game. After learning of her pregnancy, Zoey had probably started to worry about the possibility of scaring her. Interesting. In the short time they'd worked together, Zoey had twice demonstrated a tendency to protect children—first with the young girl in Niger and now with Peyton's baby.

Extensive psychological testing had revealed this trait in Zoey at the start of her career with the CIA. In fact, a stern warning had been issued to Peyton the moment she accepted her promotion as Zoey's handler: there was a strong likelihood that Zoey would disregard orders during a mission if a child's well-being was at all in question.

During her briefing, it was also revealed that Zoey had a tendency to fight for the underdog. She walked a fine line psychologically between CIA agent and vigilante. In the end, Dr. Pokale surmised that this was Zoey's greatest asset. Her natural inclination to protect the innocent was what made her an effective undercover operative.

She glanced up from the bat in her hands and met Zoey's round-eyed gaze. "If you're expecting me to say thank you for saving me from the booby trap that *you* set, think again."

"You're welcome. But there's another," Zoey admitted.

"Booby trap?"

Zoey nodded.

"Fine." She held the bat at the ready. "But I'm closing my eyes this time."

"That's the spirit." Zoey led her from the kitchen, down the hall, and into the bedroom.

Zoey took a seat at her desk and powered up her laptop. She felt the barest stirrings of guilt about her enjoyment at seeing Peyton's reaction to the demon zombie.

Peyton looked around warily. "I thought you said there was another booby trap," she said, keeping her voice down.

"There is." Zoey glanced up at her and frowned. "But whispering won't do any good. It's not like the booby trap can hear us."

Peyton pulled up a chair and took a seat beside her.

She entered her password but paused on the last keystroke. "Now would be a good time to cover your eyes."

Peyton did, without hesitation this time.

"Ears, too," she added.

"Seriously?"

"Your funeral. We've been down this road."

Peyton sighed as she covered her ears.

Zoey had programmed the image of a demon summoned up from the fiery depths of cannibal hell to flash across the computer screen at sporadic intervals. Her intent, of course, was to scare Peyton as she perused her financial records and email accounts. She'd rigged it so blood-curdling screams would accompany the image through surround-sound stereo. Bracing herself, she hit the last keystroke.

Peyton peeked one eye open and flinched as the image flashed across the screen. She uncupped her ears as soon as the screams subsided. "My God, Zoey. Where'd you even find that...that...*thing*?" she asked with a look of disgust.

"That *thing* is a Photoshop masterpiece. I designed it myself."

"No wonder you came back early. You could've literally scared me to death." Peyton stared at her, clearly in shock.

"Come on. You're tougher than that. Besides"—she winked—"you had the bat for protection."

"Then move over before I beat you with it." Peyton waved the bat in the air. "Let me finish so I can get out of this godforsaken dungeon you call a home."

"Not so fast." She held her hand up. "I have to disable the rest."

"Seriously?" Peyton lowered the bat. "How many times did you program that thing to pop up?"

"A few"—Zoey shrugged as she typed—"dozen." Peyton waited silently beside her, breathing like an angry dragon. "There," she said finally. "All set."

"You're sure?" Peyton bit her lip uncertainly. "You removed *every* image?"

Zoey nodded. "I'm sure."

"Good." Peyton made good on her threat and walloped her on the back of her head, hard, with the plastic bat.

❖

Peyton caught sight of movement out of the corner of her eye. Zoey had fashioned a white flag out of a towel and broomstick, which she now waved slowly back and forth in the bedroom doorway.

"Truce?" Zoey called out.

"On one condition," Peyton replied.

"We've been over this. No conditions."

"Then no truce," Peyton shot back.

Zoey let the flag fall to the floor and entered the room a few seconds later, wearing a sword, shield, and spiked helmet. "Game's over. Pats won."

Peyton closed the laptop and spun around in the desk chair, bat in hand. "You're putting six students through college."

"And you have a rather serious case of kinemortophobia."

"What's that?"

"You're afraid of zombies."

"Am not."

"Are."

She tightened her grip around the bat, weighing her chances of circumventing Zoey's shield to land a decent blow. "What does my *alleged* fear of zombies have to do with the fact that you're putting six kids through college?"

Zoey shrugged. "Thought we were spewing random facts."

"Almost every penny you make is going to tuition and books. No wonder you drive that abomination you call a car."

"No need to get nasty. That car's been good to me."

Peyton stared at her. It was becoming clear that this particular operative was...complex, to say the least. "Why?"

"I don't know." Zoey shrugged again. "Maybe she likes me."

"Who likes you?" she asked, momentarily confused.

"My car."

Peyton cast her eyes to the floor. She was fast approaching her threshold for games. "Give me a straight answer, Zoey. Why are you putting those kids through college?"

The helmet slid down over Zoey's eyes as she sat on the edge of the bed. She pushed it back in place with the butt of her sword. "Because I can."

She waited, hoping Zoey would decide to elaborate. There was obviously more to the story. Instinct told her there was something monumental at play here, and she was determined to find out what it was. "I'll make a deal with you. I won't put my findings in a report if you just explain what's going on here…with these kids…in this building."

"No deal."

"You and I both know this will be a red flag to the CIA. They'll suspend your assignments until they get to the bottom of this."

"They can dig all they want. Won't find anything."

"Then talk to me, Zoey."

"I have a better offer. If you stay for dinner and a movie, I'll tell you everything you want to know."

"You mean, out *there*?" Peyton asked, gesturing with her spiked bat to the rest of the apartment.

"If you're that put off by my zombie crew, we can eat dinner and watch a movie in here."

She narrowed her eyes. Couldn't be that easy. "What's the catch?"

"No catch. I just want to give you the chance to get to know me as your operative." Zoey slid open a dresser drawer, withdrew a pair of sweatpants, and tossed them on the bed. "The more you learn about me, the better our missions will go."

*Give* her the chance? Like Zoey was doing her some kind of favor? *Please*. Did Zoey believe she was that naive? She caught a whiff of a home-cooked meal through the open bedroom door. It smelled *amazing*. All other thoughts came to a screeching halt. "Did you order takeout?"

Zoey grinned. "You cook for Horace all the time. Figured it was time someone cooked for you."

Skeptical, Peyton considered the offer. Zoey had something up her sleeve. She could smell it. And it just happened to smell really, *really* good. Her stomach growled. Her mouth watered. She couldn't think straight. All she could focus on was finding the source of that delicious aroma. Her stomach growled again, much louder this time.

Zoey raised an eyebrow as they both regarded her stomach.

This baby was nothing if not persistent. She finally exhaled, knowing a lost cause when she smelled one. At this particular juncture in her life, her lack of willpower couldn't be more apparent. "Fine," she said, defeated. "But you better hold up your end of the deal, or—"

"Let me guess." Zoey started walking backward toward the open bedroom door. "You'll put it in your report."

"I wasn't going to say that."

"You totally were." Zoey turned, stepped into the hallway, and disappeared around the corner.

"No, I wasn't."

"Almost forgot." Zoey's head reappeared in the doorway. "Feejays"—she pointed—"or no dinner."

"You said no catch."

"There isn't."

"Feejays are clearly a catch."

"You'll thank me. Besides, the Feejays I'm graciously lending you happen to be my favorite pair."

Peyton glanced at the half-folded sweatpants on the bed. A huge yawning emoji covered the butt. Tiny sleeping emojis dotted both pant legs. "I am *not* wearing those."

"Up to you. But dinner will not be served without the proper attire." Zoey hastily shut the door, leaving Peyton alone with the ugliest sweatpants on the planet. She'd never be caught dead in those things.

Ever.

No matter how hungry she was.

# CHAPTER ELEVEN

Zoey stepped behind Shadow and peered over her shoulder. She watched as her protégé used a spatula to transfer the night's meal from a plastic container to a blood-red plate.

"Honey-rosemary chicken with cherry tomatoes," Shadow said without looking up. She set a plate cover over the dish, turned to face Zoey, and casually leaned against the counter. "Did she agree to your terms?"

"Not yet. She's in there cursing the Feejays as we speak."

Shadow shook her head. "Resistance is futile."

Shadow was right. Nearly everyone in the building was already hooked. Feejays were like a drug. Even Sterling—Mr. Finicky, himself—owned eleven pairs. Zoey popped some popcorn in the microwave and grabbed a bottle of beer from the fridge. "Who cooked tonight?"

"Alejandro."

She nodded and sipped her beer. Everyone who lived in the building was required to learn the fundamentals of cooking. But Alejandro took it to the next level. He had a natural skill for blending flavors that she and the others were more than happy to sample. His mind was already set on becoming a neuroscientist, but he would've made an amazing chef. "Oh, here," she said, digging into the pocket of her jeans for the key ring. She handed it to Shadow.

"Three keys?" Shadow frowned and cast a nervous glance down the hall.

"She won't set foot outside the bedroom," Zoey assured her. "The zombies are like an invisible electric fence."

Shadow held up one of the keys. "This is your apartment key." She studied the other two keys. "Shit," she said, looking up with a mix of wonder and alarm. "You were serious about the bunker for a zombie apocalypse."

Zoey nodded. "It's off the beaten path, underground, and hard to find. You'll have access to everything from food and supplies to weapons and enough ammo to bring down the government." She sketched out a map of the bunker's location on the back of her cell phone bill and handed it to Shadow. "But please don't bring down the government while I'm away. I know you're perfectly capable, and our government can be a real pain in the ass, but—"

"One problem at a time. Survive the virus first. Take down our shitty government later." Shadow nodded enthusiastically. "Got it."

"Key number three unlocks the home of someone you haven't met yet," Zoey went on. "I need you and the others to check on him every day while North is busy looking for me."

She filled Shadow in on Peyton's neighbor, Horace. Once Peyton was briefed on Zoey's decision to go rogue, protocol dictated she'd be the one assigned to retrieve her. In the CIA's eyes, Zoey was now Peyton's operative and, therefore, *her* problem. When the time came, and with no clear options for Horace's continued care, Peyton would struggle with leaving him behind. As far as Zoey could tell, Horace had no one else. He depended exclusively on Peyton.

She was about to take Peyton on a cat-and-mouse trek around the world. The least she could do was lift this one small burden from Peyton's shoulders and arrange for Horace's care. With a baby on the way, her handler already had enough to worry about.

"Have you had your flu shot yet?" Zoey asked, suddenly serious.

"Last month. You?"

She nodded. "Can you find out if there's anyone here who hasn't?"

"Our resident germaphobe beat you to the punch. He started a sign-up sheet in September. Demanded proof of immunization and threatened everyone with his famous kale soup if they didn't comply by October 10."

"God help us." Zoey put a hand over her stomach. "Not the kale soup."

"We all made a beeline to the nearest clinic."

"Everyone?"

"Everyone." Shadow bumped shoulders with her. "Don't waste time worrying about us. It's the rest of the world that needs you."

"See you tomorrow?"

Shadow nodded. "I'll help you make up with your girlfriend."

"She's *not* my girlfriend."

"You never told me what happened between you two."

"Irreconcilable differences." She shook her head, already feeling the urge to visit the shooting range with a paper cutout of Viv. "Whatever happens, please make sure I don't slip a cyanide pill in her drink." She knew she'd be tempted if she had any with her. "Or a grenade," she added. "And don't let me take her to the top of any nearby buildings under the ruse of a romantic date because I'll just pitch her over the top." She thought about it some more and sighed, deciding to come clean so Shadow could step in if she lost control. "And do *not* let me cross any busy streets with her because I'll likely push her into oncoming traffic." Unfortunately, they needed Vivian alive. She was their only hope of keeping the president in check.

Shadow raised an eyebrow. "Anything else?"

Zoey took a deep breath. She felt relieved—lighter, actually—now that everything was out in the open. "Think that about covers it."

"Rewards at the end of a difficult task have always worked for me. Tell you what, if Viv is still alive and relatively unscathed by the end of your meeting tomorrow, I'll get you that new pair of Feejays you've been wanting."

"The ones with the little poop emojis?"

Shadow nodded. "Consider them yours. All you have to do is refrain from murdering the secretary of state." They bumped fists. "Easy-peasy. You got this."

Zoey knocked softly on the bedroom door. "You decent?"

"That's a matter of opinion," Peyton answered grumpily from the other side. "Am I naked? No. Am I dressed decently enough to be seen by anyone other than the proud owner of the ugliest sweatpants on the planet? Definitely not."

Zoey cracked the door open and cast her eyes on her Feejay-wearing handler. She pushed the door open the rest of the way and savored the moment with a grin. Feejays on the bottom half. Black blazer over a burgundy-and-black-striped rib-knit shirt on the top. Peyton looked like a fashion model in the middle of a nervous breakdown.

"Happy?"

"Very." Zoey opened her closet and grabbed a gray cotton T-shirt. "Here," she said, tossing it to Peyton.

"No." Peyton let it fall to the floor.

"No?" she repeated, frowning.

"No, thank you."

"You plan on watching a movie…in the blazer?"

Peyton crossed her arms and met her gaze defiantly. "At least half of me will be dressed tastefully."

"Suit yourself," she said, stepping back to admire the new fashion statement.

Peyton cut right to the chase. "Where's dinner?"

She stepped into the hallway, lifted the tray of food, and carried it to Peyton's side of the bed.

Like a starving velociraptor that just spotted a flock of helpless sheep, Peyton never took her eyes from the chicken. "That popcorn better be yours. I didn't put these on just for you to do a bait and switch."

"Popcorn's mine, but the chocolate milk's all yours," Zoey assured her. "This dish goes best with chardonnay, but I thought milk might be better for the baby."

Peyton scooted back against the pillows and headboard as Zoey set the wooden tray over her lap. She lifted the bowl of popcorn, walked around the bed, and took her seat on the other side as Peyton draped a napkin over her lap and dug in.

"What are we watching?" Peyton asked.

"We're tackling your fear of zombies with some exposure therapy."

Peyton's eyes grew wide. "While I'm eating?"

She grabbed the remote off the nightstand, clicked on the TV, and scrolled through her library of purchased movies. "We'll start small." She selected the animated movie *ParaNorman* and played the trailer for Peyton.

"Poor kid," Peyton said as soon as the trailer ended. She daintily dabbed at the corners of her mouth with the napkin. "Destined for life as a loner. Bullied at school because everyone thinks he's weird. No friends. No hope for a decent life."

"*That's* what you got from the trailer?"

"Can't we watch something happier?"

"Zombie movies don't get any happier than that. Take it or leave it."

Peyton hesitated.

"We can watch *Rabid*. It's about a woman who loses part of her face in an accident, undergoes a radical treatment to fix it, and then starts craving human flesh."

Peyton set her fork down and squeezed her eyes shut.

"*ParaNorman* it is," Zoey said, stuffing another handful of popcorn in her mouth.

When Peyton had finished eating, she paused the movie to brush her teeth with the travel-size toothbrush that she kept within reach at all times. Zoey knew from their travels together that Peyton always brushed her teeth after every meal, a habit Zoey had developed, as well. Seeing countless cases of meth mouth when she was a kid made her just as obsessive about oral hygiene as Peyton. At least that was one thing they had in common.

Zoey took their dishes to the kitchen and then joined Peyton in the bathroom.

"Do you mind?" Peyton asked.

"You're done peeing, so what's the big deal?" She squeezed some toothpaste on her toothbrush. "Besides, this is what you do on a sleepover."

Peyton spat in the sink and looked at her like she'd just suggested sex. "I am *not* sleeping over. That wasn't part of the deal."

"We'll see," she replied through the toothpaste foam. "There's floss and mouthwash in the drawer there if you want some."

Peyton helped herself. "You're a very messy brusher."

"And you shed a lot." Zoey reached behind Peyton to pry several strands of dark auburn hair from the back of her blazer. As she did, a sizeable drop of white toothpaste foam landed on Peyton's sleeve. "Oops. Now I guess you'll have to take that off."

Peyton dried her hands on a nearby towel and shrugged out of the blazer with a look of disgust. "You did that on purpose."

Zoey held the toothbrush in the corner of her mouth as she unscrewed the cap from the toothpaste and smeared a dollop across the shoulder of Peyton's rib-knit top. She pointed. "I did *that* on purpose.

The drool was an accident." Another drop of white drool hit the floor near Zoey's bare feet. "See? Another accident."

"Are you seriously this immature?"

"Is that stick up your ass *ever* coming out?"

Without another word, Peyton turned and stormed from the bathroom.

Maybe by the time she was done brushing her teeth, Peyton would be gone and on her way home. Driven away by a little drool. Who knew it'd be that easy?

If she left, then Zoey wouldn't have to share anything about the residents in her building. If she stayed, then she was now probably wearing Zoey's T-shirt. Either way, it was a win-win.

Zoey washed her hands and opened the door to find Peyton waiting on the bed. She was curled around a navy-blue throw blanket and wearing the T-shirt that Zoey had offered earlier. The soiled blazer and rib-knit top were now folded neatly on the desk. "Comfy?" she asked.

Peyton watched her as she dimmed the lights and walked around the bed. "Why do you want me to wear your clothes so badly?"

"I'm a shareholder in Feejays. This is my marketing strategy."

"I just went through your finances, so I know that's a lie. Try again." Peyton offered her half of the throw blanket. "The truth this time."

"I've been having fantasies about you wearing my clothes since we met. I'm so turned-on I can hardly stand it."

"And I've never felt so attractive in my life. Pregnant. Bloated. Gassy. Wearing sweatpants with feet and a cotton Fruit of the Loom T-shirt."

"Gassy?" Zoey asked.

Peyton nodded and held her gaze. "And now we're sharing a blanket."

She couldn't help but be impressed. Her prim and proper handler had just joked about farting. At least, Zoey *thought* she was joking. Maybe she should get the other blanket down from the closet, just to be safe.

Peyton shifted on the bed to face her. "What's up, Zoey? Something's bothering you. I can see it."

"Right. You can tell something's bothering me because you know me so well."

"I don't yet. But I'd like to."

"Unbelievable." Zoey shook her head and sighed. "Who would've guessed? Turns out you're no different than most of the men I meet."

Peyton wrinkled her forehead in confusion. "How so?"

"You obviously have a one-track mind."

"You think I'm trying to *seduce* you?" Peyton asked, drawing back like she'd just stepped too close to a bonfire. "I'm not."

She'd succeeded in putting Peyton on the defensive. Good. "My point is, you have ulterior motives."

Peyton stared at her. "You're right. I did," she admitted. "Ever since we were paired, I've been trying to figure out how to get inside your head. Because a handler is only as good—"

"As her agent," Zoey finished. She nodded, surprised by Peyton's candor.

"But then I set foot in this apartment. At first, I thought you had an unnatural obsession with death. Maybe you'd missed your calling as a medical examiner. Or maybe you dabbled on the side as a serial torturer, committing your crimes during missions abroad to keep from getting caught."

"And you agreed to watch a movie with me?" Zoey frowned. "Alone and pregnant? At night?"

"When I walked into your bedroom, I realized what you'd done— what it all meant."

Zoey's mind reeled. Was Peyton saying what she thought she was saying? No one had ever figured it out before. She returned Peyton's gaze but said nothing, determined not to give anything away.

"As your handler, you know I'm required to review your file."

Zoey nodded. Peyton had her full attention now. Where was she heading with this?

"Sterling took you in when you were twelve. Not much is known about you before then. Whatever happened in your life had traumatized you so deeply that you couldn't remember who you were. But I think that was a ruse. I think you remembered everything but made the conscious choice to push it down in order to survive and move on with your life." Peyton paused, searching Zoey's face for a chink in her armor. "How am I doing so far?"

"You got all that…from my bedroom?" Zoey asked, pretending to be mystified as she gazed around the room.

"You protected that little girl in Niger," Peyton went on. "You returned to your apartment early to disable the booby traps and protect my baby, who also happens to be a girl."

Zoey felt her heart pick up speed. Impossible. Peyton couldn't have figured it out.

## CHAPTER TWELVE

S hadow led me to your apartment," Peyton went on. "It's obvious the two of you share a bond. She's like a little sister to you, isn't she?"

Zoey swallowed, aware that she was now drawing quick, shallow breaths. "I have no idea what you're driving at, but can you get to the point so we can finish the movie?"

"You lost someone close to you when you were young. If I had to venture a guess, I'd say it happened just before Sterling found you. You were genuinely traumatized—that much is evident from your file—but I believe you conjured up the amnesia to keep from talking about what happened. A very smart move, by the way." Peyton studied her, quiet.

Zoey couldn't bring herself to say anything. She held Peyton's gaze.

"You lost a little sister. Something awful happened to her. It wasn't your fault, but you blame yourself." Peyton reached out to touch her arm. "You blame yourself for not protecting her."

"A-plus work there, Agent North." Zoey clapped her hands in mock applause. "I mean it. That was really, really good. Unfortunately, none of it is true."

Peyton drew uncomfortably close, their faces mere inches apart. "You're lying."

Zoey could smell her minty-fresh breath and had half the mind to kiss her. Maybe kissing Peyton would derail this train of thought and put a pin in the conversation indefinitely.

"When you're lying, your orbicularis oculi tenses." Peyton reached up and tenderly touched the left side of Zoey's face. "Right here. I spotted it in Niger when I asked if you knew anything about your target's murder."

So that's why Dr. Pokale had given her the third degree in their session. Peyton must've documented her suspicions about Zoey having inside knowledge about her target's demise. *Shit*. She had to get this tell under control. Damn Sterling for keeping it to himself all these years.

"Don't lie to me, Zoey. Tell me you don't want to talk about it"—Peyton gently swept Zoey's hair out of her face—"but don't lie to me."

She held Peyton's gaze as she considered her words. The moment she shared the mere existence of her sister with someone was the moment she had to admit that Ella was gone. Forever. Before today, revealing anything about this to her handler could very well have put her career with the CIA in jeopardy. But it didn't matter now. None of it did. She was getting ready to betray their trust and use everything they had taught her against them.

"I don't want to talk about it," she whispered, haunted by the truth of her own words. Immediately, she felt the hairline cracks begin to form in the walls she'd built around the precious memories of her sister. Those were the memories she held on to the tightest. Keeping them to herself was like storing a rare-edition comic book in its cellophane sleeve. They were sacred. And she shared them with no one—not even Sterling. As far as she knew, he had no idea she'd even had a sister.

Peyton nodded as she reached out to give Zoey's arm a gentle squeeze.

"What the hell was *that*?"

"What?" Peyton asked in alarm.

Zoey held up her arm. "Did you just give me…an *arm* hug?"

"There's no such thing," Peyton said, rolling her eyes.

"There most certainly is. And you just gave me one." Zoey wiped her arm off like it had cooties from James Baggot in the fourth grade. Baggot the Maggot. Everyone except Zoey had called him that. "Congratulations. You just made an awkward moment even more awkward with that overly tender human touch."

"You're wiping off my arm hug? You can't wipe off a hug."

"I can, and I just did. It's gone. See?" Zoey held up her arm again.

"Still there. I can see it." Peyton pointed. "My hugs stick to any surface. Nonremovable for twenty-four hours."

Zoey lifted the remote and pushed *play* as Peyton settled against the pillows. The first part of her plan was working. Peyton was finally starting to loosen up. Good to know she had it in her to take a joke and tease back. Looked like there was a sense of humor in there, after all, along with the ability to play and be in the moment—something Peyton's psych assessments hadn't revealed over the years.

Pushing her handler to find out just how tightly she was wound was important for the journey ahead. If Peyton had continued to behave with unrelenting rigidity—as her personnel file indicated she would—then Zoey would've taken the appropriate measures to ensure Peyton wasn't assigned the task of capturing her. Being unable to live in the moment, play, and have a little fun could be detrimental for mother and baby during a high-stakes mission. Now she knew for sure that Peyton was capable of letting her hair down a little. This would be fun.

Peyton yawned beside her and sank deeper into the pillows. Perfect. From the looks of it, she'd soon be asleep and out of the way until morning. Zoey could finally start prepping for her new mission, and her handler would be none the wiser.

Peyton snuggled in more closely to the warm body beside hers. The skin-to-skin contact felt warm and reassuring—something she hadn't felt in a while. Unlike Ben's hairy, muscular chest, this body was smooth, soft, and smelled so tantalizingly *good*.

Wait.

Was that a breast?

She opened her eyes, met Zoey's gaze, and sat bolt upright. *No.*

Zoey sat up slowly beside her. "Hope that was as good for you as it was for me."

Peyton scooted to the other side of the bed, pulling the covers along with her. She realized then that she wasn't naked—thank *God*—but Zoey was just wearing a white tank top with lacy french-cut black panties. She tossed the covers over Zoey's bare legs, grabbed for a pillow, and hugged it tightly against her chest. Speechless, she stared at her operative in horror.

"I learned three things about you last night," Zoey said, yawning. "You weren't lying about the gas, you're really good at snuggling, and you're a big fan of boobs."

"God, please tell me we didn't snuggle all night." That was her weakness. Always had been. Whomever she fell asleep next to inevitably suffered the wrath of the snuggle. It'd been happening ever since she could remember. Didn't matter who it was. Any warm body within a four-foot radius was up for grabs. She'd stopped attending sleepovers with friends as a teenager because it had gotten totally out of control.

"Oh, we got our snuggle on." Zoey nodded with a knowing smile. "There's just *no* going back from what we did last night."

Peyton squeezed her eyes shut. This was beyond mortifying. The word didn't even exist for how mortified she felt. "Why didn't you wake me up and send me home?"

"And deny us both a good snuggle?" Zoey shook her head. "No way. That was a once-in-a-lifetime opportunity."

Then it hit her. *Horace.* She checked her watch: 5:06 a.m. She had to get home. She'd fixed dinner for him yesterday and left it in his fridge with instructions for reheating. But she hadn't checked on him last night before bed to make sure he was tucked in safely and not patrolling the neighborhood. What if he'd decided to take a late-night stroll without a coat and never made it home?

"Relax," Zoey said groggily beside her. "Horace is fine. He ate dinner, his clothes are set out, and breakfast is waiting for him on the counter."

"What? But how—"

"Shadow checked in on him last night after you fell asleep. I didn't have the heart to wake you."

"How'd she get inside his house?" Peyton put up her hand and shook her head. "Forget it. I don't want to know." She met Zoey's gaze, feeling angrier by the second. "What I do want to know is why you're playing these games with me, Zoey."

Zoey reached behind her, unplugged a small device, and lifted it from the nightstand. "Here," she said, handing it over.

Peyton glanced down at the illuminated screen to see Horace sleeping soundly in his bed. "A baby monitor?" Zoey's apartment was at least ten miles from her condo on Beacon Street. "How'd you get it to work from here?"

"It's Reboot's invention—one of the kids I'm putting through college. He's a tech wiz. He took it apart and rigged something to make it work. I don't know the specifics. If you want to ask him, be my guest. But I guarantee he'll bore you to death, and you'll come away from the chat more stupid than when you went in." Zoey stretched her arms above her head, looking as sexy as ever in a skinny-strap tank top with no bra. One strap dipped off her shoulder as she lowered her arms, exposing the top of her breast and precariously close to exposing more. Peyton forced herself to look away.

"Bottom line is he said it'll work from anywhere," Zoey went on. "That's good enough for me."

"Anywhere?" she asked. "As in…anywhere within the city of Boston?"

"This kid's way smarter than that. Pretty sure he meant anywhere on the planet. Maybe the universe. You'd have to ask him, but again, I don't recommend it."

Zoey sure was chatty this morning. "Dinner and a movie for the truth about why you're putting those kids through college." Peyton set the monitor in her lap. "That was the deal."

"Patience, my little cuddle bug. I'll tell you everything. But first, I need a shower to wake up. Didn't get much sleep last night on account of all the snuggling." Zoey stood from the bed, headed to the bathroom, and shut the door.

Peyton was about to object about having to wait when Zoey called out from the other side of the door.

"I'll make you some breakfast. That's usually a reward I reserve only for one-nighters who are particularly skilled in bed. Now, I know what you're thinking. You and I obviously didn't have sex." Peyton heard the toilet flush. "But all the snuggling we did feels somehow even more intimate. The least I can do is make you some breakfast as a thank-you. Then we can talk and eat and reminisce about our special night together."

*God, just kill me now.* Part of Peyton—the mortified part that despised the snuggle-loving traitor hidden deep within—wanted to resign as Zoey's handler on the spot, flee the scene, and move far, far away. But another, even deeper part of her wanted to find out what had prompted Zoey to put six teenagers through college. *Six.* She shook her head, trying to talk herself out of staying as she heard the shower turn on.

She realized then that she was in trouble. Learning more about

Zoey was now like a hunger she couldn't control. Peyton had never met anyone like her. She had a sudden, irresistible urge to peel back the layers of this complex, wisecracking operative and see for herself what lay underneath. It was like a physical *need*—not unlike the pregnancy cravings she'd always believed were total nonsense, until she started experiencing them. Maybe this obsession with penetrating Zoey's fortress had something to do with being pregnant. Hormones were doing strange things to her body. Were they affecting her mind, too? And why had she just used the word *penetrating*? Its sexual connotations were obvious. With all this talk about intimacy, Zoey was trying to get inside her head and had obviously succeeded.

She glanced down at the monitor. Horace sat up in bed. As unnerving as it was that Zoey knew the depth of her involvement with Horace's care, it told her two things: Zoey was extraordinarily adept at gathering intel, and perhaps more importantly, it showed she cared enough to do so. The nagging question of the hour was *why*. Had she done it to help Peyton, lighten her load, and make up for what a pain in the ass she'd been in Niger? She wanted to believe that, but instinct told her something else was at play here.

Whatever Zoey was up to, this was all part of her plan. Peyton just wasn't sure what that plan was or what—if anything—it had to do with her. All she could do now was wait and see how this played out. In the meantime, she intended to learn everything she could about Zoey. Something told her she'd need to arm herself with all the intel she could gather.

Griffin excused himself from his virtual meeting with the chairman of the Joint Chiefs of Staff to accept an incoming call from someone more important. He answered in a genial tone, "Defense Secretary Bick."

"Our weak link is growing weaker—too weak now to maintain the integrity of our circle."

"I understand, sir." Vice President Grady had just given him the green light to eject Arnie from their circle and replace him with a backup already in position at the CDC. Griffin shook his head, disappointed but unsurprised. He'd expected as much—hell, they all had—but he'd hoped Arnie would last a bit longer. "He showed up on your doorstep, too."

"Just left. I told him what he needed to hear to keep him quiet for another day or two. No guarantees beyond that." The vice president sighed. "Do me a favor, and don't tell Bellingham. She'll have a problem with this."

Secretary of State Vivian Bellingham was the only one in their circle whose heart occasionally still bled for the little guy—unless that little guy happened to be poor and Black. Then her compassion flew right out the window, and she was ruthless. Griffin wouldn't have believed it if he hadn't seen it for himself. But they weren't talking about a poor Black man. They were talking about Dr. Arnold Langston, an educated, professional *white* man. This, she'd have a problem with. He cautioned Grady, "She'll find out sooner or later."

"Later is better. She has the president's ear. If we give her the chance, she'll come up with a more colorful—and less permanent—solution for nipping this in the bud. But we both know this particular bud can't be nipped."

"It has to be cut off," Griffin agreed, nodding. "I'll take care of it."

## CHAPTER THIRTEEN

"Did you ever see *Fifty First Dates*?" Zoey asked as Peyton took a seat on the barstool at the kitchen counter.

Peyton looked warily at the life-size zombie beside her before turning her attention to Zoey. "No."

"Came out in 2004. Great movie. Drew Barrymore's character, Lucy, has amnesia. She lost the ability to store new memories after her car accident. Her family loves her very much, and all they want to do is keep her safe. They go to great lengths to manipulate her environment to keep her from finding out about her condition. They're afraid she wouldn't be able to handle it." Zoey finished pouring two glasses of orange juice, slid one across the counter, and glanced up to gauge Peyton's reaction. Beautiful as always, but the corners of her mouth were slightly turned down in a grumpy little frown.

"It's subtle," Peyton said, "but I see where you're going with this. Horace is fine. He has me. For now, that's enough."

"Horace is lucky to have you. That's not my point."

"What *is* your point?"

Zoey started dicing the red and green bell peppers for their Western omelets. "Everything's hunky-dory in Lucy's world. Years go by, and she's none the wiser—until Adam Sandler's character, Henry, strolls into her life. He meets her at a bar and falls head over heels. But when he returns the next day to see her again, she has no idea who he is. He begins the process of reintroducing himself each day, wooing her with grand gestures, determined to make a lasting impression. Unfortunately, with the dawn of each new day, she remembers nothing of the previous day and inevitably forgets who he is. In the end, Henry decides her inability to remember him shouldn't stop them from being in love and living their lives together."

Peyton's frown deepened. "I'm not in love with Horace."

"The part of the movie you'll want to pay particular attention to is the ending. Henry comes up with an ingenious solution to help Lucy remember him, even though she can't."

Peyton was quiet for so long that Zoey looked over her shoulder to make sure she was still there.

"Well?" Peyton asked, clearly annoyed. "I'm waiting."

"For what?"

"For you to tell me what Henry's solution was."

"No can do." Zoey shook her head. "I've given away too much already. You'll just have to watch the movie."

"I don't want to watch the movie."

Zoey smiled to herself as she finished dicing the peppers. It was like taking someone to the edge of an orgasm and then suddenly pulling away. "You'll want to make time for this one. Trust me."

Peyton sighed. "Why do you do that?"

"Do what?"

"Play games. Why can't you just say what you mean?"

As a former covert agent, Peyton was supposed to be good at reading between the lines. Clearly, that wasn't the case. "I'm *not* playing games." She set the knife down and turned to face Peyton. "You found out you were pregnant on the heels of losing your husband. Your next-door neighbor suffers from a form of amnesia that I wouldn't wish on my worst enemy. Instead of admitting him to a nursing home, you chose to take care of him yourself because he's like family. I respect that. Deeply. I don't know you well, but—from what I can tell—you're alone in this world, seemingly by choice. Your parents are gone. You have no siblings and no other family to speak of. For reasons I can only imagine, you've distanced yourself from whatever friendships you had before you met your husband. All you have now is Horace, this job, and that baby growing inside you." She eased her chastising tone when she saw the tears in Peyton's eyes. "If you're going to have this baby *and* take care of Horace, you need a support system. This is me reaching out to let you know you're not alone. I'll be there when you need me. Not as your operative." She paused, hoping her words carried the weight they were meant to. "As your friend."

Peyton looked away and studied the baby monitor in her hands, silent.

Zoey knew it was a lot to take in, but it was the truth. The sooner Peyton faced it, the better off she'd be. She tore off a sheet from the paper towel roll and pushed it across the counter to Peyton. "Please make note for future reference—this is a perfect example of when *not* to give an arm hug."

Peyton laughed as she dried her cheeks with the paper towel.

There. Thank God that was out of the way. Now they could get on with breakfast.

Peyton exited Zoey's apartment building and made her way to Ben's Volvo, which, to her surprise, still had all its tires. She sat behind the wheel, buckled her seat belt, and started the engine. The dashboard clock lit up: 7:56 a.m. Hard to believe almost three hours had passed since she'd woken up in Zoey's bed, copping a feel and snuggling with her operative. A flash of a memory returned to her—her cheek resting comfortably on one of Zoey's breasts, her hand on the other as the nipple hardened beneath her caress. She squeezed her eyes shut and cleared her mind of the unwelcome memory. Why was she thinking about Zoey's breasts? She had two of her own.

Her Apple Watch vibrated on her wrist, scolding her with a reminder that she was usually farther along in meeting her required minutes of exercise. She was already way behind schedule. By now, she'd have run five miles on her treadmill at home, completed a vigorous thirty-minute workout, showered, and changed. She was always ready to walk out the door by 6:20 a.m. on the nose.

Skipping her morning workout made her feel anxious. Routine brought her the comfort and structure she so desperately needed right now. A multifaceted approach of discipline, routine, and staying busy with zero downtime had been holding her together since Ben's death. If she slowed down, the grief would catch up, and then she'd be forced to face the truth. Doing so would only tarnish Ben's memory. But she owed more than that to her late husband. Didn't she?

She backed out of the parking space and headed home to shower and change. As she drove, her thoughts turned to Zoey's program, AIM—Abundance in Mindfulness.

She'd learned over breakfast that Zoey had started the program when Sterling purchased her condemned apartment building thirteen years ago. He'd made the necessary repairs to Mattapan Heights, and Zoey had moved in on her eighteenth birthday.

Zoey handpicked every kid, teenager, and young adult in her building. Rather than picking the brightest of the bunch as Peyton would have done, she intentionally went straight for the troublemakers—the kids that the system had run out of options for and didn't know what to do with. Ironically, those were the kids Zoey sought out.

She took them in, talked to them, learned what made them tick, and, over time, helped them discover their passions. Sometimes it took a while, but once they figured out what really made them excited, she took it and ran with it. Whatever they decided they wanted to do in life, Zoey vowed to support it, no matter how farfetched it seemed. One by one, she filled the apartments in her building with kids who eventually found their purpose and worked hard to fulfill it.

The rules were simple: no criminal activity, and each kid had to do their part to pay it forward. Zoey made it clear to all of them that they owed her nothing and never would. They were encouraged to invest whatever good fortune they experienced later in life into their communities, in whatever ways inspired them most.

Sterling's building provided each kid with a safe place to build their own cocoon. With time, patience, hard work, and Zoey's dedicated support, they morphed into scientists, engineers, professors, journalists, politicians, doctors, lawyers—the list went on. According to Zoey, no one had ever dropped out of the program.

AIM was now pretty much running itself. As time wore on, a hierarchy of sorts had evolved where the older kids looked after the younger kids, all without being asked. They were a family, Zoey explained. They knew they could count on her to be there for them, no matter what. More importantly, the bonds they formed with each other were strong and stretched far beyond the walls of Sterling's dilapidated building.

Zoey made the same pledge of unwavering support to every kid who came to live there. She was convinced that's all they needed—to know someone would always be there for them and support them on their journey. Whatever that journey might be. The rest was up to them.

It occurred to her then that Zoey had just done the same for her during their chat in the kitchen. Zoey made it clear that her offer of friendship and support extended beyond the bounds of their professional relationship as operative and handler. It had been many years since anyone had reached out to her like that.

Peyton pulled to the side of the road as tears blurred her vision. Zoey's words returned to her...*I don't know you well, but—from what I can tell—you're alone in this world, seemingly by choice. Your parents are gone. You have no siblings and no other family to speak of. For reasons I can only imagine, you've distanced yourself from whatever friendships you had before you met your husband.*

Zoey had hit the nail on the head, as astute as ever.

Peyton withdrew a travel pack of tissues from the glove compartment and wiped at her tears. A futile act. They just coursed down her cheeks even faster.

She'd been an introvert for as long as she could remember, preferring books and solitude over social engagement. But she was also fortunate to be part of a cherished group of friends who understood and accepted her for who she was—girls she'd known and grown up with since kindergarten who never allowed her to stay away too long. The four of them even attended the same college and shared adjoining dorm rooms. They coaxed her out of her shell more times than she could count. Despite her best efforts to resist their adventures and focus solely on her studies, she never regretted joining in—not once.

All of that changed when Ben entered the picture during her junior year.

Was she really doing this? Here? Now? Confronting the truth of her marriage to Ben was on her list of things to do *eventually*. She just hadn't envisioned doing it on the side of the road, sobbing as cars sped past. And she was on her last tissue, for God's sake. All she had left was a roll of paper towels in the back seat.

Well, it looked like now was as good a time as any. She had to process these feelings somehow, and quickly, because she couldn't drive anywhere until she could see again. *Damn you, pregnancy hormones.*

❖

Zoey pulled up in front of Battery Wharf Hotel, an upscale hotel perched along Boston's waterfront that was just a three-minute walk from the Freedom Trail. She and Viv had made the mistake of walking that trail together one evening after a particularly satisfying romp in one of the hotel rooms above. Halfway through, they realized their differences were severe enough to warrant separate cab rides back to the hotel. The sex had been great while it lasted, but there was just no going back after that.

She climbed out of her Toyota and handed her keys to the valet attendant. She didn't bother educating him on how to start her finicky car. If he was any good, he'd figure it out himself. If not, then her car would still be there when her meeting concluded, and she wouldn't have to wait for it.

Vivian was already waiting for her at the bar, drink in hand. Silky golden locks framed a deceptively angelic face with full lips and large blue eyes with long lashes. She was much fuller and curvier than Zoey, her breasts always bursting forth from the tight quarters of their lacy double Ds with a sigh. As usual, everything about Viv's appearance was in perfect order—nails, hair, makeup. Everything. Right down to the Neiman Marcus plum-colored tweed skirt suit, matching Fendi handbag, and Louis Vuitton slingback pumps.

The sight of her made Zoey want to barf. She made an unintelligible sound of disgust as she strode to the bar.

"Feejays," Shadow reminded her through her earpiece.

"Feejays," she whispered back, more for her own benefit than Shadow's.

Viv sipped her wine and met her gaze as she took a seat on the barstool beside her. The bar had been emptied of its patrons as a standard security precaution. Bodyguards were already in position at both entrances, and the bartender had been replaced by an imposter.

Zoey nodded a tightlipped greeting to the handsome young man she recognized behind the bar. He traveled everywhere with Viv and wore many hats: chef, bartender, massage therapist, yoga instructor, nutritionist, fashion consultant, and hairstylist. Zoey had always suspected he'd be willing to fill *any* role. Judging from the way his gaze lingered on Viv, she could now add boy toy to that list.

She and Viv watched in silence as he gracefully filled a frosted glass with Sam Adams, set it on a napkin in front of Zoey, and retreated to the far corner of the bar, presumably out of earshot.

Viv was the first to break the ice. "I was surprised to hear from you."

Zoey took a long drink from her glass and turned to meet Viv's gaze with all the sincerity she could muster. "I've always hated the way we left things," she lied.

"Really?" Viv raised an eyebrow. "You were spewing some pretty vile things at me the last time I saw you."

Zoey nodded. "I'd like to apologize for that. My behavior that night was inappropriate and uncalled for." With any luck, Viv would leave it at that, and they could move on.

"I appreciate your apology. I really do." Viv sipped her wine. "To put this to rest, however, I'll need to know what, specifically, you're apologizing for."

"Specifically?"

Viv nodded, her gaze forthright.

She took another long drink as Shadow whispered in her ear. "Just say whatever she wants to hear."

Zoey set her glass on the bar top. "Everything that came out of my mouth that night was—"

"Asinine, moronic, weak-minded?" Viv finished with a snicker.

Zoey took yet another long drink as Shadow whispered in her ear, "Go with it. Admit you were an ass and move on."

"Yep," Zoey said on the heels of a small belch. "All that and more."

"So you agree with me now? You've come to see the light?"

*Fuck.* How was she going to do this? She drained her glass, aware she'd likely need ten more beers and a handful of shots just to get through the next few minutes of this friendly chat. Zoey nodded, unable to bring herself to speak. Maybe, by some miracle, that small gesture of simply agreeing would be enough. But something told her Shadow was about to get an earful.

## Chapter Fourteen

Peyton tossed her last tissue in the car's trash can, reached into the back seat for the roll of paper towels, and tore off a sheet to blot her cheeks and nose. The full-size sheet was obviously overkill. She smiled sadly, realizing Ben must've bought this roll for his car. They'd had an ongoing dispute for years about which was better—full-size sheets or sheets with perforations that allowed you to decide on the fly. She was a firm believer in having choices and loved the perforated lines that allowed her to wipe her spills accordingly. He, on the other hand, was a firm believer in tradition. He'd grown up with full-size paper towel sheets, and that was that. Since she was the one who did most of the shopping for groceries and household products, their home was usually stocked with her preferences. Ben, of course, had gone along with it. But he'd quietly stocked his own car with the paper towels he really wanted.

The realization just made her cry harder. In that moment, the guilt she felt over forcing half-size paper towel sheets on her husband for the duration of their marriage was almost too much to bear. How could she have done that to him? She shook her head as sobs wracked her body. She was a monster, plain and simple.

She blew her nose in the enormous paper towel. Keeping extra tissues on hand for the rest of her pregnancy might be a good idea. She was crying more and more these days.

Peyton took a deep breath and mustered the courage to face the demons of her past—the *real* reason she was so upset. She thought back to the night before college graduation. Lizzie and Grace had gone to a movie, so she and Callie were alone in the house. They'd danced around a friendship with countless flirtatious moments for years. That night, after a few beers on the porch and a friendly game of Truth or Dare, they ended up in bed together.

It was the first—and only—time Peyton was intimate with a woman. Every caress, every kiss, every moan of pleasure was burned into her memory, not because it was the most incredible sex of her life, but because she'd realized then that she was in love with Callie.

Peyton squeezed her eyes shut, willing the memory to fade. She hadn't allowed herself to think about that night since it happened. She'd worked hard to push the memory of Cal's touch deep into her subconscious. But the memory was still very much alive, just as vivid and strong as the night they'd made it.

She and Cal never discussed what happened between them because Peyton made sure they weren't alone long enough to talk about it. Eventually, she convinced herself that their choices that night were triggered entirely by fear. Fear of the unknown. Fear of the separate paths that she, Callie, Lizzie, and Grace were getting ready to take. No matter the reason, the fact remained that she had cheated on Ben. Ben proposed to her a short time later, and that was that. She never looked back.

At least, that's what she'd been telling herself all these years. But the truth was coming out now, whether she wanted it to or not. She never felt for Ben what she'd felt for Cal. She'd eagerly accepted Ben's proposal, not because she loved him but because she had an overwhelming need to prove that she wasn't in love with a *woman*.

Peyton wasn't even sure why she was so uncomfortable with her sexuality. She hadn't been raised by homophobic parents. When they were alive, her parents would've loved, accepted, and supported her, regardless. She didn't doubt that for a second. It boiled down to the expectations she'd placed on herself. At some point along the way, she'd decided being bisexual didn't match up with who she felt she *should* be.

She realized then that her greatest regret was abandoning Cal. When they parted ways after graduation, she avoided Cal's calls and texts for years before Cal finally gave up. It was a mistake she'd never have the chance to correct. Callie was killed by a drunk driver four years after graduation.

Peyton cried even harder there in Ben's car on the side of the road.

For the best friend she lost. For the chance at love she never took. And for all the things she wished she had said to Cal.

Her friend Lizzie had reached out to Ben and asked him to break the news. Peyton had shut all of them out—Grace, Lizzie, and Callie. She kept them on the outskirts of her marriage as if they were a threat to the life she was building with Ben. In some ways, they were. The three of them knew her so well. If she had kept them close and allowed them the access to her life that they were accustomed to getting, they would've forced her to confront the truth.

Dammit. What *was* the truth?

Her marriage to Ben was a coverup. There it was. How could she have done that to him? A part of her had grown to care for him deeply. But he'd deserved more than that. He'd deserved to be loved the way she'd loved Callie.

Another realization struck like a rattlesnake. She was wildly attracted to Zoey.

What kind of monster did that make her? Her husband of thirteen years had just died, for God's sake. He was a good man who'd loved her through and through. They agreed early on not to have children, but he would've been over the moon about this baby. How could she feel attracted to *anyone* so soon after his death, while carrying his child? How could she betray Ben's memory like that?

Feeling attracted to someone wasn't usually within the scope of the average person's control. But she wasn't the average person. It boiled down to a simple case of mind over matter. Willpower and discipline. That's what would get her through this.

She flashed back to the ultimatum Zoey had given her—Feejays or no dinner—and the promise she'd made to herself that she wouldn't wear them, no matter what. Peyton glanced down at the Feejays that were still on her body. If this was any indication of her willpower with Zoey, then she was in serious trouble.

Okay, Feejays were one thing. Feeling attracted to her operative was another. She could feel attracted all she wanted, but that's where it ended. She promised herself she would never, ever act on it. Period. End of story.

As to what to do with the rest of it—the question of her sexuality in the face of losing her husband, finding out she was pregnant, and being assigned as Zoey's handler—it would all have to wait. She'd put it on a mental back burner for the time being. Right now, she needed to get home, shower, change, and head to the office.

She tore off another paper towel and blew her nose loudly. Time to gather herself together and get on with the day.

❖

"It's good you understand now that you're fighting a lost cause." Viv shook her head and sighed. "No matter what you do, some people will always be a drain on government resources. Last I heard, they were your pet project in that Mattapan hellhole you call home. What happened? One of them finally hold you up at gunpoint and rob you?" She didn't even wait for an answer. "Drugs. It's always drugs with them."

*Here we go.* Zoey chugged the last of her beer and waved the boy toy over for another.

"The mission objective has changed." Shadow's voice was surprisingly calm. "You'll only get our agreed-upon reward if you murder her."

Viv dabbed at her lipstick with her napkin. "They get into a gang, sell drugs on the street, and then knock up some teenage neighborhood hussy. Instead of giving the baby up for adoption and finishing school to break the cycle of poverty, she has the baby while he's in jail."

"Cyanide," Zoey coughed into her hand.

"Too quick," Shadow whispered. "I like pushing her from the top of a building better."

"She's lazy—too lazy to work," Viv went on, "so she does what her mama did and applies for welfare. She ends up with a free ride—free rent, free food, free medical care—as long as she keeps popping out those babies from different daddies."

Shadow conceded. "On second thought, I don't care how you do it. I'll buy you Feejays for life if you just cap her ass now."

"You're wasting your time on them." Viv took another sip of wine, pinkie extended. "They're too busy milking the government and feeling entitled to whatever they get. Boohoo. Let's be honest, poor people are too stupid to end their own cycle of poverty."

And there she was—the woman who'd finally revealed her true colors on their walk together along the Freedom Trail. Zoey despised prejudice of any kind, but this was particularly disturbing. Vivian was, after all, one of the highest-ranking members of the United States government. Sitting so close to the vilest human being she'd ever met made her long to break the law in ways she'd never before considered.

Shadow's voice sounded in her ear. "Those bodyguards look slow. You'll have plenty of time to escape after you sever her carotid with your pocketknife. I can have a getaway car ready and waiting for you outside in two minutes."

"Those people have spent generations taking advantage of our government. But the government is finally putting its foot down. They'll get what's coming to them. I've made sure of that."

Zoey's mind raced, and she didn't like where it was heading. Time to do what she did best: use her tools to her advantage, and get on with the mission. "I heard," she said cryptically. "So that was your idea." She nodded.

Viv narrowed her eyes and studied her but said nothing.

"You guessed right," Zoey went on. "A group of kids I was helping turned on me. They ambushed me, tied me up, and pistol-whipped me when I refused to give them the password to my bank account." She pushed her hair aside to reveal a prominent scar near her temple—put there by her own mother in a fit of rage after she discovered that Zoey had flushed her heroin down the toilet. "I was naive to think anything I did for them would make a difference. I bent over backward for those kids, gave them all the tools they needed to be successful and make their own way in life. But you're right, they don't want to work. They're inherently lazy. That sense of entitlement has been passed down for too many generations. One way or another, they're stealing from us—either at gunpoint or through the welfare system." She took a long drink of her beer and shrugged. "I heard about what you decided to do to take care of the problem. I wanted to apologize for the things I said that night. More to the point, I wanted to tell you that I support what you're doing."

Viv looked away. "I have no idea what you're talking about."

"Bird of Prey," Zoey prompted.

Viv stared at her.

Zoey prayed her hunch was wrong, but she had to venture out onto the thinnest branches to find out for sure. "Stocking pharmacies, clinics, and doctors' offices in poor neighborhoods around the country with the *real* flu vaccine was brilliant. Everyone else gets the good stuff—the vaccine that'll protect them from the deadliest virus known to man." She shook her head. "An ingenious solution."

The words felt disgusting in her mouth—a betrayal to Sterling, Shadow, her kids at Mattapan Heights. Part of her worried about what Shadow was thinking—and feeling—on the other end of the earpiece. If her suspicions about the vaccine were true, then they were in a lot more trouble than she'd originally thought. Not only would she and Shadow have to deliver the vaccine's formula to the rest of the world, but they'd also have to fix what the US government had done to its own people.

"If there's any truth to your theory—and I'm not saying there is—it would be a gross misuse of power."

"A gross misuse of power is holding a gun to my head and demanding money."

"How did you hear about this alleged virus and plans to exterminate our own people?" Contrary to her words, there was no concern whatsoever in Viv's voice or expression.

"You know what I do for a living. It's my job to gather intel and dig up secrets." She shrugged. "I'm just better at it than most."

"And what are you planning to do with this information?"

"I'm doing it now." Zoey met Vivian's gaze and leaned in for a slow kiss. Long seconds ticked by as their tongues danced in a familiar rhythm. She pulled back and gently caressed Viv's cheek with her thumb. "Just letting you know I'm here…for whatever assistance you might need along the way."

Vivian licked her lips seductively. "Make sure you get your flu shot at a *reputable* clinic this year," she said, all but confirming Zoey's theory. "It takes about two weeks to build immunity. You still have time but not much. Get it soon."

# CHAPTER FIFTEEN

Zoey unlocked the door to her apartment and stepped inside. Shadow was already sitting at the dining room table, laptop open. "What's with the radio silence?" she asked, withdrawing the earbud.

"Took mine out before." Shadow pointed to the tiny earbud on the kitchen counter. "Vivian's a noisy kisser." She wrinkled her nose in disgust, her eyes glued to the screen of her laptop as she typed away furiously. "How'd you pull that off without throwing up in her mouth?"

"Remember that scene in *Alien 3* where the alien licks and nuzzles Sigourney Weaver?"

Shadow nodded, still typing.

"That was my inspiration."

"Sigourney would be proud."

"Did you get the audio file I sent?" Zoey had recorded her entire conversation with Viv.

"Already uploaded to our website."

"We have a website?"

"Dozens, actually. All duplicates of the original. They're not published yet, but they're all linked. If our government takes one down, the next one goes up automatically to keep the stream of information intact and accessible to the public."

"And when are we planning to publish these websites?" Zoey asked, mildly alarmed at the prospect of this thing going public before they were ready. Global panic would inevitably follow the release of such sensitive information. She'd prefer to have completed her mission abroad before that happened.

"Not sure yet. We'll know when the time is right." Shadow hit *enter* and swung the laptop around. "Here's the travel itinerary I've mapped out for you."

Zoey pulled up a chair, took a seat, and studied the world map on the screen.

"You'll be traveling in a clockwise fashion," Shadow said. "Since you obviously can't hit every country in the amount of time we have, I've prioritized your pit stops according to region, population, and a country's ability to distribute international aid."

There were ten countries highlighted. Each was assigned a number.

Shadow tapped on the numeral one hovering over Canada. Their population, global power ranking, and a list of other relevant data popped up in a separate window, along with a photo of their Minister of Public Safety and Emergency Preparedness. "You'll be meeting with Robert Bellair," she said, pointing to the photo. "I'm already piggybacking his cell phone and tracking his GPS coordinates. I'll provide you with a meeting point when the time comes—somewhere off the grid so you can feed him the intel in private." She closed the popup for Canada and glanced at Zoey. "Go ahead. You can scroll through the rest."

Zoey tapped on the numeral two hovering over France. A popup with similar data appeared.

"From left to right," Shadow went on, pointing, "you'll hit Canada, France, Russia, China, Australia, Egypt, Nigeria, South Africa, Brazil, and, lastly, Mexico."

It certainly wasn't everyone, but it was a start. They had to start somewhere.

"I'm guessing you won't make it through all ten countries before our government figures out what you're up to. Someone will leak news of the virus along the way. I'm digging into backgrounds and selecting each contact carefully, but it's impossible to predict human behavior from afar without investing hours of research. Since we don't have that kind of time right now, I developed a set of criteria that each of your contacts must meet. It'll minimize the chance of information leaks, but it doesn't eliminate the risk completely. When news of this virus gets out—because it *will*—our government will come after you. Hard. I suspect they'll do everything humanly possible to discredit you, deny the truth, and try to get in front of this thing by quashing it. Our goal here is to get this vaccine to as many world leaders as possible *before* that happens.

"Once the cat is out of the bag," Shadow went on, "it'll be both a blessing and a curse. We can publish our website at that point—that's the blessing. Foreign governments will be granted access to the information needed to make the vaccine. As long as the world believes you, countries can then start working in tandem to distribute the vaccine globally." She paused and took a breath. "Hopefully in time to save the majority of the human population."

"As long as the rest of the world believes me," Zoey repeated, nodding. Her mind had already gone down this road. Secretary of Defense Griffin Bick would likely step in the moment her mission abroad went public.

Viv had confided during their meeting that Bick was heading up Operation Bird of Prey. Zoey wasn't surprised that Bick the Dick had found a way to dip his greedy fingers in the president's agenda. Sterling had shared the details of his run-ins with Bick over the course of his career. Sterling had no respect for the man. Bick was a shallow, power-hungry predator. When President Cooper appointed Bick, Sterling predicted he'd use his influence to secure a lifelong seat at the head of the table. Looked like Sterling's prediction was right on the mark.

Once Operation Bird of Prey was leaked to the public, Bick's position could include everything from outright denial of the existence of the virus to blaming Zoey for creating it. He might even claim the vaccine she was spreading was itself the virus. That's truly all it would take to halt the inoculation process in its tracks. By the time each country's people realized she was telling the truth, they'd be infected, and their fate sealed. According to Vivian, there was no chance of recovery once infection occurred. The vaccine had to be administered *before* exposure. Then the body needed two weeks to make the necessary antibodies.

All she really needed to save the human population was enough time. Whether or not each country opted to heed her warning, make the vaccine, and inoculate their people was ultimately their decision and totally beyond her control.

Zoey thought about the flash drive Sterling had given her. She'd opened it, but everything on it had looked like gobbledygook to her.

She had a feeling it would make more sense to Bug, their resident microbiology nerd. "Did Bug take a look at the flash drive?"

"You were right," Shadow said. "It's the formula to make the vaccine."

"Nothing about Operation Bird of Prey?" She hadn't seen anything, but she wanted to be sure.

Shadow shook her head. "Just the formula."

"Are you putting that formula on the website?" she asked, forcing her mind to steamroll over the giant potholes in their plan. Perhaps they could fill those potholes in time. Knowing Shadow, she was already working on them.

"Yes and no. The formula will be there, but it'll be hidden. Our website has a back door that can only be unlocked with a code. Each contact you meet with will be assigned a list of contacts in neighboring countries that they must forward the code to."

"Feels like we're planning a surprise party and asking the whole world to keep it a secret. This should be fun." She sighed. What could possibly go wrong?

"Each code is trackable, so I'll be able to see if, when, and where they send it." Shadow shrugged. "It's not much, but it's all we can do right now with the resources we have."

"Resources," Zoey repeated, chuckling. "Meaning *you*." She was impressed by the progress Shadow had made in such a short time. "You've accomplished a lot in the last fifteen hours. Did you sleep at all last night?"

"Grabbed a catnap before your meeting this morning with the devil incarnate. I can sleep when I'm dead." Shadow swung the laptop around and resumed her feverish typing. "Which'll be soon if I don't keep working on this."

"Have you eaten anything?"

Shadow shook her head. "No time."

"There's always time to eat." She stood and headed to the kitchen, intent on making Shadow her favorite meal. She set baking powder, flour, salt, and sugar on the kitchen counter and went to the fridge to grab milk, butter, and eggs. Her stomach growled as she mixed the ingredients together and studied her compadre from afar. Shadow had the soul of a warrior, the mind of a con artist, and the heart of a poet.

Zoey knew that, underneath it all, there was still a kid who craved the simple pleasures representative of the childhood Shadow never had—things like chocolate chip pancakes loaded with syrup, whipped cream, and rainbow sprinkles.

"You know," Shadow said, her eyes never straying from the laptop, "I could get more done if we brought some of the others into the fold."

Zoey had been thinking the same. Numerous gifted young minds resided in this very building, many of them perfectly suited to various aspects of the mission. She hated the idea of putting her kids in harm's way. By all accounts and purposes, they were her family. She'd taken them under her wing, vowing to support and protect them to the best of her ability. But it was quickly becoming apparent that she and Shadow would need more help. Recruiting her kids for this mission would more than double their chances of success. Knowing Shadow, she'd probably already done the math down to the tiniest fraction of a percent. She nodded. "I agree."

"There's a list in the junk drawer."

"Of what?" she asked absently, already second-guessing her decision.

"Of everyone we need. Just give me your stamp of approval, and I'll brief them on the mission. Everyone will work remotely. We'll set up shop in the locker—the one you gave me a key to last night. It's off the grid and perfect for what we need. Does anyone else know about that place?"

"Just Sterling." She and Sterling had started building it when Zoey was fifteen. They called it *the locker*, but it was more like a bomb shelter. Built underground, it was located on a remote piece of land in Foxborough, Massachusetts. Sterling had purchased the land through a shell company so the sale could never be traced back to him. It had taken them over a decade to finish construction, then another few years to collect all the essential items they'd need to survive a zombie apocalypse. Theoretically, they could live there for years without needing to come to the surface for anything. Except, maybe, for the occasional glimpse of sunlight.

Shadow didn't ask about Sterling. She knew Zoey trusted him, and that was obviously good enough for her. Shadow was—and always had been—very efficient with her time. She wouldn't waste valuable energy second-guessing Zoey's judgment. Zoey wished she could say the same for herself. With so much on the line, she seemed to be doing a lot of second-guessing these days.

She pulled open the junk drawer and perused Shadow's handwritten list of fifteen names—all of them essential. This was everyone she would've chosen. Shadow had been on the job less than twenty-four hours and was already kicking ass as her handler. She shook her head, amazed, and steered her thoughts back to the other looming issue at hand. "We need to make sure everyone here gets revaccinated."

"At a reputable clinic," Shadow finished, making air quotes. "Already on it. The tricky part will be making sure our brothers and sisters in every low-income community around the country get it, too." She slapped the laptop shut. "At first, I was trying to devise a strategy that would encourage people to circumvent neighborhood clinics, pharmacies, and doctors' offices in favor of being vaccinated somewhere *outside* of their own neighborhood. But that would be a tedious uphill battle and likely yield limited results." Shadow met her gaze with a mischievous grin. "Then I thought of something *way* more fun."

Zoey's mind had been chewing on this problem since her meeting with Viv. She wondered if Shadow was about to propose the same harebrained solution she had come up with on the car ride home—steal the millions of doses that the government had undoubtedly already made and earmarked for worldwide distribution. Instead of selling it to governments abroad, she and Shadow would distribute it to their own people here in the US. They could give whatever vaccines remained to the poorest countries that didn't have the resources to make their own. It would be a grand vaccine heist—maybe the grandest heist in world history. "Robin Hood," she said, returning Shadow's gaze with a grin of her own. They'd be stealing from the rich to give to the poor.

Shadow nodded. "Exactly."

# Chapter Sixteen

Showered and dressed, Peyton studied herself in the mirror as her chin quivered. She hardly recognized the raw, vulnerable woman standing before her. Her eyes were puffy, red, haunted. No matter what she did, the tears just wouldn't stop flowing. She shook her head, angry with herself for letting her emotions get the best of her.

There was no way she could show up at the office looking like this and crying like a blubbering idiot. She called in sick, changed into her workout clothes, and decided to hop on the treadmill for a run. Pushing herself physically might prompt her body to release the endorphins it needed to help her get back on track.

She quickly realized that running while crying was as compatible as eating while chewing gum. Her tears and drippy nose pummeled the treadmill belt like fat raindrops on pavement. The treadmill's wet surface soon grew slippery—too slippery to run on—so she finally gave up and stepped down.

What was wrong with her? Was this what the rest of her pregnancy would be like? She needed to get a handle on this crying thing. Fast.

Peyton reached into the past once again and instantly grasped the source of her grief—she couldn't fix her mistakes. Ben and Cal were both dead. She would never be able to apologize and set things right. With both of them gone, how could she ever find closure?

She glanced down at her stomach. The only way she'd be able to make amends with Ben was raising his baby in the best way she knew how, by giving their daughter all the love she'd secretly withheld from him.

But what about Callie? The thought that Cal had died without knowing the truth of how she felt made her soul ache. There was no fixing that.

Peyton unlaced her running shoes and paced the living room. She needed to take action, do *something*. What if she called Lizzie and Grace? She could apologize and come clean with the truth. It wasn't closure exactly, but it would be a step. It was something.

Something was better than nothing.

She dialed Lizzie's cell, left a message, and did the same for Grace. There. Now all she had to do was wait. And find a way to stop crying.

Peyton took her second shower of the day, dressed in navy-blue silk pajamas, and set her Bluetooth in her ear as she tried to figure out how to pass the time until Lizzie or Grace called back. She glanced at the clock: 11:09 a.m. Both were likely working and wouldn't call until this evening. What was she supposed to do with herself until then? More importantly, how was she going to calm herself down and get these waterworks under control? This—whatever *this* was—was now approaching crisis mode.

Fluids. That's what she needed. Was it possible to cry herself into dehydration? Probably not, but it was better to be safe.

She was managing small sips of water between sobs when her Bluetooth announced an incoming call. She set her glass on the kitchen counter and accepted the call with a loud sniffle. "Hello?"

There was a pause on the other end. "Peyton? Is that you?"

It took her a second to realize the voice on the other end wasn't Lizzie's or Grace's. Zoey was the last person she'd expected to hear from today. She squeezed her eyes shut. Tears flowed freely down both cheeks. "It's me," Peyton confirmed, aware she sounded hoarse, congested, and not herself at all.

"Alvarez said you called in sick. You okay?"

"I'm fine." She wasn't expecting anyone from the office to call—especially Zoey—and hadn't taken the time to manufacture an illness. She'd never had a reason to lie about being sick and suddenly found herself stumped. She was mentally and physically exhausted, her brain too consumed with grief to think straight.

"Everything okay with the baby?"

It was difficult to eke out even a one-word answer between sobs. "Yes."

"Are you...*crying*?"

"No," she lied, willing her tears to stop just long enough for her to get through the call. "Bad cold." She muted her Bluetooth as another sob escaped her lips.

"I just saw you three hours ago. You were fine."

She unmuted the Bluetooth. "Allergies," she said, muting the call once again to blow her nose.

There was a long pause on the other end. Zoey obviously wasn't buying it. "Do you need anything?" she asked. "Is there something I can do to help?"

She wiped her cheeks and unmuted the Bluetooth. "Thanks, but I have"—she drew in a shuddering breath between sobs and silently cursed herself for being so transparent—"everything I need."

A long, awkward silence crept over the line. Peyton couldn't bring herself to fill it. She was mortified, embarrassed, and ashamed of her emotional fragility. She just wanted the phone call to end.

"I'm here if you need anything," Zoey offered, sounding more than a little concerned. "Call me, day or night. I mean it."

"Thanks. Bye." Peyton had already disconnected the call by the time she realized she'd forgotten to unmute the Bluetooth for those last two words. She'd just hung up on Zoey without a proper good-bye.

She collapsed on the sofa, pulled the throw blanket over her head, and wept.

❖

Zoey ended the call and met Shadow's gaze.

"That sounded cheerful." Shadow raised an eyebrow. "She okay?"

"I don't know," she said, frowning. But that wasn't true. She did know. Peyton obviously wasn't okay.

Shadow took another bite of her pancakes. "You like her."

"Replacing *like* with *tolerate* would make that statement more accurate." Zoey stared at the map on the laptop. She pried her thoughts from her handler and steered them back to the mission at hand.

"What are you waiting for?" Shadow asked. "Go. Make sure she's okay."

"No time for that. Billions of lives hang in the balance, remember?" She zoomed in on Shadow's notes alongside Austria. "What do you have against Austria?"

"Nothing," Shadow replied, chewing. "That's the name of the town."

"Fucking, Austria?"

"Technically they changed their name to *Fugging* a few years back, but humor me. Local residents are referred to as *Fuckingers*. It's a small town. They have three signs posted with their town name. I was hoping, you know, if you have some time to kill when you're passing through France, maybe you could pay them a visit and take a photo for me."

"We're about to face off with a virus that threatens human extinction, and you're thinking about—"

"Fucking," Shadow finished, nodding. "How could you *not* think about fucking at a time like this?"

Zoey rolled her eyes.

"All I'm saying is, we can't let the entire fucking culture die out." Shadow set her fork down, pushed the empty plate aside, and pulled her laptop closer. "Check on North. I'll keep working on this."

Zoey hesitated. There was still so much to do. "Fine." She stood and met Shadow's all-knowing gaze. "For the record, though, it's not Peyton I'm worried about."

"Holy town of Fucking." Shadow leaned back in her chair with a look of disbelief. "You let her take the Feejays?"

Zoey nodded, genuinely concerned for their welfare. "She was still wearing them when she left. What was I supposed to do?"

"Don't look at me. You dug your own hole on this one." Shadow shook her head and sighed. "We obviously can't get this mission underway until they're safely back in your possession."

"Obviously." It felt good to have a handler who truly understood her.

"Then you have no choice. Go rescue your Feejays under the pretense of being a concerned colleague."

That she could do. Zoey hurried to her bedroom, lifted her giant boom box from the closet shelf, and then grabbed her coat and car keys on her way out the door.

❖

Peyton woke up to the sound of the doorbell. She'd fallen asleep on the couch. With the blanket over her head, no less.

She glanced at where her Apple Watch should've been, but she'd forgotten to strap it on after her shower. How long had she been asleep? She could tell from the darkening room that the sun was nearing the end of its shift. Hours wasted. At least sleep had granted her a blessed reprieve from the incessant crying.

Much to her chagrin, her eyes welled up again as soon as her feet hit the floor. She grabbed the tissue box from the coffee table and stood. Curiosity propelled her toward the door, but there was no chance she'd be welcoming anyone inside today. Not even Horace. She could only imagine what she looked like right now—swollen eyelids, wrinkled pajamas, hair pasted to the sides of her face with dried tears.

The doorbell rang again.

A singsong voice called out from the other side of the door, "Cuddle bug, are you in there?"

She tiptoed over and peered through the peephole. One enormous eyeball peered back. Yep. Definitely Zoey.

"Your car's here, so I know you're home."

Peyton decided silence was her best option. For all Zoey knew, maybe she'd left the house to take a walk around the neighborhood.

Zoey finally backed away from the peephole. "Fine. Have it your way." She disappeared around the corner and returned with a boom box on her shoulder. She threw a thumbs-up at the peephole, grinned, and pressed *play*.

"Lean on Me" blasted through the speakers. It shook the door against which Peyton was leaning and vibrated the floorboards under her feet. She had to put a stop to this before someone called the police. But she'd promised herself she wouldn't open the door. For God's sake, she was wearing pajamas without a bra.

Bill Withers belted out the lyrics at full volume as she grabbed a broom from the closet and hurried up the stairs to fetch one of Ben's white T-shirts. She tied the T-shirt to the end of the broom, opened the upstairs bedroom window, and waved the broom furiously back and forth in a gesture of surrender.

The music stopped.

"You shouldn't be around me right now. I'm not feeling well," she called down, hoping that would be enough to send Zoey on her way.

"Last I checked, crying wasn't contagious."

She faked a coughing fit.

"Lousy performance." Zoey shook her head. "You really should've prepared better. Next time, go to Soundsnap, type *woman coughing with phlegm* in the search bar, and download one of the audio files there." She winked. "Works like a charm."

"I'm in my pajamas," she pleaded.

"We're *way* past pajamas." Zoey set the boom box down and gazed up once again. "You got to second base with me last night, remember?"

She shook her head. How could she forget?

Zoey stuffed a hand in her coat pocket. "What do we have here?" She pulled out a key and held it up.

"That better not be a key to my house." The tears halted momentarily as anger washed over her.

"Listen, if you want to cry alone, that's fine." Zoey slipped the key back inside her pocket. "What I really came here for is the Feejays. Just toss them down, and I'll be on my way."

Peyton frowned. Could it really be that easy?

"If you return my favorite Feejays, unharmed, in the next two minutes, you'll never see me again."

"Never?" Peyton asked, feeling hopeful for the first time all day.

"You'll never see me again *today*," Zoey clarified. "Assuming you make a miraculous overnight recovery, I'll grace you with my presence at work again tomorrow."

"They're in the other room. Give me a minute." She started to turn away from the window but thought better of it and turned back. "If you use that key to unlock my door, the Feejays stay with me, and I won't treat them kindly." She gave Zoey the sternest look she could muster with swollen eyelids. "Have I made myself clear?"

"Crystal." Zoey leaned over, hefted the boom box back onto her shoulder, and pressed *play* once again.

"Lean on Me" resumed blasting through the second-story window, pummeling her eardrums like tiny fists. Zoey's song choice was clever. It would almost be sweet, if she actually meant it. But Zoey was clearly here for the Feejays and not out of concern for her welfare. Just as well. She didn't have the energy to fend off an unsolicited friendship with her subordinate.

Peyton fished around in her hamper, pulled the Feejays out, and folded them neatly in her lap. She returned to the open window and looked down. The boom box was still on the front stoop, but Zoey was gone.

She nearly jumped out of her skin when Zoey joined her at the window to survey the front stoop below. "I don't think I'm down there anymore."

Peyton stood, took several steps back, and hugged the Feejays protectively against her chest.

"You're squeezing too hard." Zoey nodded at the Feejays. "They can't breathe."

"I'm not wearing a bra," she blurted in her own defense.

Zoey set her hands on her hips. "If I were you, I'd use the Feejays to cover my face. Breasts without a bra I can handle. But your face...it reminds me of *Beauty and the Beast*. Usually, you're the beauty." She grimaced. "Today...well."

Peyton felt her chin start to quiver. She buried her face in the Feejays and sobbed.

"Hey." Zoey stepped over and set a hand on her shoulder. "I was kidding. That was supposed to make you laugh. You're beautiful," she said gently.

Peyton couldn't bring herself to speak. She was now past the point of no return. She'd never felt this kind of soul-wrenching sadness. What in the world was happening to her? Felt like she was free-falling into an abyss of despair. Right in front of her operative.

Zoey led her to the bed, kicked off her shoes, and climbed in alongside her. She wrapped her arms around Peyton and held her as she sobbed into the Feejays.

## CHAPTER SEVENTEEN

Zoey watched Peyton's chest rise and fall steadily for long minutes. Peyton was sound asleep. Save for a flickering candle night-light in the corner, darkness held the room almost as tightly as she was holding Peyton. She took one last whiff of the incredible-smelling woman in her arms. God only knew when Peyton would let her get this close again, so she savored the moment before finally releasing her to slip out of bed. She covered her with a throw blanket from a nearby armchair, stepped to the window, and looked down. The neighbor's porch light illuminated her boom box, still right where she'd left it.

The Peyton she'd come to know so far was tougher than this. Maybe the pregnancy hormones were taking their toll. Maybe the death of her husband was finally settling in, and this was just a normal part of the grieving process. Maybe the idea of having his baby without him was sending her into a tailspin of anxiety. Or maybe it was a combination of everything. Regardless, Peyton clearly needed a friend, now more than ever.

Zoey decided that she'd do everything in her power to be there for Peyton and support her in whatever ways she could. She stuffed her hands in the pockets of her jeans and watched the passing traffic on the city street below. With her new mission on the horizon, living up to that promise would be tricky. But not impossible. She'd find a way to make it work.

"You're still here," Peyton called out groggily behind her, sounding surprised as she sat up in bed.

"I'm not leaving without them." She nodded at the Feejays in

Peyton's arms. "But they're in no shape to travel right now, not after what you did to them."

"You forfeited these when you unlocked my door without my permission."

"Who said anything about unlocking your door?"

Peyton frowned. "But you said you had a key."

"I lied. That's the key to Horace's place next door."

"Then how'd you get in here?"

"I picked the lock." She shook her head. "What kind of covert agent would I be if I couldn't pick a lock?"

"Whatever." Peyton folded the Feejays into a neat little square. "They're mine now."

They could fight over custody later. She sat on the edge of the bed. "How're you feeling?"

"Better now. Thanks. You can go."

"Want to talk about what's going on?"

"Not with you."

"Why?" she asked, offended.

"Because you showed up uninvited and then broke into my home, for starters."

"Out of concern."

"For your Feejays," Peyton shot back.

They stared at one another across the bed. Neither budged. "I must warn you, I'm the reigning champ."

Peyton frowned. "Of what?"

"Of every stare-down challenge since I was six," she boasted. "Are we allowed to blink?"

"Here." Peyton handed her the Feejays as her eyes filled with tears. "Just leave." She stood from the bed, grabbed a fresh pair of silk pajamas from a dresser drawer, and retreated to the bathroom.

Zoey heard the shower turn on and glanced down at her body. She and Peyton had strikingly similar builds and probably wore the same size. She'd never been a fan of silk, but who was to say she wouldn't like it? She hurriedly shed her clothes and helped herself to a pair of dark red pajama bottoms and a matching, long-sleeved top. Fancy gold cording lined the collar and cuffs.

She withdrew her cell from her coat pocket and texted Shadow. *Still here. Feejays safe.*

Shadow replied with a relieved emoji. *Horace fed n walked*, she texted back. *He's playing chess w Big D now.*

Shadow had obviously sent Big D to care for Peyton's forgetful neighbor. One less thing on Peyton's plate tonight. Sometimes it took a village.

Zoey ordered a pizza and switched on the bedroom TV. She found *Fifty First Dates* on Netflix and made herself comfortable in bed while Peyton finished her shower.

The bathroom door finally swung open, and Peyton stepped out. Wet hair clung to the sides of her face and neck. A box of tissues was tucked under one arm. She stopped dead in her tracks, her gaze as penetrating as a coroner's bone saw. "Are those my pajamas?"

Zoey nodded. "Fair is fair."

"What's that supposed to mean?"

"You wore mine last night, so I'm returning the favor." She stood from the bed. "And look, no bra."

"Why in the world would I object to you wearing a bra?"

"Levels the playing field. You don't have to feel self-conscious and hide behind the Feejays anymore."

"I have a better idea." Peyton's neck and cheeks flushed with anger. "If you leave—like, *now*—then I can be alone and braless in my own home."

"Nope." Zoey climbed back in bed and pulled the throw blanket over her legs. "I'm staying."

"Zoey, I don't want you to stay. I want you to go."

"A wise fortune cookie once told me… *You get what you need, and you need what you get.*"

Peyton set the box of tissues on the nightstand and crossed her arms. "And what is it, exactly, that you think I need right now?"

"A friend," she said sincerely. "Let me be that friend for you. If you don't want to talk about what's upsetting you, I won't push. Instead, I'll try to make you laugh. If that doesn't work, I can make you so angry that you forget why you're sad. And if *that* doesn't work, well…then I'll just hold you while you cry."

"Why?" Peyton's tears returned with a vengeance. "Why are you doing this?"

Zoey stood, walked around the bed, and set her hands on Peyton's shoulders. "Let's get one thing straight. It's not because I like you. It's more out of a sense of obligation than anything else." She released Peyton's shoulders and shrugged. "Whenever I bring someone into the Feejays club, they become my responsibility."

"And what do you get in return?" Peyton asked with fresh tears on her cheeks.

"The satisfaction of you breathing easier because you know someone's in your corner. Someone who'll be there for you, no matter what." The doorbell rang. "Ooh. That's the pizza."

Peyton stared at her. "You ordered pizza?"

"Green peppers, black olives. Just the way you like it." She stepped over to the closet, opened the door, and lifted Peyton's plush white robe from the hook.

"That's the way *you* like it. I prefer plain cheese, remember?"

Zoey shrugged into the robe and tied the belt around her waist. "Which is why I'll pick off the unwanted toppings for you, Your Highness." She looked around. "Where's your wallet? I need to pay the driver."

"You expect me to pay for a pizza that I didn't order with toppings I don't even like?"

"I'm putting six kids through college, remember?" Zoey winked. "Kidding. I already paid. Just thought that jolt of anger might help you put a cork in the crying."

Peyton met her gaze, dry-eyed and now visibly annoyed. "It did."

Peyton followed Zoey downstairs and veered off to the kitchen as Zoey continued to the front door. She grabbed the plates and napkins for a second round of dinner in bed.

She never ate in bed, and now she was doing it two nights in a row. But the alternative was worse. The thought of sitting at the dining room table and having a civilized conversation in her current state of mind was unfathomable. She felt her anger ebb as grief threatened to rear its ugly head once again. Zoey rounded the corner wearing her robe—the robe she hadn't even bothered asking to borrow—and *poof*, the anger was back. Problem solved.

Zoey set two large pizza boxes on the counter.

"Two pizzas?" she said, surprised.

Zoey lifted the cardboard lid to reveal a cheese pizza. "You didn't seriously believe I'd force my toppings on you, did you?"

And, just like that, the tears returned. "Damn you."

"Ask me how I knew where your robe was," Zoey pressed.

She pulled a tissue from her pocket to soak up the tears. "How?"

"When I found out you were assigned to me, I picked your lock and went through all of your belongings. Even your underwear. I particularly liked the animal-print thongs. The tiger was my favorite. I was trying to find something I could use to blackmail you into opting out as my handler—you know, in case we didn't get along. Now I know where *everything* is." She paused and narrowed her eyes. "Even your vibrator."

The anger swam back into focus. "I don't have a vibrator."

"Dildo?"

Peyton blotted her nose and shook her head.

"I didn't find either one," Zoey admitted. "That was just a test."

They carried their pizza and bottles of water upstairs, settled on the bed, and watched *Fifty First Dates* as they ate. Peyton's cell phone rang halfway through the movie. She glanced at the caller ID and nearly jumped off the bed. Lizzie.

Zoey aimed the remote at the TV and pressed *pause*. "Everything okay?"

"Fine," she said, struggling to slide the Bluetooth in her ear. "I need to take this." She went to the walk-in closet that she once shared with Ben, stepped inside, and closed the door. "Hi, Lizzie."

"No one calls me that anymore. It's just Liz." Lizzie cleared her throat. "Are you okay? You sounded upset when you left me that message."

No time for pleasantries. "I cheated on Ben in college. Callie and I slept together. I was in love with her," she blurted. She couldn't stand the thought of keeping it inside a moment longer. She had to get everything out in the open. "I'm sorry I never told you or Grace. Most of all, I'm sorry I never told her. She deserved better than the way I treated her. All of you deserved better." Peyton was surprised to find that the boa constrictor inside her chest instantly released its grip. For the first time all day, she could breathe. She'd been stuffing this down for so long that she hadn't realized how physically and mentally taxing it was. The sadness and regret were still there—they'd probably always be there—but sharing the truth with someone who knew and loved Callie as much as she did made those feelings more bearable. "I don't expect you to forgive me," she went on. "I'm not even asking for forgiveness. I just wanted you to know the truth."

Lizzie didn't skip a beat. "It's okay, Peyton. Callie told us. We knew why you shut us out of your life with Ben. Cal insisted you'd eventually make your way back to us. Looks like she was right."

"She did?" Peyton asked, surprised by Callie's faith in her.

"She was adamant. Grace was pissed, but Callie talked her down. She explained your side—made us understand how hard it was for you to come to terms with everything. She made us both promise we'd take you back if you ever asked."

Peyton didn't know what to say. It was a lot to take in, and she was too busy crying. But this wasn't the panicked crying she'd been doing on and off all day. This felt different—a healing cry. Like opening the windows of a long-abandoned house on a sunny spring day.

"Cal loved you. Grace and I love you, too, just as much now as we did back then. Don't waste your time trying to make up for the past. What's done is done. Just move on, find peace, and be happy. That's what Callie would want for you." Lizzie paused and took a breath. "More than anything, that's what Grace and I want for you, too."

She finished her call, wiped her tears, and opened the closet door to find Zoey with two bowls of popcorn in bed. "Hope you don't mind," she said, chewing. "I helped myself."

"What else is new?" She climbed in bed, grabbed a handful of popcorn, and pushed *play* to resume their movie.

Zoey picked up the remote and paused the movie. "Who's Callie?"

"An old friend," she answered, taken aback.

"And you're in love with her?" Zoey asked around a mouthful of popcorn.

Peyton started choking. She took a drink of water to clear her throat and stared at Zoey. "Do you even know what boundaries are?"

Zoey shrugged. "I can't help it if my hearing is above average."

"How much did you hear?"

"Enough to know that the closet was the perfect place for that phone call. Are you out now?"

"Obviously. I'm here in bed with *you*, aren't I?"

"I meant, are you out of the closet?" Zoey pressed. "As a lesbian."

Peyton rolled her eyes and took another sip of water.

"Oh. I get it. You made a joke." Zoey nodded in approval. "That was funny."

"Can we please get back to the movie?" Now she knew how Zoey must've felt during their chat the night before, when Peyton had pushed her to talk about the death of her sister.

"My, how the tables have turned," Zoey replied with a wry grin, as if reading her mind. "Why didn't you tell me you were struggling with this? Wouldn't I be the most logical person to share this with?"

"Why? Because you're gay?"

"Do you know any other lesbians?"

Truth be told, she didn't. It was a valid point. But discussing her sexuality with her operative would cross countless professional boundaries. Then again, she was sitting in bed with said operative, eating popcorn without a bra. How in the world had she let it get this far? "Fine." She shut off the TV, set her bowl of popcorn on the nightstand, and turned to face Zoey. "I'll tell you about Callie if you tell me about your sister."

# CHAPTER EIGHTEEN

Secretary of Defense Griffin Bick pushed his chair away from the dinner table, thanked his wife for a delicious meal with a peck on the cheek, and retreated to his study. He poured himself some bourbon, started a fire, and stared at the flames from his favorite leather armchair, mulling over the latest development with Operation Bird of Prey. He'd listened to the recording of Vivian's conversation with her assumed lover too many times to count. The conclusion he'd come to was disturbing.

His cell phone vibrated in the pocket of his robe. He glanced at the caller ID: John Polluck, his right-hand man. Polluck was fast, thorough, and discreet. He'd always done whatever Bick had asked of him. Thankfully, Polluck's conscience never stood in the way of carrying out a job. "Bick," he answered.

"I have a name, sir," Polluck said, wasting no time on pleasantries. "Zoey Blackwood. She's an undercover operative for the CIA."

"Any relation to Sterling Blackwood?" he asked.

"Sterling was Agent Blackwood's handler until he retired eight months ago. He's also her adoptive father."

If what Griffin suspected was true, this could throw a wrench in their plans. "Bring them both in." He sipped his bourbon. "By force, if necessary. And keep this under the radar, Polluck."

"Roger that, sir. I'll collect them. Tonight."

❖

Zoey finished chewing her popcorn, swallowed, and met Peyton's gaze. Before tonight, she'd never even considered talking about what happened. To her knowledge, no one in her life had ever figured out she had a sister. What kind of hypocrite would she be if she pushed Peyton to talk about something that was difficult if she wasn't willing to do the same? "What do you want to know?"

Peyton regarded her, quiet for a moment. "What was her name?"

She stared down at her hands. "Ella." Saying her sister's name aloud made her chest ache with longing. "My mother had an old record player when I was growing up, one of the few possessions she didn't sell for drugs. Ella Fitzgerald was singing 'Love Is Here to Stay' when my mother gave birth in our apartment." She met Peyton's gaze, haunted by the memories of her mom's strangled cries and tormented groans during childbirth. "She was in no shape to think of a name when my sister finally made her debut, so I named her."

"It's beautiful," Peyton said, quiet as she waited for Zoey to go on.

"I was eight. The minute I held her, I knew she was my responsibility. All my mother cared about was getting her next fix. She'd managed to stay clean through most of her pregnancy, but I knew that wouldn't last long after the baby came."

Her mother had been a drinker and recreational drug user as far back as Zoey could remember. She cranked her habit up a few notches after Zoey's father walked out on her fifth birthday. They never saw him again, but it was no big loss. The few memories Zoey had of her father involved chain-smoking, profanity, and late-night arguments that ended in physical altercations with her mother. Zoey was never sure who was the instigator. Her mother had received her fair share of black eyes and fat lips, but she always gave as good as she got. After Zoey's father left, her mother traded in her bartender job at the local strip club for a full-time gig as a heroin addict. She'd disappear for days at a stretch, leaving her without food or money. Zoey was forced to become resourceful at a young age in order to survive. By the time her sister came along, she was good at providing for herself. Ella's arrival just gave her more incentive to keep going. Without a doubt, she knew she wouldn't be who she was today if her little sister hadn't come along when she did.

Even after all these years, Zoey still remembered every detail of her sister's life. "I stole enough baby formula to keep Ella growing and enough diapers to keep her from getting a rash. Things got easier when she started eating solids at six months. I potty trained her when she was two." She smiled, remembering how excited Ella was to wear big girl underpants. "Took her three days to learn how to pee in the potty. She never had an accident after that, not one." A huge burden had been lifted when Zoey realized she didn't have to steal diapers anymore. They were so big and bulky and hard to conceal. She'd stolen thousands of diapers over a two-year period and still found it hard to believe that she never got caught.

"What about school?" Peyton asked, scooting closer. "What did you do with Ella when you went to school?"

"I stopped going." She shrugged, realizing her story must've sounded unimaginable to someone like Peyton. "But I stole a stroller, walked to the library every day, and read everything I could get my hands on." That's where she'd honed her speedreading and memorization skills. She consumed as much material as possible in the time allotted, before the deafening wails of a ravenous infant pierced the sacred library stillness. She'd been fully aware that she had to keep up with her education if there was any hope of giving Ella a better life.

Caring for a baby twenty-four seven when she was just a child was one of the hardest things she'd ever done. But she never resented Ella. The thought never even occurred to her that life would be easier without her baby sister. On the contrary, raising Ella had brought so much joy, love, and wonder into her world.

Zoey was quiet as she summoned the courage to finish her sister's story. Seconds stretched into minutes. Peyton waited patiently beside her and didn't push. Thankfully, there were no arm hugs tonight.

She took a deep breath. "We lived in Dorchester at the time. Rough neighborhood. A lot of gang activity. I figured out early on that I couldn't keep stealing from the same places, so I mixed it up as much as possible to minimize my chances of getting caught. I was crossing the street at Fields Corner, and Ella was holding my hand. There was a drive-by shooting. She bled out in my arms there on the sidewalk. She was three."

Peyton apparently couldn't hold herself back any longer. She reached out to bestow the dreaded arm hug. "I'm so sorry."

She'd waited with Ella until the coroner took her away. That was the last time she saw her favorite person in the world. When she returned home later that day, her mother didn't even seem to notice Ella was missing. A month later, she found her mother on the bathroom floor, unresponsive, cold to the touch, and barely breathing. She'd held her mother's head in her lap, smoothed back her hair, and whispered in her ear that everything would be okay. It took her over an hour to die— the longest hour of Zoey's life, by far. But it was the only gift she could give her mother and, she knew, the only gift her mother could give her.

Peyton was crying again. Zoey looked down. At some point— she wasn't sure when—Peyton must've reached out to hold her hand. Their fingers were entwined. Instead of pulling away, she found herself holding on a little tighter. Peyton's touch was warm. Soft. Comforting.

"The amnesia," Peyton said, nodding. "It all makes sense now."

Zoey's career with the CIA would've been over before it even began. She might've saved her mother's life by calling for an ambulance. Instead, she'd made the decision to let her mother die. Not once had she ever regretted that decision. Even now, she knew it had been the right one.

"I'm truly, truly sorry," Peyton said with a reassuring squeeze. "What happened to Ella is awful, but it wasn't your fault. Tell me you understand that."

"She was my responsibility. Of course it was my fault." She pulled her hand away, angry with Peyton for denying the obvious.

"But she *shouldn't* have been your responsibility."

She'd always known her childhood was harsh, darkened around the edges by her mother's neglect and fervor for self-destruction. She thanked her lucky stars all the time that her mother never pimped her out. That was a line even she never crossed. "Ella was the best part of my life. Without her..." She trailed off, too choked up to go on.

"You wouldn't be who you are today," Peyton finished. "It sounds like you did an extraordinary job raising her. You gave her everything your mom couldn't give you."

"But it didn't matter. I got her killed that day, Peyton. I knew Fields Corner was dangerous. It was no place for a three-year-old, and I took her there anyway."

"To steal food so she could eat," Peyton countered. "It was an accident. Accidents happen. Taking responsibility for an accident gives us a sense of control. That guilt is a chain that binds us to the past. It connects us in a very real way to the ones we love. It's our way of keeping them here, our way of keeping them connected to us. You've lived your whole life fighting for the underdog, Zoey. You're a protector, through and through. That's the core of who you are. But you have *nothing* to atone for. It's time to let go of that guilt because it's not yours to carry." Peyton reached over and took Zoey's hand once again. "You did right by Ella. You should be proud."

They sat for long minutes, side by side. Zoey held Peyton's hand and openly grieved for her sister. It felt good to share her journey with someone. It felt good to say Ella's name and have someone hear it. After all these years, it felt good to finally get the chance to say good-bye.

Peyton reached for the box of tissues on the nightstand and held them out to Zoey. "How'd you meet Sterling?"

"You've read my file." She grabbed a tissue and blew her nose. "You already know that story."

"You're right," Peyton admitted, taking a tissue to wipe her own tears. "But I want to know the real story."

She and Peyton locked gazes. Zoey felt their connection deepen. Peyton's intuition seemed to rival even Shadow's. "I started picking pockets in downtown Boston after my mother died." Since she was only eleven at the time and couldn't legally work to earn money, she'd continued down the criminal path, promising herself she'd stop as soon as she turned eighteen. "One of my targets turned out to be Sterling." Zoey shrugged guiltily. She could only imagine what was running through Peyton's mind as she confessed the sins of her past.

## CHAPTER NINETEEN

Z oey thought back to the night she'd met Sterling. She was twelve. He was waiting for her in the driveway of the house she'd broken into the week before. The homeowners were vacationing in Spain. Zoey recognized him immediately when he stepped out from the shadows. His first question surprised her. "How long have you been doing this?"

She held her ground, refused to run. The owners weren't due back for two more weeks. She had other travel plans lined up when her stay here came to an end, but she had no intention of being homeless until then. Living on the streets of Boston in December was no picnic. "How long have I been doing what?"

"Ignorance doesn't suit you. Take pride in your work." He stepped closer and looked her over. "You have a natural talent."

She held his gaze and decided to turn the tables. "Why were you pretending to be someone you're not?" The man standing in front of her was a far cry from the filthy homeless guy she'd seen—and smelled—yesterday. He'd cleaned himself up and was now wearing an unbuttoned black trench coat over an expensive-looking suit and tie.

"What gave me away?" he asked.

"Your fingernails. There was dirt underneath them." She pointed to his freshly scrubbed hands. "You obviously scraped your nails along the ground to make them look the part, but there were no signs of vitamin deficiency that real homeless people have." She withdrew the flashlight from her pocket and shone it on his nails. "They aren't cracked, chipped, or yellow. No ridges or white spots. And those perfect half-moons mean you probably get regular manicures." She switched off the flashlight and looked up at his dark-as-night face, his features barely discernable from the shadows.

"I'm an undercover operative with the CIA," he said, his gaze unwavering.

"Do all men in the CIA get manicures?"

He hesitated. "Probably not. But they should."

"Why?" She examined her own nails, filthy from a long day of fishing around in other people's pockets.

"Because it always pays off to go the extra mile. Case in point," he said, gesturing back and forth between them.

She read between the lines and knew what he was inferring. She'd considered him a worthwhile target because his well-manicured nails signaled wealth, thereby contradicting the rest of his appearance, which just made him a much more interesting target. If she hadn't stolen from him, he wouldn't have gone looking for her, and they wouldn't be standing here having this conversation right now. *Case in point* was his way of saying he was glad they'd met. This man was honest, complicated, intriguing. She liked that.

She decided to see his honesty and raise him one. "I'm a twelve-year-old orphan, thief, and professional pickpocket. This isn't my house. I'm just staying here while the owners are on vacation. I get my leads from a local travel agency and bounce from house to house so I can have a place to shower, eat, and sleep." She thought for a moment and decided to allay any possible misgivings. "I never take anything, and I always clean up before I leave, so no one even knows I was there."

He was quiet as he scrutinized her with intelligent eyes. She got the feeling that he was trying to decide what to do with her. She glanced down at his Italian loafers and figured she could outrun him if it came to that. But something told her it'd be better if she stood her ground.

Finally, he nodded and extended a hand to shake hers. "Sterling."

"Zoey," she said, meeting him halfway. They eyed one another suspiciously.

"Can I have my wallet back now?"

"Depends," she answered.

He raised an eyebrow. "On what?"

"Will you be pissed if I said I already used your Amex?"

"Depends," he answered back.

"On what?" she repeated.

"What did you use it for?"

"I booked a flight to Florida and bought a ten-day, all-inclusive trip to Disney World. Hotel, spa, prepaid meals, the works." Zoey watched as he traded his poker face for a scowl. She tended to have that effect on people.

"For how many?" he asked.

"One," she said matter-of-factly.

He shoved his hands in the pockets of his trench coat and sighed. "Sounds expensive."

"It was."

"When do you leave?"

"Tuesday."

He looked off into the distance. "I think I can swing some time off from work. I'm due for a vacation."

"I didn't invite you."

"You won't get very far as a minor. Might make it to Florida. Might even make it to the hotel room, but someone's bound to notify child services sooner or later. If you want to be stuck in Florida until your eighteenth birthday, be my guest. But I must warn you—bad hair days are in your future every summer with all that humidity."

She narrowed her eyes. "How bad?"

"Albert Einstein bad."

She looked down at the ground as she considered his offer. "Are you a pedophile?"

"Nope." He swept his trench coat aside, unbuttoned his suit jacket, and pointed to the CIA shield clipped to his belt. "I'm the good guy. Well, most of the time," he added with a wink. "Here." He unhooked his shield and handed it to her. "Hang on to this for me. Make sure I'm legit before you agree to anything." He turned and started to walk down the driveway.

"Wait." She hurried after him. "You're not going to arrest me?"

"Not when there's a trip to Disney World on the table."

Made sense. "But how will I find you again?"

He set a hand on her shoulder. His touch was firm, reassuring. She realized then that he was the first man she'd ever met with whom she felt safe. "You'll figure it out," he assured her.

And he was right. She did. It wasn't easy—he'd gone to great lengths to conceal his identity and home address. She decided the best way to find him was to visit some local nail salons. How many impeccably dressed Black men got manicures? She made up a lie about trying to find her long-lost grandfather and used biracial parents to explain the difference in the color of their skin. Thankfully, she hit the jackpot with number fourteen.

The manager told her that Sterling came in every other Monday, so she bought some binoculars and waited all day in a café across the street. When she saw the light brown Studebaker Commander park at the far end of the lot, she knew it had to be him. She waited for Sterling to disappear inside the salon before crossing the street.

Zoey picked the trunk's lock with ease. He drove to his Wellesley home with her in the trunk of his car as Billie Holiday sang "I'll Be Seeing You" on the radio. She made note of his address and returned the next day to search his home and find out as much as she could about him. Satisfied that he wasn't a pedophile—his only flaw was his affinity for escargot and caviar—she left his CIA shield and wallet on the kitchen counter with a pair of Mickey Mouse ears.

They met at Terminal B for Southwest Airlines at Logan Airport the following Tuesday.

Peyton chimed in, "Wait a minute. You stole his wallet, charged his credit card, and left irrefutable proof that you broke into his home… and he rewarded you with a trip to Disney World?"

Zoey smiled proudly.

"*That* explains a lot." Peyton rolled her eyes. "No wonder you think the rules don't apply to you."

"They don't," she admitted in all seriousness. She picked up her bowl of popcorn and set it in her lap. "Okay. I'm ready."

"Ready for what?" Peyton asked, frowning.

"Your turn." She tossed a piece of popcorn in the air and caught it on her tongue. "I want to hear every juicy detail about your sordid affair with Callie. Don't leave *anything* out."

Peyton felt her cheeks grow warm as she shared her story.

"Wait. You left all the good stuff out." Zoey set aside her empty popcorn bowl. "Did you and Callie go all the way?"

"I can't believe we're talking about this."

"You're embarrassed?" Zoey grinned as she held Peyton captive in her gaze. "You're so cute right now. I can hardly stand it."

Her cheeks burned hotter by the second. "You're not making this easy."

Zoey laughed. "I'm not trying to."

Peyton turned and swung her legs over the side of the bed, intent on putting some distance between them. She felt Zoey's hand on her arm.

"Don't go. I'm sorry."

She looked over her shoulder and narrowed her eyes in silent accusation. "Why does it matter?"

Zoey released her. "Why does what matter?"

"How far I went with Callie."

"What matters more is how uncomfortable you are talking about it," Zoey said in all seriousness. "Why is that?"

Peyton shifted on the bed and leaned back against the headboard as she thought about the question. "I'm ashamed," she said aloud, more to herself than to Zoey.

"Ashamed," Zoey repeated. There was a long silence between them. "Of what?" she asked finally.

"Callie died without knowing the truth of how I felt about her."

"She knew," Zoey said emphatically. "When you have that kind of connection with a woman, both of you know. Both of you feel it."

They locked gazes. The air between them sizzled. Peyton felt her heart rate accelerate.

"You'll make a connection with another woman," Zoey assured her. "It won't be the same as the one you had with Callie, but it'll be just as beautiful."

"Nope." Peyton broke their eye contact and sat up straight. "Not a chance."

Zoey sat up alongside her. "Exactly what are you saying no to?"

"Dating. In case you've forgotten, I'm *pregnant*. With my late husband's baby."

"And?"

"That takes me off the market."

"Why would being pregnant take you off the market?"

"Who in their right mind would want a widow who finally came to terms with being gay four months into her pregnancy?" She rolled her eyes. "Talk about baggage. I'm the walking definition."

"The trick is finding someone who's *not* in their right mind." Zoey bumped her playfully on the shoulder. "Someone like me."

"Funny."

"It wasn't a joke," Zoey said in all seriousness. "There's something between us."

"Nothing will ever happen between us."

"But you're not denying the fact that there's something there." Zoey nodded in understanding. "Well, I guess that's a start."

"We're not starting anything."

"We just did."

"Did not."

"Did." Zoey lifted the remote, pressed *play*, and settled back against the pillows without another word.

She stole a glance at Zoey in the dark and wondered what it would be like to kiss her.

❖

Zoey woke up with Peyton wrapped around her. She lifted her head from the pillow and checked her watch: 1:03 a.m.

Peyton's hand was cupping her left breast. She smiled and tried not to laugh. This one was definitely a boob girl.

She began the arduous task of extricating herself from Peyton's limbs. After long seconds with little progress, she checked to make sure Peyton had the standard-issue two arms and two legs. It felt like she had a very pleasant-smelling humanoid octopus holding her hostage. She finally managed to wriggle free, stood beside the bed, and studied Peyton in the dark.

Peyton was attracted to women. Wow. There was definitely something between them. Their physical chemistry was palpable. Holding Peyton as she'd cried herself to sleep earlier that day had felt, well, strangely *good*. Their bodies fit well together. The memory of Peyton sitting beside her in bed as she shared Ella's story brought goose bumps to her arms and legs. With their shoulders touching, they'd held hands as she grieved for Ella. For the first time since her sister had died in her arms twenty-five years ago, Zoey felt less alone.

Tonight's soul-baring session now tethered them emotionally. Physical *and* emotional chemistry was a dangerous combination.

Her Apple Watch alerted her to an incoming text from Shadow. Four simple words: *Sam Bruno, Search Party.*

Zoey tried to recall the song. She stood in Peyton's bedroom, closed her eyes, and quietly whispered the lyrics to "Search Party," snapping her fingers to the imagined beat.

The song was about searching for someone on the run. A warning from Shadow. She was letting Zoey know that someone was looking for her.

She paced Peyton's bedroom barefoot as she thought back to her meeting with Vivian yesterday morning. Vivian must be under surveillance. Someone from Operation Bird of Prey didn't trust her. If she had to venture a guess, the most likely suspect was Bick the Dick. He was, after all, heading up the operation. Now that he'd figured out who Zoey was, he wanted to find out how much she knew, where she'd acquired the information, and what, if anything, she planned to do with it. She was now on the government's radar.

Zoey knew she was safe for the moment. No one would suspect she was here. But they might go looking for her at Sterling's house. Out of habit, she started to dial his cell but stopped short when she remembered her promise to him. They were to have no further contact until her mission was over. It had to be that way, for Sterling's safety and for the safety of his Iranian informant. Sterling was officially retired now. There was a good chance the government would leave him alone if she kept her distance until this thing was over. Besides, if push came to shove, she knew Sterling could take care of himself.

For the time being, Zoey needed to push thoughts of her mentor aside and focus on getting this mission underway. Everything was about to kick into high gear.

She texted Shadow back. *Dolly Parton, Dark as a Dungeon.* Shadow needed to gather the team and get to the locker.

Shadow sent a reply. *Sugarland, Already Gone.*

She shook her head, amazed yet again by Shadow's level of preparedness. How could she have thought for one second that Shadow would be caught off guard by the news of someone searching for her less than forty-eight hours into their mission? Knowing Shadow, she probably saw this coming a mile away. The question was, why hadn't *she*?

She sat on the edge of the bed and brushed Peyton's hair aside to see her face more clearly. This was the reason, right here. Time somehow slowed when she was in Peyton's presence. She'd forged a bond with this beautiful and difficult woman. Severing that bond now was out of the question. Zoey knew herself too well to believe she had any control over what was happening between them. For her sake and for Peyton's, she'd just have to make her brain work double-time at half capacity. That's all there was to it. Because Peyton would likely be occupying her thoughts from this point forward.

She quietly changed back into her clothes and, since Peyton still had possession of her Feejays, decided to abscond with the silk pajamas. She found some paper and wrote Peyton a quick note.

*Hate to snuggle and run, but duty calls. Whatever you hear about me, take it with a grain of salt. FYI: you might need the whole saltshaker. I'll be in touch soon, my little cuddle bug. –Z*

*P.S. Keep the Feejays and boom box. For now. Please take good care of them.*

*P.P.S. I've borrowed your car in exchange for the Feejays and boom box.*

*P.P.P.S. The car wasn't enough, so I also kept the pj's.*

She made her way downstairs in the dark and found the keys to Peyton's Subaru on the kitchen counter. Peyton had been driving Ben's Volvo since his death, so she probably wouldn't miss it. Now that Zoey was on the government's radar, she couldn't risk driving her own car.

She climbed behind the steering wheel, started the engine, and texted Shadow. *Cody Johnson, On My Way to You.*

She knew she couldn't risk returning home to pack for her travels. She'd meet Shadow and the rest of the team at the underground locker in Foxborough. Everything she needed was there.

## CHAPTER TWENTY

Zoey pulled off the dirt road, located the truck-sized boulder that served as her landmark, and climbed down from the Subaru. Still a mile from the locker, this was where she and Sterling had decided to build their underground garage. It was large enough to store four vehicles and accessible only if you knew exactly how to find the metal door.

She dimmed the car's headlights and used the flashlight on her phone to illuminate her path. There, about twenty feet from the large boulder, was a much smaller one. She rolled it aside to reveal a brown metal door. The massive door, which she'd cleverly concealed with dark-green moss to make it indistinguishable from the surrounding terrain, could only be unlocked with a special magnetic key.

She inserted the key and yanked upward, pulling the huge metal door in the opposite direction until it rested flat against the earth. She hopped back in the Subaru and carefully inched forward into the underground darkness, relieved to find three other vehicles already parked inside. Shadow had obviously transported the rest of their team and found this place with no problem.

She grabbed the hat, gloves, and scarf from the passenger's seat, grateful that Peyton had left them behind. It was a bone-chilling seventeen degrees outside tonight, and all she had with her was her coat. She pulled the hat over her head, slid her hands into the gloves, and wrapped the scarf snugly around the exposed skin on her face and neck.

Zoey closed her eyes and inhaled deeply. The scarf still smelled like Peyton. One day, maybe she'd unlock the secret behind the intoxicating aroma that followed Peyton everywhere and lingered on everything she touched. She opened her eyes. On second thought, maybe she didn't want to know. A little mystery was good for the soul.

She ascended the ramp, set the metal door over the gaping hole in the earth, and doused the flashlight on her phone. The sky was clear tonight. She stood in place and let her eyes adjust to the darkness. The moonlight would illuminate her path through the forest. Fortunately, Massachusetts hadn't gotten its first snowfall yet—a good thing since she was wearing only sneakers.

She knew her way by heart and jogged along the trail with ease, covering the mile-long trek in eight minutes. Shadow was waiting for her in the darkness beside the entrance to the locker.

"Dolly Parton?" Shadow asked when Zoey stepped into view.

"Sugarland?" she shot back, freeing herself from the scarf as she followed Shadow down the stone staircase and into their underground hideout.

"I was sticking to the country theme you started," Shadow said, closing and locking the door behind them. "I have a crush on Jen."

"Jennifer Nettles?" Zoey asked. "The lead singer?"

Shadow nodded. "Hottest country singer in…ever."

"I didn't know you liked country."

"I didn't know you liked Dolly."

"Big hair. Big boobs." Zoey shrugged. "What's not to like?"

Shadow slipped a cell phone from her coat pocket and handed it to Zoey. "Reboot worked his magic on this. It's untraceable to everyone but me." She pulled an identical phone from her other pocket. "I have its twin, so we're linked. No matter where you travel in the world, we'll be able to communicate freely."

They were standing in the main room now. She and Sterling had designed the blueprints together. The space was quaint but comfortable. A large sectional sofa faced a ventless stone gas fireplace in the center of the room. There was a spacious kitchen on one side and a full bathroom on the other. A long hallway that probed deeper into this subterranean world led to four bedrooms, an office, an exercise room, and a massive storage room that held enough food and supplies to last several years.

Zoey shrugged out of her coat, kicked off her sneakers, and sat on the sofa in front of the fire to warm her fingers and toes. "Has Phisher made any progress?" Phisher had once operated a genius—and highly illegal—phishing scam that had earned her a small fortune before Zoey caught up with her.

"She found an email from a CDC virologist," Shadow answered, "but it was heavily redacted."

Zoey needed something to prove that a deadly virus was about to be unleashed by the US government. Having credible documentation in hand to show her contacts would definitely help. She needed irrefutable proof that Operation Bird of Prey was underway, something other than her word. If she'd had more time, she would've penetrated the Pentagon by posing as a DOD employee, gaining entry to their database, and gathering the proof with her own two hands. Walking into the hornet's nest was usually right up her alley, but there was simply too much at stake right now to warrant making such a risky play. Now that they knew who she was, it was best to lie low and get out of the country as soon as possible.

"Don't worry. We'll find a way to get you what you need," Shadow said, as if reading her mind.

"Is the whole team here? Everyone from the list?"

Shadow nodded. "I was monitoring the audio and video feeds back home when this guy showed up." She pulled up a video on the new phone, pushed *play*, and handed the phone to Zoey. "Do you recognize him?"

She shook her head and fast-forwarded through the video. Her stomach somersaulted as she watched a sniper cell storm the lobby of their building. They swept through the building with military precision, kicking in apartment doors on each floor as they went. She'd installed security cameras in the hallways years ago. She watched as all of her kids were forced from their apartments into the hallway, bleary-eyed and still in their pajamas, where they were shoved face-first against the wall.

Zoey's vision blurred. She was unable to stop the tears. These were *her* kids. *Her* responsibility. And she had done nothing to protect them from this.

"Everyone's fine." Shadow hit *pause*. "Before I left, I told them the raid was coming. The older kids bunked with the younger ones so they wouldn't be afraid."

"I should've been there." How could she have left those kids unprotected? "You'll never have to pick up my slack again, Shadow. That's a promise."

"There was no slack to pick up," Shadow said. "We're a team. Remember?"

Zoey stood from the sofa and started pacing. She refused to let anyone shield her from blame. This one was squarely on her shoulders. She had half a mind to hunt down every member of that sniper cell and make them pay for what they did.

Shadow persisted. "You were doing what you always do."

"Putting my family in danger?" she hissed.

Shadow stood, blocking her path. She looked Zoey square in the eye. "North needed you, and you were there. That's what you do." She set a hand on Zoey's shoulder. "That's what you've done for all of us—every single one of us. Now we're here for *you*. We're *your* team. Letting us do our jobs doesn't mean you're not doing yours."

She held Shadow's gaze and steadied her breathing. There was an element of truth in Shadow's words. Zoey was accustomed to being a one-woman operation. Sterling had always been there to guide and oversee her missions, but ultimately, she executed them alone. For the first time in her career—maybe for the first time in her life—she'd have to cast that mentality aside and be a team player. She couldn't do this alone. She wiped the tears from her cheeks with the back of her hand. "That was a decent first pep talk."

"Thanks." Shadow let her hand drop from Zoey's shoulder. "Wrote it about an hour ago. I knew you'd give yourself a serious ass-whoopin' when you saw that video." She shrugged. "There's a longer version of the pep talk if you care to hear it."

She put up a hand. "I'm good."

Shadow reached behind the sofa, lifted a black duffel bag, and handed it to her.

"Don't tell me. You packed for me while you were writing that speech." She shook her head, amazed. "Can I get a well-done Shadow with a side of overachiever sauce?"

"Clever. I see what you did there. What would you be?"

Zoey pushed up her shirtsleeve to examine her own skin tone. "Medium?" She frowned. "Minus the overachiever sauce."

Shadow pointed to the bag. "Everything you'll need is inside."

"Is there anything you haven't prepared for?"

"Hope not. The world's counting on us," Shadow said with a sigh. "Runway's meeting you at Norwood Memorial Airport to take you to Canada. Your flight leaves in three hours."

Zoey had spent a small fortune helping Runway get his pilot's license six years ago. Now he flew commercial all over the world.

"Be careful out there, Z. Don't know what I'd do if anything happened to you."

"With you running point, the bad guys don't stand a chance." Zoey set the duffel bag on the sofa and leaned in for a hug.

She bid Shadow good night, and then showered, changed, and grabbed a catnap before trekking back to the underground garage. She considered taking one of the other SUVs parked inside but ultimately decided against it. The likelihood that Peyton had a GPS transmitter on the car played right into her plan. Assuming Peyton would be assigned to look for her, she needed a logical place to start. Parking near the airport would give Peyton the breadcrumb she needed.

When someone was searching for you, Zoey knew it was best to keep them close. Not so close that they'd find you but close enough that you could keep an eye on them from afar.

❖

Secretary of Defense Griffin Bick checked his watch: 3:56 a.m. He shoved his hands in his pockets for warmth as he strode across the dirt lot to a concrete building. It was a brisk thirty-nine degrees. He'd worn civilian clothes for today's meeting but had intentionally left his coat in the car—a necessary precaution against the inevitable spattering of blood. For this reason, he kept a stash of clothes in his trunk and regularly replenished it.

Griffin swiped his keycard, stepped inside the building, and listened to the echoes of his footfalls on the concrete floor. Like his good coat, his shoes were something he was unwilling to soil because they were simply too expensive. He summoned the subterranean elevator with the press of a button, leaned against the concrete wall, and slid a blue surgical bootie over each of his loafers. There. He stood and gave himself a thumbs-up. Good to go.

The harsh hum of a motor drowned out the sounds of his excited breathing as the elevator cage ascended from the depths below. He'd always loved coming here. The dungeon-like feel of this place perfectly suited his needs. More importantly, it never failed to lift him out of a foul mood. With so much on the line, it'd be easy to slip into a place of uncertainty and self-doubt. But he was about to eliminate the source of that uncertainty. Sterling had been a thorn in his side for years. Griffin was thrilled at the prospect of being rid of him, once and for all.

The elevator cage announced its arrival with the bone-crushing sound of metal against concrete. He watched as his right-hand man shoved the steel gate aside with effort. Griffin nodded a tight-lipped greeting, stepped inside, and waited for Polluck to close the gate behind him.

The dim elevator light flickered. He studied the smears of blood on Polluck's white coveralls and nodded, pleased that there was significantly more than usual. Per his instructions, Polluck had not held back. "Still nothing?" he asked.

Polluck pressed *S* for the subterranean level and turned to face Griffin with small, hard eyes and his perpetual five-o'clock shadow. "Not a peep, sir. Sterling's one tough sonofabitch. I had plans to cut out his tongue, but then I realized that'd be counterproductive."

Goose bumps broke out on Griffin's arms as he envisioned Sterling without a tongue to deliver his clever quips.

Polluck muscled the gate aside as their ride came to a bone-jarring end. He stood back and waited for Griffin to step out first—a sign of respect. Polluck always seemed to know and readily accept his place in the hierarchy. If he could just find ten more Pollucks, his workload would be much lighter. Good help was hard to come by in this line of work, particularly help that was willing to go the extra mile and get their hands dirty.

Polluck made no effort to hide the fact that he took pleasure in torturing detainees, which just made Griffin trust him more. He often found himself admiring Polluck for his unabashed honesty. Hey, everyone had a vice. Some vices were just more socially acceptable than others. If Griffin didn't regularly replenish the stock of detainees, he had no doubt that Polluck would be abducting and torturing innocent civilians on the sly. The way Griffin saw it, he was actually doing a good deed by sparing the world at large from Polluck's insatiable need for... He paused, unable to pinpoint what aspect of the process appealed most to Polluck. Blood? Agonizing screams? Cries for mercy? Prolonged torture? Maybe a combination of all four. He was never sure what made Polluck tick, exactly, and he didn't care enough to ask. Perhaps, like Griffin, he found the idea of ultimate control intoxicating.

With Polluck behind him, Griffin made his way through a maze of damp, dimly lit tunnels until he reached cell nine. He withdrew his key card from his pocket and glanced down at his gunmetal V-neck sweater and navy linen-blend slacks. He was starched and wrinkle-free from head to toe. Unlike Polluck, he didn't bother with coveralls. Ending someone's life was a very intimate experience, far too intimate for coveralls. Wearing the blood of the deceased was Griffin's way of showing ultimate dominance, like an alpha wolf pissing all over a lowly omega packmate. He took a deep cleansing breath, swiped his keycard, and stepped inside.

Sterling met his gaze—naked, bloodied, and battle-scarred but as alert as ever. His forehead, arms, torso, and legs were tethered to the interrogation board with leather restraints, his usually vibrant black skin now a dull ashen-gray, presumably from blood loss. Shock would be setting in soon. He was already starting to shake.

Griffin walked around him in a slow circle. The beauty of the interrogation board was that it allowed a detainee to be placed in any position: upright, flat, upside-down. If he chose, Griffin could even spin detainees around and around until they vomited or passed out from a bad case of vertigo.

"Finally," Sterling muttered, flashing a brave but bloody smile. "I was starting to worry you'd miss my send-off."

"Wouldn't dream of it." Griffin clasped his hands together behind his back and kept his gaze on Sterling's. "I trust the accommodations are meeting your expectations?"

"Exceeding them," Sterling shot back.

Griffin smiled, nodded, and then cut to the chase. "Where is she?"

"In the shadows, like I taught her. You'll never find her, Bick."

"Oh, I assure you, we *will* find her. Delta Force is tracking her as we speak."

"They're good but not as good as Zoey. She'll always be a step ahead." Sterling puckered his plump lips and spat with vehemence, like a spitting cobra about to be decapitated by the gardener's shovel. Bloodied saliva landed on Griffin's blue surgical bootie. "When her mission's done, she'll send someone for you and Commander Slice and Dice over there"—he pointed to Polluck with the one remaining finger on his right hand. "The someone she'll send will be very, very angry."

Griffin glanced at Sterling's genitals. "You've got balls to threaten me like that."

"Just giving you a heads-up on what's to come." Sterling managed to shrug through the restraints. "I know my kid. She's quicker and smarter than you and me combined. If I were you, I'd get my affairs in order while you still have time."

"Great!" Griffin clapped his hands loudly and then rubbed them together in mock-excitement. "Okay, I think that about wraps things up," he said, undaunted by Sterling's pathetic diatribe. The former CIA legend had been reduced to a dying man, grasping at straws. "Last chance to tell me where she is. If you choose not to talk, you can die knowing your daughter will be tortured in ways that'll make your injuries look like paper cuts." He threw a thumb over his shoulder at Polluck. "Commander Slice and Dice has particularly sadistic desires when it comes to detainees of the opposite sex." He glanced at Polluck. "No offense intended."

"None taken, sir," Polluck replied, stone-faced.

"Female visitors are so few and far between," Griffin went on, "so he has to make them last, you see." He held out his hand.

Polluck stepped toward him and placed a Smith & Wesson in his palm.

"I'll be sure to tell your beautiful daughter that her suffering was your doing." Griffin made a point of checking the chamber for bullets. He raised the gun's muzzle and smiled. "Last chance."

Sterling closed his eyes and spoke in French, his dialect as flawless as a native Parisian's.

Griffin silently translated: *You stole my wallet and my heart and made my journey worthwhile.* A sentimental utterance that was obviously not meant for him. Whatever. He shrugged and pulled the trigger, over and over again, until the sound of empty clicks echoed off the concrete walls.

## CHAPTER TWENTY-ONE

Peyton rapped lightly on the open office door as her boss glanced up from his computer.

Alvarez slid his glasses off, stood, and waved her in. "Feeling better?" he asked with a look of concern.

"Yes, sir."

"Good." He slid his hands in his pockets. "Get the door, please."

She closed the door, shrugged out of her coat, and took a seat in the leather chair opposite his desk. She watched his jaw muscles tense. Something had happened. "You said it was urgent," she prompted. "Is this about Blackwood?"

He met her gaze. "Why do you ask?"

"She hasn't checked in yet today." Zoey's cryptic note had given her a heads-up that something was brewing. "I've tried calling, but she's not answering. Goes straight to voice mail."

He sat, rested his arms on the desk, and laced his fingers together. "Blackwood's in trouble. I need you to find her."

"What kind of trouble?"

"Defense Secretary Bick called me this morning. At *home*," he added, making his point that this was, indeed, urgent. "Said Blackwood's a threat to national security."

Peyton frowned. A threat to national security? She uncrossed her legs and leaned forward. "How?"

"He wouldn't give me the specifics. A Special Forces unit is attempting to locate her as we speak."

"Attempting to locate her," she repeated as she felt her frown deepen. "And just what are they planning to do with Blackwood when they find her?"

He sighed but didn't answer, his eyes sharp and quietly tormented.

Peyton sat back in her chair, confused. "Why are you telling me this?"

"I'd like you to find her," he said firmly, "before they do."

In all her years of working for him, Alvarez had always been the proverbial rock. She'd never seen him like this. "You're worried about her."

"Damn right I am." He stood from his chair, shoved his hands in his pockets, and paced behind his desk. "Blackwood's one of our best. I don't know what she's done, but I want the chance to talk to her first—*before* the DOD gets their hands on her. I need to find out what's going on. Whatever she's caught up in"—he stopped pacing, ran a hand over his graying mustache, and locked his gaze on hers—"I wish she'd brought it to me first." He shoved his hands back inside his pockets and resumed pacing. "I'm assuming she's on foreign soil, but I have no clue where she is or where the hell she's headed."

Zoey had obviously kept them both in the dark. "You said a Special Forces unit is looking for her?"

He nodded, still pacing.

"Which one?"

"Delta Force."

*Delta Force*. An elite, highly trained special operations force comprised of only the toughest and brightest. "Who's on my team?" she asked, assuming she'd be leading a team of operatives to rival the vast resources of the DOD.

"You." He stopped pacing and met her gaze with a force that was startling. "You're it, North. I can't afford to let this get out. If word gets back to the DOD that we're trying to find Blackwood before they do, my entire career goes up in flames."

She raised an eyebrow. Pitting Peyton against Delta Force was like assigning a security guard to the White House to stave off a nuclear bomb attack. "If you don't mind me saying, sir, I think your faith in me is misplaced. I don't know Agent Blackwood well enough to anticipate, well, *anything*. Like you, I have no idea what she's doing or where she's going."

Alvarez studied her. He studied her for so long that she began to feel self-conscious. Was he questioning her truthfulness? He finally let his gaze drop, reached for the dark-blue CIA mug on his desk, and took a sip. He set the mug down and cleared his throat. "God knows, Blackwood can be slippery," he admitted with a fleeting smile. "But you've managed to hold on to her the longest since her previous handler retired. Dr. Pokale saw something between the two of you in your meeting last week. She thinks there's definitive chemistry there, enough for a successful, long-term partnership."

Peyton stiffened at the word *chemistry*.

"I know you, North," he went on. "Your work in the field is rock-solid. If there's any chance of beating the DOD to the punch, you're it. And if you're caught, I'll take the fall for this. I give you my word that your career will not be impacted." His expression softened as he stepped around and leaned against the corner of his desk. "But I also know you just lost your husband, and I'm asking a lot. You can walk away from this." He shrugged. "No questions."

Peyton felt the weight of this decision like a cinder block in her lap. What in the world had Zoey gotten herself into? Both the woman and the operative Peyton had come to know went to great lengths to protect the underdog and the people she cared about. Now the DOD was claiming that Zoey was enough of a threat to national security to warrant sending Delta Force after her. She couldn't imagine Zoey doing *anything* to compromise the safety of innocent people. Zoey wouldn't put anyone's life at risk, except, maybe, her own. She stood. "Blackwood's my operative, my responsibility. I'll retrieve her."

Alvarez nodded, visibly relieved. He walked to the other side of his desk. "Check in with me when you can to keep me apprised." He scribbled a phone number on a yellow sticky note and handed it to her. "Call me if you need anything, day or night."

"I'll do everything I can to find her, sir."

"I know you will," he said, absently running a hand over his mustache.

Peyton slipped the number inside her pocket, grabbed her coat, and turned to leave.

"North?"

She looked back over her shoulder. "Sir?"

"If the DOD finds her first, my impression is…we won't get her back."

They locked gazes from across the room. Peyton nodded. She understood him perfectly. Delta Force would likely capture, detain, and then terminate Agent Zoey Blackwood.

❖

Zoey gave Canada's Minister of Public Safety and Emergency Preparedness a thumbs-up as he drove away. She'd envisioned a lean, bespectacled nerd with an extra pair of glasses in one shirt pocket and a pen with a pocket protector in the other. But the man who showed up for their meeting forty-seven minutes late with a still-drying dollop of mustard on the front of his wrinkled button-down shirt fell slightly short of that vision.

The day was overcast and gloomy—a perfect backdrop to her somber meeting with Slobby Bobby. She noticed one of his taillights was out as his SUV ambled down the dirt road, in no particular hurry. Why would Canada put *that* guy in charge of safety and emergency preparedness when he clearly couldn't even run a safety check on his own vehicle? "Bet he stops at that all-you-can-eat buffet in the center of town on his way back to his office."

"I just reviewed Bob's GPS coordinates for the last few weeks." Shadow sighed defeatedly. "He's a regular there."

"Ace job picking my Canadian contact," Zoey chided.

"I'll add all-you-can-eat buffets to the list of disqualifying factors when selecting your contacts from now on."

"No worries. Rookie mistake." Zoey withdrew the flash drive from her coat pocket and turned it over in her palm. Her decision to hold off on sharing news of the virus with Bob had been the right one. They needed to find someone else. And fast. They also still needed some actual proof that Operation Bird of Prey was underway. "Any progress yet with—"

"No," Shadow answered, cutting her off. "Phisher's still combing through employee emails at the CDC, but she thinks it's a lost cause. What she really wants is your permission to hack into the DOD. She believes what you need is in there."

"No." Zoey wouldn't even consider the request. Hacking into the DOD was just too dangerous.

"If your contacts have nothing to go on but your word that this virus is real, they won't start manufacturing the vaccine."

"There has to be another way," she insisted.

"There isn't." Shadow paused. "Unless you want us to abduct the director of the CDC. I did a quick analysis, and I think we could easily get him to talk—"

"No hacking into the DOD, and *no* abductions. Find another way." She ended the call but kept the earpiece in place. Shadow had made her promise to keep it in at all times. The earpiece was programmed to connect to Shadow's automatically if Zoey uttered their agreed-upon safe word: *zombie*. The reverse was also true. Shadow and the rest of the team would likely never be found in the underground locker, but all mothers had the right to be nervous when it came to the safety of their kids.

Those kids weren't really hers, of course, at least not biologically. Mentoring the kids in her building was probably the closest she'd ever get to being a parent. Without a doubt, she knew her love for those kids was just as fierce as it would be if she'd given birth to them herself.

Zoey realized something she'd never thought much about before now—she longed to be a mother. For the first time since Ella's death, the idea of holding a baby and raising it as her own was immensely intriguing.

She shook her head. It didn't take a shrink to figure this one out. Peyton's pregnancy had obviously triggered her own maternal instinct. But something told her it went even deeper than that. She'd opened up to Peyton and shared her sister's journey. Talking about Ella had healed a very deep wound.

Was the sudden onset of these maternal feelings brought on by the fact that Peyton was facing motherhood alone? Was she trying to rescue Peyton? She was well aware of her compulsive need to heal the broken. Setting out on a mission to heal a broken spirit was her typical MO.

But Peyton was far from broken. She was smart, assertive, stubborn, and gorgeous. A little emotional, yes. But broken? Hardly. It seemed her developing feelings for Peyton had less to do with rescuing her and more to do with, well, doing what most animals were inevitably driven toward: finding a mate and starting a family. The idea of wooing Peyton—the same intensely competitive woman assigned to her capture—made Zoey's heart beat faster.

She checked her watch. The primary mission, of course, would remain unchanged—deliver the vaccine's formula to as many world leaders as possible in the coming days. Who said she couldn't have a little fun along the way? But first things first. "Save the human race," she whispered, reaching inside her coat pocket for the car keys.

It was like having to eat dinner before dessert.

And Peyton was definitely the dessert.

Peyton parked on the street in front of her condo and climbed down from Ben's SUV. With her keys in hand and her mind preoccupied with Zoey, she nearly tripped over the young man sitting on her front stoop.

He looked up from his physics textbook and withdrew his earbuds. "Agent North." He stuffed the textbook inside his backpack, scrambled to his feet, and towered over her, even though he was standing on the step below hers.

She recognized him immediately. He'd been one of the sentries at Mattapan Heights the night she'd searched Zoey's apartment. "Can I help you?"

"Zoey sent me." He reached into the pocket of his jeans and handed her a note. "She asked me to give this to you."

"You're one of the sentries," she said, studying him. "From the other night."

He nodded. "Don't worry. I'm not here to collect on the credit card, Subaru, or your 401(k)." He grinned. "Name's Darius, but everyone calls me Big D."

With good reason. He was easily six eight and pushing three hundred pounds. Curious, she unfolded the note.

*Big D has agreed to look after Horace while you're out of town. You can trust him. –Z*

She glanced up. "Have you met Horace?"

"Yes, ma'am. I brought him pizza for lunch, and then we played a game of chess." Big D frowned. "I want to say it was a competitive game, but truthfully, he wiped the floor with me."

"How often will you check in on him?"

"I was planning on twice a day, but I'll visit as often as you want."

She nodded, deep in thought as she glanced up and down the street. "How'd you get here, Darius?"

"A train and two buses, ma'am." He hesitated, looking concerned. "Is something wrong?"

Zoey trusted him. Instinctively, she knew she could, too. "How old are you?"

"I'm turning nineteen next month."

"Do you have a driver's license?"

He nodded. "Zoey said you might give me the third degree." He reached inside his backpack, pulled out his wallet, and withdrew his driver's license.

She stole a quick glance before handing it back. "Here," she said, holding out the keys to Ben's Volvo. "This should make getting back and forth a little easier. I'll give you a credit card for gas, food, and anything else you might need to take care of Horace."

Darius's eyes grew wide as he gazed back and forth between the keys and the Volvo. He made no motion to take them, so she stepped forward and dropped them inside his open backpack. "I'm heading out of town," she went on. "Not sure how long I'll be gone. Can you stick around while I pack and then give me a lift to…" She trailed off, unsure of where she was going, exactly.

"Your next destination?" he finished.

She frowned. "Did Zoey happen to mention where that would be, Darius?"

"No, ma'am. But she did give me this." He withdrew a small pouch from the front pocket of his backpack and handed it to her.

She pulled the drawstring and peered inside. Coins. Lots of them. From different countries. She stuffed the pouch inside her coat pocket and met Darius's gaze. "Anything else?"

He shook his head, zipped his backpack, and slung it over one shoulder.

Darius followed her inside, seated himself at the kitchen table, and diligently resumed his studies. Peyton handed him a bottle of water and some chocolate chip cookies and then hurried upstairs to pack.

She sat at her desk in the corner, emptied the pouch, and spread out the coins. Ten coins from ten countries: Mexico, Brazil, Australia, Russia, France, Nigeria, Canada, China, Egypt, and South Africa. Zoey was obviously planning to visit these countries, but why? She opened her laptop, brought up a world map, and gazed back and forth between the coins and the map on the screen.

If Peyton was planning a trip around the world, she'd visit Canada first and proceed in a clockwise fashion. She arranged the coins in the most logical order for travel from the US: Canada, France, Russia, China, Australia, Egypt, Nigeria, South Africa, Brazil, and, lastly, Mexico.

What could these countries possibly have in common? Zoey wasn't fleeing from the US. She was visiting these countries to give them something. But what? Information, most likely. Why would Zoey go to the trouble of visiting each country in person when she could so easily convey the information in an email, phone call, or text? Maybe Zoey was trying to pass along an object of some kind.

What was so important that Zoey would put her hard-won career on the line and her life at risk? More to the point, what would be considered enough of an infraction to put her on the DOD's most-wanted list?

These were questions Peyton would have to contemplate later. Time was of the essence now. She needed to focus on the task at hand.

She'd never packed for a ten-country trip before. The temperature and climate differences were extreme. In the end, she decided the best plan was to keep it simple. She had everything laid out on the bed in five minutes: two casual outfits for hot weather, two for cold, and two for everything in between. After thinking it over, she added one business suit, one set of workout clothes, a pair of boots, a pair of sneakers, and sensible square-heel dress shoes. She grabbed her prepacked toiletry bag, passport, and Glock.

Wait. Pajamas. She'd forgotten to pack them—her subconscious mind at work, believing she wouldn't have time to sleep. But it was especially important to take care of her body right now. Even though her baby wasn't yet born, her job as a mother had already started. She tossed two pairs of silk pajamas on the bed, along with Zoey's prized Feejays and a gray *Star Wars* T-shirt. Peyton wasn't sure why she was packing the Feejays. It just felt wrong to leave them behind.

She retrieved her black suitcase from the master bedroom closet, folded all her clothes into neat little squares, and stacked everything inside the suitcase in the order she would most likely use them.

She zipped up the suitcase, set her hands on her hips, and took one last look around her bedroom. No matter what Zoey did to get on the DOD's shit list, she knew she'd do whatever was necessary to keep them from finding her.

Peyton realized then that she was in trouble. She was heading into this mission without the cool detachment and total objectivity that usually accompanied her. Objectivity was an essential tool for any mission, and she'd always leaned on it like a wooden staff on a treacherous hike. When a mission grew personal and feelings got involved, the chances of successfully completing said mission decreased substantially. The only thing that Peyton had to her advantage was her awareness of this fact.

From this point forward, it would be imperative that she be honest with herself every step of the way—particularly about her developing feelings for Zoey. Because ignorance and denial were the cornerstones of peril for any CIA handler.

## Chapter Twenty-two

Zoey hadn't planned on staying overnight in Canada, but she didn't have much of a choice. She couldn't, in all good conscience, leave Canada's fate in the hands of Slobby Bobby. And she couldn't proceed to France and return to Canada later—it was simply too risky to double back when the DOD was looking for her. Her best bet was to stay put until Shadow could find proof that Operation Bird of Prey was real.

So, where to bunk for the night? She drove east, chose a quaint bed-and-breakfast near the edge of town, and parked a few blocks away. With some extra time on her hands, maybe she could squeeze in a run. She withdrew the night's necessities from her duffel bag—workout clothes, sneakers, pajamas, toiletries, and an outfit for tomorrow—and tossed them inside the empty backpack that Shadow had packed for her. Always best to travel light and leave as many of her belongings behind as possible. If the DOD caught up with her, she could sneak out of the bed-and-breakfast with only the clothes on her back, get to the car, and make a clean getaway. Lugging the duffel bag around would only slow her down. She tossed it in the trunk, slung the backpack over her shoulder, and traveled the rest of the way on foot.

Peyton thanked the pilot as she stepped off the plane and onto the tarmac. She'd traced the GPS in her Subaru to a small airport in Mansfield, Massachusetts. She couldn't help but feel insulted by the giant breadcrumb Zoey had left for her to follow. The eight-ounce bottle of maple syrup that was duct-taped to the steering wheel might as well have been a roadmap with a neon arrow pointing to Canada.

She stepped up to the rental car counter and withdrew her ID, one of many aliases she'd used as an undercover operative. "Excuse me," she said with a feigned look of worry. She slid her driver's license across the counter. "My sister came through here a few hours ago. We're supposed to meet up, but she forgot her phone. I can't reach her." She held up the two cell phones she'd brought with her for the trip. "My height, dark hair, dark eyes. She's quite beautiful." Peyton felt her cheeks flush at that last remark, but the rental car agent seemed not to notice as he picked up her ID and studied it.

"I remember her. Sisters, huh? Wow, you two look *nothing* alike." He glanced up from her license. "But you're equally beautiful," he said, sliding her ID back across the counter. "For the record, I'm not flirting." He pointed to his wedding band and flashed a genuine smile. "That observation came from a happily married man."

"Do you happen to know where she was heading?" Every rental car was GPS-equipped, which allowed the companies to track their vehicles. She crossed her fingers, hoping he'd offer to look it up.

"Didn't say where she was going." He narrowed his eyes and thought for a moment. "But I can check in our system to see where the car is now."

Bingo. Peyton watched his fingers closely and memorized each keystroke as he typed.

Username: *CanadaCars*

Password: *FindMyCar*

Easy enough. Now all she had to do was download the app on her cell. By entering the same username and password, she'd be able to track Zoey's whereabouts in real time.

"Car's in Ottawa—4750 Bank Street, to be exact." He studied the computer monitor and looked up. "I think she's parked at Hunter's."

"Hunter's?" she repeated, the irony of the name not lost on her.

"It's a restaurant and pub. Best burgers around." He checked his watch. "If you leave now, you can be there in ten minutes."

Peyton rented a car and made it there in eight. She pulled to the side of the road and checked the app on her phone. Zoey's car was very close, just around the corner.

Her stomach somersaulted at the thought of seeing Zoey again. What should she do upon finding her? Cuff her and haul her back to headquarters for a sit-down with Alvarez? She hadn't planned this far ahead and suddenly wondered why. Had she believed that she wouldn't be able to find Zoey, or was there a part of her that had hoped she wouldn't? Whatever the case, she needed to come up with a game plan fast.

She sat in the car for several minutes, running through different scenarios. There were so many variables. Would Zoey put up a fight? Probably not. But she might attempt to flee. Peyton glanced down at her sneakers. She was prepared to give chase. She was pregnant, but she was still as fast as she'd ever been. Should she handcuff Zoey? If she proceeded to return Zoey to headquarters, what were the chances they'd be intercepted and detained by Delta Force before they reached their destination? Should she actively go undercover and take Zoey with her to evade capture?

Crap.

Why hadn't she worked through this during the hour-long flight to Canada? That had been the perfect opportunity to formulate a more definitive plan. Instead, she'd wasted an entire hour on...on...*what*? She frowned. Thoughts of Zoey. That's what. Her mind had wandered against her will as she'd imagined Zoey's tongue inside her mouth, Zoey's breasts against her own, the sensation of Zoey's fingers inside her...

Disgusted by her lack of professionalism, Peyton realized her daydreams had become X-rated overnight, likely triggered by surging pregnancy hormones and her long-suppressed attraction toward women. She needed to get her mind out of the gutter. Stay focused. Complete the mission.

She closed her eyes and took a deep breath.

Zoey was unpredictable. Peyton realized then that making a plan of any kind in this situation was solely for her own benefit, to give herself the illusion of control. When it came to Zoey, having control over *anything* went right out the window.

*Okay, Peyton. Breathe. You can do this.* There was, in fact, an upside to this mission. It was an opportunity to work on something she'd been fighting against her entire life: being fully present and reacting in the moment without a plan. It all boiled down to one thing. She had to learn to trust herself. She'd know what to do when the time came. Wouldn't she?

All she had to do now was open the door, step out of the car, and take each moment as it unfolded. She reached for the door handle and froze. She despised the unknown. Diving into a mission minus the exhaustive preparation work she usually did was like…leaving the house without making the bed.

She remembered the time Ben had challenged her to go a whole day without making their bed. She'd managed to leave the bed unmade and head to work as usual, but no matter how hard she tried, she couldn't hold herself back from returning home and making it during her lunch hour. Was she totally incapable of functioning without the illusion of having control?

"I'm a total control freak." There. She'd said it. Never before had those words come out of her mouth. She felt the vicelike grip of panic ease just a bit.

She looked down at her hand on the car door handle. Time to dive headfirst into whatever waited for her around the corner. She could do this. She had to. Deep breaths.

Peyton unbuckled her seat belt, climbed out of the car, and looked up and down the street for any signs that she was being followed. She cautiously stepped to the sidewalk and rounded the corner, keeping an eye out for Zoey's rental car. There. Parked outside Hunter's, just like the rental car agent had said. Perhaps Zoey was inside, grabbing a bite to eat. Could it really be that easy?

She glanced at her watch. It was closing in on seven p.m. Mouth-watering aromas of roasted garlic and fresh-baked bread wafted over her as she walked to Hunter's front entrance. Her stomach growled insistently, reminding her that she hadn't eaten anything since breakfast. She'd been too hyped up to think about food. Now that food was within her reach, she suddenly couldn't think of anything else.

Peyton opened the door and stepped inside. The place was packed and bustling with activity. The noise of too many people talking at once made her long for earplugs. Every seat was taken at the bar, and every table, occupied. She searched for Zoey as she stood in line, wishing she'd brought a headscarf to obscure her from Zoey's watchful gaze. Why hadn't she thought to pack a scarf? She felt herself starting to obsess about the scarf—a minor detail but one she never would've overlooked in the past. Dammit. This oversight was just more evidence that she wasn't at the top of her game.

Zoey had likely chosen a table with the best view of the door, to keep track of the comings and goings of patrons and identify possible threats. She surveyed the crowd of faces.

Zoey was nowhere to be found.

She should leave now…*before* Zoey spotted her. She could wait near the rental car and surprise Zoey when she returned. Her stomach growled in protest, but she had a job to do. She'd eat later, when the time was right.

She was just turning to leave when she felt a tap on her shoulder.

"Mrs. Cuddlebug?"

Peyton spun around and met the young hostess, eye to eye.

"Mrs. Cuddlebug?" she repeated.

Peyton refrained from rolling her eyes. She nodded.

"Your wife was here earlier and showed me your picture. She reserved a table for you. Your dinner's ready."

"My dinner?" she asked, confused.

The hostess smiled knowingly and glanced at her stomach. "She shared the news about your pregnancy—congratulations, by the way—and gave me specific instructions not to let you leave without eating. She told me to use a bouncer to keep you here, if it came to that." The hostess frowned when Peyton stared at her. "Your wife was joking, of course. We don't have a bouncer."

Peyton willed herself to set aside her frustration and stay focused. Be in the moment. Go with the flow. She *was* hungry. Ravenous, actually. Besides, Zoey was probably long gone by now. The rental car was nothing but a decoy. She should've known better. Zoey was too smart to be caught so easily. "I'm all yours," she said with a defeated sigh. "Lead the way." As she followed the hostess to the back of the restaurant, it dawned on her that Zoey had referred to her as her wife. Obviously her idea of a joke.

Was it possible that Zoey was feeling the same stirrings of attraction? No. Ridiculous. She was pregnant, for God's sake. What was Zoey's plan? Woo Peyton while she was on the lam? The laughter that threatened to bubble up from within caught in her throat as she took a seat in the booth. A bouquet of fragrant red roses sat in the middle of the table. She stared at them, frozen. A miniature card had been tucked inside the bouquet.

The hostess glanced at the flowers and smiled again, even more broadly this time. "Your dinner will be right out."

Zoey was using Peyton's recent confession about her sexuality to manipulate her and throw her off balance. Her in-depth review of Zoey's file had revealed one thing, loud and clear—she was the type of operative who would use anything and everything to gain the upper hand during a mission. That's all this was, a tactic.

She shook her head, impressed by Zoey's resourcefulness but insulted at the same time. The question was, how far would Zoey actually take this? If what happened in Niger was any indication of how far she was willing to go to ensure mission success, then the answer was…all the way. She frowned as she envisioned Zoey having sex with her male target. Peyton had to hand it to her, though. She was a great performer. Her throaty sounds of pleasure were very convincing.

And incredibly sexy.

Well, no matter what, she would never let things get that far. She'd play along and make Zoey believe she was a sucker for romance. Let Zoey feel like she was roping her in for the con, and then, when Zoey least expected it, she'd slap the handcuffs on and haul her back to headquarters.

She grinned. Handcuffs. *Yes.* No more second-guessing about how to capture Zoey when the time came. Handcuffs were definitely needed. For one thing, they set clear boundaries, both physical and mental. They would also keep Zoey from touching her. In her current state of pregnancy, with her hormones raging, she was starting to feel like a feline in heat. The handcuffs would be her safety valve.

Peyton reached for the card inside the bouquet, feeling more confident about her plan by the second. She slipped the card from the tiny envelope.

*Go to the barmaid—the hot one with big boobs. Follow her to the back office, 8:00 sharp.*

She turned the envelope over, but there was nothing more. If this was Zoey's attempt at romance, her skills were sorely lacking. She frowned. Was Zoey trying to hook her up with the barmaid?

Peyton glanced at her watch. She had forty-five minutes to kill before her rendezvous with the well-endowed barmaid. As if on cue, a young man pushed through the swinging kitchen doors and made a beeline for her table. He carefully set the tray down and smiled uncertainly. "I usually bring the salad first, followed by the soup, and then the main dish. But I was told to bring everything out at the same time."

"Thank you," she said, setting a napkin over her lap as he served her a garden salad, a sliced baguette, autumn squash soup, and gnocchi with sage, butter, and Parmesan. Zoey had obviously taken the time to research not only her favorite foods, but how she most enjoyed to eat them. Instead of feeling like her privacy had been breached, she felt grateful that Zoey had taken the time to do the research.

Peyton loved to mix hot with cold, crunchy with chewy, sweet with salty. A forkful of a cold salad followed by some hot soup, a bite of bread, and then a taste of the flavorful main dish. She craved discipline, order, and routine in all areas of her life, except this one. When it came to eating a meal, she preferred to mix things up and keep her tastebuds on their toes, not knowing what to expect from one moment to the next. In some ways, she realized she was a walking contradiction and found it interesting that Zoey had already figured this out about her.

She finished her meal and made her way to the bar at 7:58 p.m. Every barstool was occupied, but the room was absent of conversational banter between patrons. The bar's large-screen TV held nearly everyone's gaze. She didn't know much about hockey, but it was clearly a source of great pride and entertainment for Canadians.

The barmaid glanced in her direction, nodded, and wiped her hands on a dish towel. She stepped around the bar and led Peyton to the back office. "Here." She handed Peyton a small key and pointed to a group of lockers on the wall. "Locker three."

"What's in locker three?"

"A surprise." The barmaid shrugged. "From your wife."

Peyton frowned. The wife thing again. Her knee-jerk reaction was to deny that she was married to Zoey, but she held her tongue, stepped over to the locker, and inserted the key. The screaming demon face that Zoey had rigged to spring up from her kitchen cabinet flashed through her mind.

Zoey wouldn't try to scare her again, would she? She closed her eyes, took a deep breath, and nudged the door open with the toe of her sneaker.

## CHAPTER TWENTY-THREE

Peyton held the locker door open with the toe of her sneaker and peeked inside. A fuzzy brown teddy bear peered up at her. She stared back at him, waiting.

The barmaid piped up behind her, "Unless something's changed in the last ten years, I'm pretty sure stuffed animals can't walk. You'll probably have to reach inside and pull him out."

She glanced over her shoulder at the barmaid. "Do you mind?"

The barmaid pointed a finger at herself. "You want *me* to get the bear for you?"

Peyton nodded.

"You're acting weird." The barmaid sidled up beside her. "Is there a bomb inside the locker?"

"No bomb." Peyton shook her head. "But there might be a zombie."

The barmaid paused in thought. "I don't think a whole zombie would fit inside that little locker."

"True. Probably just the head."

"Can a zombie live without a head?"

"Zombies are already dead, so technically, I guess they could."

Neither of them moved. They both stared at the locker.

"I didn't think zombies were, like, real," the barmaid admitted.

"They're not. But my...*wife*...thinks it's funny to hide them and have them jump out at me."

"I saw your wife. If she wasn't so totally hot, I'd advise you to get a divorce." The barmaid rolled up her sleeves, grabbed an empty paper towel roll from a nearby recycle bin, and used it to poke at the teddy bear until he tipped over.

"Ouch!" came a voice from inside the locker.

The barmaid leaped back, chucked the paper towel roll, and ran from the room.

Peyton sighed. So much for her barmaid in shining armor. She reached in, grabbed the talking bear, and held him up for inspection. He was heavier than he should've been. He'd been fitted with a wireless video camera and microphone—a nanny cam.

"What's my favorite dessert?" the bear asked in a cute voice that was clearly Zoey's.

"What?" she asked, rolling her eyes.

"Blue-bear-y pie."

She turned the bear around, peeled apart the Velcro backing, and removed the cell phone that Zoey had hidden inside. The phone instantly vibrated with an incoming call.

She tapped *accept* and held it to her ear.

"I have more," came Zoey's voice on the other end.

"More what?"

"Bear jokes. Would you like to hear them?"

"I'll pass, thanks." She tucked the teddy bear under one arm and made her way through the restaurant.

"How was dinner?"

"Delicious," she said truthfully, pushing her way through the double doors and stepping out onto the sidewalk. "Where are you?"

"Obviously not where you expected me to be."

"Obviously."

"Where are *you*?" Zoey asked.

"You know exactly where I am," she said, annoyed.

"And so does Delta Force. Look across the street. Second floor, northeast corner. Do it discreetly."

Peyton glanced upward as someone moved out of view in the window.

"Snipers are in position on the rooftop. Their orders are shoot to kill on sight."

Peyton felt the blood drain from her face.

"They're after me, not you," Zoey added quickly. "They're

tracking you, hoping you'll lead them to me." She sighed, and Peyton swore she could hear Zoey rolling her eyes. "Way to spot a tail, by the way. There were four more inside Hunter's, but you were too consumed by that bottomless pit you call a stomach to notice."

"I'm eating for two," she said defensively.

"Ditch your phone and Apple Watch. Keep the bear."

Peyton preferred her Apple Watch over the bear, but she already knew the reason behind the suggestion. Delta Force was piggybacking her signal. "What about this phone?"

"Clean and untraceable. Keep it. I'll be in touch."

She was about to ask why she needed the bear since she was keeping the phone, but the answer came to her. Zoey was obviously planning to use the nanny cam to keep visual tabs on her. She was essentially trading one party's surveillance for another. She frowned, momentarily conflicted. Instinct told her to stay as far away from Delta Force as possible. The lesser of two evils in this scenario was definitely Zoey.

She unlocked the rental car, climbed inside, and started the engine. Delta Force believed she was unaware that they were watching her. They would stay at a respectable distance to keep her from spotting the tail. She planned to use that to her advantage.

She drove west for twenty miles to Homewood Suites, checked in, and unlocked the door to her room. She left her iPhone, Apple Watch, and rental car keys in the nightstand drawer, turned on the TV, and promptly exited the room. She was making her way down the rear staircase with the bear tucked under her arm and her suitcase in tow when Zoey's phone vibrated in her pocket. She halted in her tracks, dug the phone out of her pocket, and accepted the call. "I'm a little busy here."

"Proceed to the first-floor exit. Obsidian-blue Honda Odyssey. Second row, fourth space from the left."

"A minivan?" she whispered.

"With a five-star safety rating."

"How am I supposed to feel like a badass in a minivan?"

"That growing life in your womb makes your safety paramount."

"There are plenty of sportier vehicles that are just as safe. You did this on purpose."

"Sorry to break it to you," Zoey went on, ignoring her, "but your badass days are now officially over. If any such days existed."

Peyton reached the minivan, opened the driver's side door, and tossed her bag on the passenger's seat. "What's that supposed to mean?"

"Exactly what you think it means. You're too much of a rule-follower to be a badass. A badass, by definition, does *not* color inside the lines. I bet you've never colored outside the lines, not even when you picked up your first crayon as a kid."

"For your information, I was planning to leave the rental car here at the hotel and steal a car. If grand larceny isn't a badass move, then I don't know what is."

"You mean, *borrow* a car. Knowing you, you already had a plan in place to return it." Zoey laughed. "With a formal letter of apology, a full tank of gas, and compensation of some kind," she added.

Peyton was quiet. She had planned to return the car to its rightful owner with a thank-you note and a sizable gift card to compensate them for their trouble. She sat in the driver's seat, more than a little miffed, her hopes of being a badass ripped out from under her like a magic flying carpet in midair. "Keys?"

"Inside the bear. Just push the button to start the engine."

"I've driven a keyless car before." She started the engine, not feeling like a badass at all. "Where am I going?"

"I reserved a room for you at the Fairmont Le Chateau Montebello, about an hour's drive from your current location. Address has already been loaded into the car's navigation system, and, wait for it..." Zoey inserted a dramatic pause as Peyton felt her patience wearing thin. "The reservation is under *Leia Solo*."

She couldn't help but smile at the reference to the *Star Wars* characters, Princess Leia and Han Solo. It almost made up for the minivan. "Are you meeting me there?"

"For snugglefest, round three?" Zoey sighed. "I'm afraid not, my little cuddle bug. The bear will have to do for now. Speaking of our furry friend, he's holding an earpiece for you. Right paw. You'll want to wear that at all times."

Great. As if the bear wasn't enough to keep her under surveillance. "Why?" she asked, annoyed all over again. She was starting to feel like a puppet.

"It's programmed to recognize a safe word, in case you run into trouble."

"And what'll happen if I use the safe word?" She dug out the earpiece and stared at it in the palm of her hand. Tiny and beige, it would be difficult—if not impossible—to spot in someone's ear, if they had her skin tone.

"Use the safe word, and I'll come for you. No matter what. That's a promise."

"Great. So, what's the magic word?"

"Yoda."

Another *Star Wars* reference. "Yoda." She paused. "Yoda. Yoda. Yoda. There, I said it. Come find me so I can arrest you, take you back to headquarters, and get on with my life."

"I'm giving you a way to call for me," Zoey explained. "No questions asked. Just know—if you use that, you'll likely be putting me in our government's crosshairs."

"In other words, you're giving me the gift of getting you out of *my* hair, once and for all."

"I'm at your beck and call. Yours for the taking. Ready to pounce on a moment's notice. Here whenever you need a—"

"Booty call?" Peyton finished, rolling her eyes.

There was an awkward silence. "I was going to say *friend*."

She squeezed her eyes shut, mortified, and felt her cheeks instantly grow hot.

"But booty call works better," Zoey quipped. "I imagine one night with you would be worth the risk of life or limb."

Peyton remembered the coins from different countries Zoey had left behind. She hurriedly changed the subject. "When are you leaving for France?"

"Soon. I've booked a flight for you. Departs at 7:51 a.m. from YUL and arrives at CDG in Paris at 8:36 p.m."

"What name did you put me under?"

"Luke Bacca."

Yet another clever combination of *Star Wars* characters: Luke Skywalker and Chewbacca. "Funny," she said as she familiarized herself with the minivan's console. "Give me the name. I'll need time to create a passport."

"Passport's already waiting for you at the Fairmont. I also took the liberty of having the proper attire delivered to your room."

"Proper attire?" she asked, suddenly curious. "For what?"

"Your new identity. It's a good thing you don't look pregnant yet."

"You can't be serious. You expect me to travel as a *man*?"

"It'll give us something to look back on and laugh about when we're old. Something tells me we'll need things to laugh about to keep us from strangling each other after retirement. More importantly, this'll keep you under Delta Force's radar. Make sure you prop the bear somewhere close as you don your disguise. I can give you some pointers on the mask and makeup if you—"

Peyton disconnected the call and shut off the cell phone. Damn. She wasn't in the mood for this.

Zoey's voice sounded on the seat beside her. "Shutting off the phone was pointless. I can still talk through the bear."

Peyton threw the minivan in drive, lowered her window, and held the bear over the blacktop as she accelerated. "Keep talking, and the bear dies."

"You wouldn't."

She summoned her evilest grin and looked into the bear's eyes. "I *so* would."

Silence. "Fine. I'll stop. Just don't hurt the bear."

Peyton flashed the bear a victorious smile, tossed it in the back, and started on the long drive to her hotel. Halfway there, when she was certain no one was tailing her, she pulled to the side of the road and called Alvarez. Time to check in and give him an update.

But it wasn't Alvarez who answered. Peyton momentarily froze. Had she misdialed?

"Please don't hang up, Agent North. It's Meredith Pokale. Alvarez gave me this phone and asked me to step in. I was hoping you'd call soon."

If that was true, it was out of character for Alvarez. He never passed the buck or wiped his hands of an operative. And, if he had, why would he hand her off to a CIA psychologist instead of a fellow operative?

"The DOD is monitoring Alvarez closely," Dr. Pokale went on. "Too closely. He couldn't risk leading them to Zoey. When I approached him and shared what I knew, he requested I take his place. The DOD has no idea I'm involved."

"Okay," Peyton said skeptically. "I'm listening."

"Sterling's dead. Executed by Defense Secretary Griffin Bick. Zoey's next, if you don't find her."

Peyton remained quiet. She swallowed the lump in her throat. The relationship between Zoey and Sterling transcended the bounds of agent and handler. This news would rock Zoey to her core. "What do you want from me?" she asked, sensing a quid pro quo.

"Find Zoey. Pass along the news of Sterling's death."

"Then my mission hasn't changed. I'm to retrieve Agent Blackwood and return her to headquarters."

"No," Dr. Pokale said firmly. "I need you to put that aside for now."

"And do what?" she asked, thoroughly confused.

"Declare an armistice."

"An armistice?" Peyton repeated.

"Find Zoey, deliver the news of Sterling's death, and then let her go. I need your word that you won't take her into custody—at least, not yet."

"Why would I agree to that?"

"Because I won't give you her coordinates until you do."

"You know where she is?" What in the world was going on here?

"I know this is hard." Dr. Pokale sighed. "But I'm asking you to trust me."

## CHAPTER TWENTY-FOUR

Zoey checked in at the bed-and-breakfast, paid for her one-night stay in cash, and requested the room at the top of the stairs to keep track of the comings and goings of all visitors. She accepted the room key from the clerk, hurried up the stairs, and quickly familiarized herself with all escape routes. With one last look around, she committed everything to memory—the placement of the furniture, the framed photos on the walls, the creases of the folded-down sheets and blankets on the bed. All of it. If anything was disturbed upon her return, she'd know. She changed into her workout clothes, laced up her sneakers, pulled her hair in a ponytail, and threw on her favorite Asics running hat.

A seven-mile run through unfamiliar streets was just what she needed. Cold air lashed at her face as daylight waned and darkness staked its claim on the quaint Canadian town. Dusk was her favorite time of the day—a time when she could blend in with her surroundings and watch the world from the safety of the shadows. A part of her always breathed easier when the sun went down.

Zoey sprinted the last half mile back to the bed-and-breakfast and then walked the surrounding streets to cool down. A handful of cars had been parked along the street in her absence, but nothing appeared out of the ordinary. She entered through the back door, used the rear staircase to reach the second floor, and unlocked her room, scanning everything with lightning speed as she stepped inside.

Good. Everything was exactly as she'd left it.

Satisfied that the DOD wasn't likely closing in anytime soon, she undressed and showered. She was rinsing the conditioner from her hair when she heard the loud *click* of a door closing—*her* door, if she wasn't mistaken. Whoever was inside her room now wasn't attempting to mask their presence.

She kept the shower running, carefully stepped onto the tile floor, and grabbed her Glock off the bathroom vanity. She hadn't envisioned running naked from the DOD, but she was willing to do whatever was required to carry out her mission.

She took a breath, raised her weapon, and nudged the door open with one wet foot. There, sitting cross-legged in an armchair about ten feet away, was the CIA's sexiest handler. Peyton had found her? Impossible. She squeezed her eyes shut and then opened them again.

"Still here," Peyton said with a sad smile.

She surveyed the room. Peyton's coat and Glock were laid out on the bed. She'd even unloaded the Glock and set the cartridge of bullets on the nightstand.

Peyton held her palms up in a gesture of surrender. "I'm unarmed."

She lowered her gun but kept her grip firm. "Anyone with you?"

Peyton shook her head, her gaze forthright, unwavering.

She stood in place, mystified as the water dripped from her body onto the bare wood floor. She held the Glock against her leg. How the hell had Peyton found her?

"Perhaps you'd like a moment to put some clothes on," Peyton prompted.

Zoey didn't budge. She pushed all modesty aside, set her weapon on a nearby table, and walked boldly over to Peyton. Naked or not, she was confident that she could take her handler in hand-to-hand combat if the need arose. "Stand up."

Peyton complied with the same sad smile.

"Anything else on you?" she asked, puzzled by the somber mood.

"No." Peyton raised both arms and nodded, silently consenting to a body search.

She patted Peyton's arms, hips, back, and stomach before running her hands down each of her legs. "Bra?" she asked, standing.

Peyton unbuttoned her blouse and held it open, revealing a lacy, push-up tiger-print bra.

She took a step back, satisfied that Peyton had nothing else on her. No one from the DOD had kicked in the door to her room yet, a good sign that Peyton hadn't been followed. "How'd you find me?"

"I'm not here to take you into custody." Peyton began buttoning her blouse, her gaze on Zoey's. "We need to talk. Then I'll leave and resume my mission tomorrow."

"An armistice?" she asked, intrigued.

Peyton nodded. "But put some clothes on first. I can't focus with you"—her gaze dropped and traveled the length of Zoey's body—"like *that*."

So many clever quips were there for the taking, but she decided to hold her tongue. There was an air of urgent seriousness about Peyton tonight, more than the usual party-pooper seriousness that she wielded like a weapon during their missions. Something had obviously happened. Something big.

Zoey returned to the bathroom, shut off the water in the shower, and threw a T-shirt over her head. She felt very patriotic as she stepped into the brand-new Feejays Shadow had packed for her. Dozens of tiny American flags adorned each pant leg. Shadow was paying tribute to the greatness of their country—her idea of a joke. She returned to the room and took a seat on the bed across from Peyton. "I'm all ears."

Peyton paused, took a breath, and then spoke in French with a fluency that caught Zoey off-guard.

Peyton spoke, aphorism after aphorism, and Zoey translated silently.

*Fix your sights on the greater good.* The first of Sterling's favorite phrases.

*Dedicate your life to truth.* Zoey could almost hear Sterling in the background, encouraging her to repeat each phrase, again and again, until she had no discernable accent.

*Tempt fate fully or not at all.*

Sterling had tutored Zoey in many languages. He'd insisted on perfect enunciation with fluent reading and writing skills. Fortunately for both of them, Zoey possessed a natural aptitude for languages and an ear for subtle dialects. She waited but said nothing. There was one more phrase Peyton had left out.

"And the last is my personal favorite," Peyton admitted with a sigh.

*Never fart while hiding in a closet.*

Sterling had painstakingly selected the first three phrases as code and then, to his eternal regret, allowed Zoey to pick the last. Hearing all four phrases spoken aloud was a message to trust the person reciting them. But it also meant Sterling was in trouble.

Zoey's mouth went dry. She couldn't bring herself to speak. She felt the blood drain from her face as she sat on the edge of the bed. If she was right about Sterling—she prayed she wasn't—Peyton would be passing along one final message. She had no idea what that message would be, but that's what she and Sterling had agreed to if something ever went wrong.

Peyton held her gaze and passed one final message from Sterling. *You stole my wallet and my heart and made my journey worthwhile.*

A part of Zoey had believed—had *hoped*—that Sterling would outlive her. It was always too painful to imagine it any other way. "Who?"

"I'm told it was Agent Thirteen who prepped him and Defense Secretary Bick who delivered the kill shot."

Zoey had been in the CIA long enough to know that Agent Thirteen didn't officially exist. It was a blanket term that undercover operatives used for the anonymous soldiers recruited by defense intelligence to perform two key functions: stay under the radar and obtain critical information by any means necessary. "And you know this how?" she pressed.

"Sterling had an ATI put in a few weeks ago. When he was abducted, it started recording and transmitting the data."

An Audio Tooth Implant. Zoey shook her head in disbelief. *Smooth move, Sterling.* "Where was the data transmitted?"

"To an email address."

"Whose?" she asked, curious to know who Sterling had entrusted with such sensitive information.

"Meredith Pokale's."

Zoey was momentarily stunned. "Dr. Poke?"

Peyton nodded. "She forwarded it to you but wanted me to warn you *not* to open it."

Sterling had obviously predicted his own murder but had done nothing to protect himself. She suddenly understood what he wanted her to do. She grabbed her cell from the nightstand drawer and checked her email.

"It's not something you should hear, Zoey." Peyton sat beside her on the bed. "Sterling wouldn't want that."

But that's exactly what Sterling had intended all along. He didn't necessarily want *her* to hear it. He wanted her to get it to the people who would hold Griffin Bick and Agent Thirteen accountable. Once again, Sterling had sacrificed himself for the greater good.

She typed *Make Them Pay* in the subject line and forwarded the email to Shadow without opening it. Shadow would know what to do. Zoey didn't need to hear the recording to know that Sterling had faced his own death the same way he'd lived his life: with grace, integrity, and honor.

She hung her head, squeezed her eyes shut, and quietly bid farewell to the man who'd proved himself worthy of her trust, respect, and admiration too many times to count. She needed her wits about her now more than ever before, but *this*...this was a huge blow. For the first time in her life, she wasn't certain she could go on.

Her body shook with sobs. Peyton gathered Zoey in her arms, smoothed her wet hair, and whispered words of reassurance as she wept.

❖

Griffin accepted the incoming call as he drove. "Bick," he answered. He was alone in his Land Rover and could talk freely over the car's Bluetooth.

"Team Cobra reporting in, sir."

Delta Force. He recognized the commander's voice at once. "Have you acquired the target?"

"Negative. But we have eyes on North. We're confident North will lead us to the target."

"Ticktock," he replied, annoyed by the delay. He ended the call, pulled to the side of the road, and texted his wife. *Working late. Don't wait up hon. Love you.*

Griffin wasted no time in dialing his new intern's cell. He needed a release. Bad. He imagined his cock filling Robin's beautiful mouth and swelled at the thought. She agreed to meet him back at the office to assist him with a last-minute project. He'd use every trick in his playbook to make her feel valued, indispensable, special. Then, he would seduce her—reluctantly, of course, because she knew he was married. Showing the proper amount of inner conflict and vulnerability always made women fall to their knees for him. Literally. He was sure Robin would be no different.

He checked the time on the dash: 6:21 p.m. If his calculations were correct, he'd be inside Robin's mouth in about two hours, finally getting the release he so desperately needed and the reward he so richly deserved.

He'd be sure to take his time with Robin. Coach her gently. He wasn't just a taker. He was a giver, too. By the time he was finished with her, she'd know how to give the perfect blow job and please any man who came her way.

❖

Zoey woke up to the smell of pizza. How long had she been asleep? Peyton had declared an armistice until tomorrow, but something told her the clock was ticking down. She glanced at her watch: 12:24 a.m.

Peyton set a takeout pizza box on the table. "Good. You're awake."

She sat up in bed, suddenly ravenous. She hadn't eaten anything after her run. "Is that my last meal before you haul me in?" she asked, mentally calculating how fast she could grab her sneakers, Glock, backpack, and a few slices of pizza on her way out the door.

"The armistice is in effect until—"

"Tomorrow, I remember." Zoey swung her feet over the side of the bed. "Technically, that's now."

Peyton handed her a paper plate with two slices of pizza and sat down beside her. "Relax, eat, refuel. No fun in catching you if you're not a hundred percent." She took a bite of her pizza. "I gave Meredith my word."

"Doc Poke suggested the armistice?"

Peyton nodded, chewing.

Interesting. Zoey suddenly wondered what else Shadow would find in the email from Dr. Pokale. Was she trying to help with this mission?

"Is she helping you?" Peyton asked, as if reading her thoughts.

She shrugged and answered around a mouthful of pizza, "I honestly don't know. Did she share anything else with you?"

"She wouldn't answer my questions. Said it was too dangerous for me to know anything more." Peyton frowned, clearly frustrated. "Why can't you just tell me what's going on?"

"Same reason," she admitted. "I'm not willing to put your life on the line, too."

Peyton set her empty plate aside, stood, and crossed her arms. "Shouldn't I be the one making that call?"

"Too late. Call's already been made."

"Why? Because I'm pregnant?" Peyton started pacing in front of her. "Last I checked, I'm every bit the operative you are. Being pregnant doesn't make me incompetent."

Zoey stood, reached out, and grabbed Peyton's arm. "You'll just have to trust that I'm doing what's right."

"If you're so sure about that, then tell me so I can be useful."

"The DOD needs to believe you're looking for me. If they realize you've stopped, then they'll think you're helping me. Their orders will change from surveilling you to executing you on sight. I can't live with that on my conscience. It'd also put a huge damper on my plans." Zoey stepped closer. They were now mere inches apart.

Peyton's breathing visibly quickened. "What plans?"

Zoey watched as Peyton's pupils dilated, a sign that she was sexually aroused. "To seduce you."

❖

Peyton stared at Zoey's lips. She couldn't stand the tension any longer. She sidled closer, slid her hands up Zoey's back and neck, and pulled her in for a slow, sweet kiss.

Their tongues danced in a seductive rhythm that felt both playful and competitive. Zoey's hands began exploring her body as Peyton did the same. She slipped her hands inside Zoey's T-shirt, caressed her breasts and nipples, and was rewarded with a gasp of pleasure.

She felt herself grow wet with desire as Zoey began unbuttoning her blouse. "Wait," she said, breathless. She set her hands over Zoey's to stop her. "I can't." It took every ounce of willpower to break their connection. She took a step back. "How could you put me in this position?" she asked angrily, buttoning her blouse.

Zoey raised an eyebrow. "*You* kissed *me*, remember?"

"Did not."

"Did."

Peyton thought for a moment and set her hands on her hips. "Dammit. You're right. That was me. Sorry."

"No need to apologize. You're a great kisser."

She started tucking in her blouse. "This was beyond unprofessional. I'll make sure it never happens—"

Zoey swiftly closed the gap between them and set her lips over Peyton's, cutting her off in midsentence. They kissed once again. But this kiss was exploratory and deliberate with a tenderness that made Peyton want to cry. *This* was what was missing from her marriage with Ben: a sweet, insatiable hunger that shot straight to her core.

Zoey released her and stepped back. "There. Now we're even."

Peyton didn't trust herself to do anything but make a hasty exit. She shrugged into her coat, holstered her weapon, and left without saying another word.

## CHAPTER TWENTY-FIVE

Zoey woke up alone. She sat up in bed and gazed around the room. Peyton had stayed true to her word, observing the rules of their armistice. But Zoey needed to get a move on. She wasn't going to press her luck by staying here a moment longer.

She climbed out of bed and headed to the bathroom to wash her face, brush her teeth, and freshen up. Dressed, she leaned against the sink and shook her head. She could hardly believe Sterling was gone. The world felt...*different* without him. It would take her some time to come to grips with the fact that he was no longer in it.

She popped in her earpiece and dialed Shadow's cell. She was anxious to find out if Doc Poke was offering to assist her with the mission. "Did you open the email I sent?"

"I did. The woman who sent it—"

"Dr. Poke."

"I like her," Shadow admitted. "I checked her out—up, down, and sideways. She's legit."

"Good." Zoey had no reason to doubt Shadow's assessment of the CIA shrink. Shadow was thorough, and Zoey trusted her instincts. "Did she offer to help?"

"On one condition."

"What?"

"That you stop calling her Dr. Poke. Her name's Meredith. Mere, for short."

"Fine. Done."

"I just got off the phone with her and finalized your itineraries.

You'll be leapfrogging one another from country to country. Mere's taking Canada, Russia, Australia, Nigeria, and South Africa."

"That leaves me with France, China, Egypt, Brazil, and..." Zoey strained to recall the list as she yawned.

"Mexico," Shadow finished impatiently. "This changes your departure and arrival times. I'll send you an updated itinerary within the hour. I'm so sorry," she said abruptly. "About Sterling."

Zoey swallowed the lump in her throat. She couldn't bring herself to speak about his death. Not yet. She'd honor Sterling by doing exactly what he taught her and put her feelings on hold until this mission was over.

❖

Peyton opened her eyes and flicked her wrist, momentarily forgetting that her Apple Watch was in the nightstand drawer at a different hotel. She refrained from peeking at the clock and closed her eyes again to take a guess at the time. It was her secret superpower. Regardless of the time of day, she almost always came within three minutes of the actual time. Felt like...five o'clock, give or take a minute. She glanced at the digital clock on the nightstand: 4:59 a.m.

She sat up in the king-sized bed and switched on a small owl-shaped lamp. The memory of kissing Zoey crashed down around her like a thunderous tsunami. God, that kiss. She'd allowed Zoey to kiss her even after she'd apologized and promised that it would never happen again. For a moment, Peyton had totally lost control.

She took a deep breath and gazed around the hotel room. Mahogany-stained, hand-hewn logs comprised the wall across from her. On her left, red plaid curtains covered twin casement windows that offered an unobstructed view of the river below. One corner of the room held a reading nook with a comfy armchair, fur-lined throw pillows, and a green plaid blanket. Floor-to-ceiling shelves filled with hardcover books adorned the opposite corner. The overall decor was rustic, earthy, warm, and soothing to the soul. Zoey would like this. Had Zoey ever stayed there?

Peyton realized there was a part of her that didn't want to leave this room. There was a part of her that didn't want to get up and face the day...as a man. *Damn you, Zoey.*

Sure, traveling undercover as the opposite sex was a strategic move that would likely keep her off the chessboard or, at the very least, make her an invisible pawn in this high-stakes game of cat and mouse. But something told her the true motive behind her temporary gender reassignment had nothing whatsoever to do with strategy. This was purely for Zoey's entertainment.

The passport that Zoey had left for her was more than satisfactory. All the tools she needed to transform herself into a man had been boxed, gift-wrapped, and left on the bed.

In all her years as a CIA operative, she'd never gone undercover as a man. It came as a relief that her disguise had already been planned for her. The only thing left for Peyton to figure out was the voice. It was time to embrace her more masculine side.

Over the course of her thirteen-year marriage to Ben, she'd often felt irrationally envious of his penis, particularly when they were in the middle of making love. She couldn't help but wonder what it would feel like to be inside a woman. Pretty damn good, she imagined. Interestingly enough, that's what would usually push her over the edge with Ben and allow her to orgasm.

Did her longing for a penis mean that she wanted to be a man? It was something she'd never before considered. Peyton sat in bed and tried to imagine what it would feel like to have a totally different body: hairy arms and legs, barrel chest, deep voice, testicles, the whole nine yards. She wrinkled her nose at the thought. No. Definitely not. She loved her body. But if she could *borrow* a penis for occasional use—minus the scrotum because it had always weirded her out—well, that penis would likely become her new best friend.

She sighed. If only such a thing was possible.

Peyton stood from the bed and stepped to the bathroom to shower and begin her adventure. Pretending to be a man for a day, she decided, might actually be fun.

## CHAPTER TWENTY-SIX

Zoey lowered the binoculars and whispered to Shadow at the other end of her earpiece comm. "Right on time. Looks like he's alone."

"If by right on time you mean fifty-five minutes early, then yeah," Shadow whispered back.

"He's always exactly fifty-five minutes early. And why are you whispering? I'm the only one who needs to whisper."

"It's called sympathy whispering." Shadow paused. "Why fifty-five minutes and not an hour?"

"Superstition. Claims bad things happen if he doesn't stick to fifty-five." Zoey raised the binoculars again and studied the surrounding landscape. Sacha had worked for MI6 as a senior intelligence officer and, like Sterling, had recently retired. They'd conducted numerous missions abroad, side by side. Even though Zoey had never met Sacha, she felt like she knew him from all the stories Sterling had shared over the years. "Patch me through to him," she whispered, sweeping the binoculars from left to right, looking for anything out of the ordinary. As far as she could tell, he was alone. She watched as he activated his earpiece to accept the incoming call. "Why don't grasshoppers watch soccer?" she asked, following the script to let Sacha know that the source of this contact was Sterling.

"They watch cricket, instead." Sacha's French accent dripped from every word like wax from a fast-burning candle. "Why are centipedes forbidden to play football?"

"Takes too long to tie their cleats," she replied, still watching him.

He narrowed his eyes and slid his hands in the pockets of his trench coat. "I'm not convinced this is you, old friend—unless your voice has gone up several octaves since retirement."

"I'm here to pass along a—"

"I'm leaving if you don't show yourself in thirty seconds." He disconnected the call, climbed inside his SUV, and started the engine.

Damn. She glanced longingly over one shoulder, wishing she'd parked a bit closer. No time to retrieve the car now. She hopped down from the concrete wall and sprinted along the blacktop as fast as her legs would carry her. She was well aware that this was her best—and only—shot with Sacha. She needed his help to carry out this mission.

Zoey was still two hundred yards away when the trunk of Sacha's SUV started to rise. She halted in her tracks and raised the binoculars. Two massive rottweilers turned their heads in unison and set their gaze upon her like missiles locking on to a target. The sight of them made her heart pick up speed. She'd left her Glock in the car on purpose. Showing up armed to a meeting created an atmosphere of distrust.

She scanned the surrounding terrain. Launching an ambush here was virtually impossible. The land was barren—mostly rocks, low-lying brush, and scattered tufts of grass. Shadow had chosen this location precisely because it offered superb visibility. But that was working against her now. There was nothing she could climb to escape the four-legged missiles Sacha was preparing to launch. If she sprinted back the way she came, she'd never make it.

"Shit," she said aloud.

Shadow's voice sounded in her ear. "What's going on?"

"Two attack dogs, coming in fast."

"On it. Give me a sec."

"No worries." She looked on as both rottweilers leaped down from the SUV and galloped toward her in a fury of snarls, bared teeth, and flapping, salivating jowls. "Take all the time you need."

"You have your phone?"

"Sure do." She dug it out of her pocket without taking her gaze from the dogs. "Did you want to talk to them?"

"Hold it up."

She did, half expecting to hear Shadow recite the *down* command in every language imaginable. But she heard nothing. Zoey glanced at the phone. Was Sacha jamming the signal?

The dogs were closing in fast. Thirty yards. Twenty yards. Ten. Damn, they were huge. Maybe she could take one in a fight-to-the-death challenge, but she didn't stand a chance with two. "I leave my entire Feejay collection to you," she said, squeezing her eyes shut as she readied herself for the oncoming assault.

But none came.

"Do I still get the Feejays?" Shadow asked, sounding rather smug.

Zoey opened her eyes. Both dogs were sprawled on the ground, pawing frantically at their ears. "What—"

"Ultrasonic soundwaves. I'm connecting you to Sacha now. Talk fast before their eardrums burst."

Sacha was already stepping down from the SUV and peering in her direction as he accepted the call. "Don't hurt them."

"Call off the attack."

He withdrew a silver whistle from the pocket of his trench coat, held it to his lips, and blew two short bursts. "Done."

She took a few steps back and braced herself as the dogs righted themselves. They zeroed in on her with predatory focus.

Sacha blew the whistle again—one long burst this time. The dogs returned to him at once. "What do you want?" he asked through the earpiece as one dog sat on his left and the other, on his right.

"To keep my limbs, for starters. Can you please put those things away?"

He homed in on her with his binoculars. "Not until you tell me who you are and why you've sought me out."

"First, I'm unarmed." She lifted her shirt and turned in a full circle. "Second—"

"You're Sterling's kid," he said with a tone of disbelief.

She nodded. "Zoey." She felt a lump in her throat at the mention of Sterling's name. "Zoey Blackwood."

"Bloody hell," came his response as he hung his head and leaned back against the SUV. "He's dead, isn't he?" He turned to the dogs and spoke in his native tongue. "Amie."

*Friend.* The dogs instantly relaxed.

She took his cue and jogged over, quickly closing the gap between them. The dogs pranced excitedly in place and wagged their stubby tails at her approach.

"Ruger," Sacha said, pointing to the rottweiler on his left, "and Remington." He gestured to the dog on his right.

"Ruger and Remington," she repeated. Perfect names for this particular arsenal. Both dogs met her gaze with curiosity as their stubs wagged in earnest. "Thanks for not eating me."

"Who killed him?" Sacha asked, the tears in his eyes replaced with a shrewdness born of loss few could fathom. Sacha's wife and daughters had been murdered decades ago, prompting his lifelong career. Having nothing to lose made him one of the most effective intelligence officers MI6 had ever seen. According to Sterling, it also made Sacha one of the most dangerous men on the planet. "Tell me everything."

She did. They both leaned against the SUV in silence. One of the dogs nudged her hand with his massive head, asking her to stroke him. She obliged as she waited for Sacha to say something. Anything.

"Oh, I get it," Shadow said finally in her ear. "We're giving the geriatric, retired intelligence officer time to contemplate the end of the human race and come up with a solution that us young, quick-minded folk haven't thought of yet." Shadow had no patience for someone who couldn't keep up with her ability to process information at warp speed. "Tell you what, I'll get cracking on our next crisis—global warming— while Sacha takes his sweet time processing at the speed of a sloth." She sighed, clearly annoyed. "The silver lining to having a sloth on our team? I'll have plenty of time to grab a nap after I solve the climate crisis."

Minutes ticked by, filled only by the sound of Shadow's dramatic sighs on the other end of the comm. Her protégé was nearing the end of her rope. "Interesting fact: the average sloth takes one full minute to cover a distance of just six feet."

More silence. Sacha was so still and his breathing so shallow that Zoey wondered if he'd somehow mastered the art of sleeping while standing.

"They move so slow," Shadow went on, "that the fur on their backs is home to algae, fungi, and six different species of sloth moths."

Zoey followed Sacha's gaze but couldn't pinpoint anything of interest in the distance.

"Does Sacha's hair have a greenish tint? Are there any moths fluttering around his head?"

Ruger and Remington panted beside her. "They're thirsty," she said finally, searching for an opportunity to make sure Sacha was still alive.

"Bowls are in the back," he replied without looking over.

She lifted the tailgate, found two stainless-steel bowls, and filled them with water from a nearby jug. The dogs sat a few feet away and waited like gentlemen. She set the bowls on the ground and backed away quickly, half expecting to be mowed over by their exuberance and obvious thirst. Both dogs remained seated. They gazed longingly from the bowls to her face. "Go ahead," she said. "Drink." Neither dog moved. She turned to Sacha. "Do they want me to test it first to make sure it's not poisoned?"

"You put their bowls down incorrectly," he said gruffly without taking his eyes from the horizon. "Ruger's goes on the left. Remington's, on the right."

"But the bowls are identical."

"Not to them."

She knelt in the dirt, rearranged the bowls, and watched as they lapped up the water with gusto. Who knew dogs could be so particular?

Sacha finally emerged from his trance, uncrossed his arms, and met her gaze. "All set."

"Great." She forced a smile. "Glad we had this little chat."

He slid his hands in the pockets of his trousers. "Do you want to hear my plan for saving billions of lives or not?"

# Chapter Twenty-seven

Peyton stood from her seat and slung her bag over one shoulder as the announcement sounded for first-class passengers to begin boarding. She waited in line, her gaze on the floor to avoid eye contact and discourage unwanted conversation from fellow passengers. When she got to the front of the line, she handed her boarding pass to the flight attendant. At least Zoey had splurged for a first-class ticket.

The flight attendant flashed her a genuine smile, seemingly oblivious to her disguise. She wore a Scally cap, black-framed glasses, and a neatly trimmed beard. Red plaid suspenders held up a very comfortable pair of Dolce & Gabbana stonewashed jeans. She'd rolled up the sleeves of her pale gray button-down shirt to reveal colorful, full-sleeve tattoos on both arms, which, she hoped, drew attention away from the fact that her arms were hairless and slender. It had taken her nearly three hours of painstaking work to don this disguise.

"Welcome, Mr. Bacca."

Peyton met the flight attendant's gaze, nodded, and moved along. She might look like a man, but she definitely didn't sound like one, at least not to her discerning ears. No matter how hard she tried, she just couldn't get a handle on the voice. She'd stared at her reflection in the hotel mirror earlier that morning and experimented with different combinations of low timbres and scratchy tones. Zoey had watched through the eyes of the teddy bear perched on the dresser beside her.

*"God, no," Zoey had said, clearly frustrated.* "Who talks like that? You sound like an old man with no teeth."

Peyton kept trying, but no matter how hard she tried to switch it up, there was little variation to her voice. It boiled down to a choice between the toothless old man or a prepubescent teenage boy.

"I'm not giving up." Peyton checked the time. "I still have fifteen minutes to figure this out."

"Fifteen years wouldn't help. You're hopeless."

She glanced down at her chest. Her breasts were nowhere to be found. She missed them. "What did you expect? I can hardly breathe in this chest wrap."

"How come it looks like you have no package?"

"What package?" she asked, confused. "Am I supposed to carry a package?"

"Your penis, Peyton. Where's your penis?"

"Oh." She glanced at the box on the bed and grimaced. "I am not wearing that...that...thing."

"Committing fully to a new identity as an undercover operative is an important step toward ensuring mission success. You know that as well as I do."

Peyton crossed her arms. "I was never trained to carry that particular weapon."

"That's not just any weapon," Zoey said in all seriousness. "That's Twinkie the Dinkie, a state-of-the-art pocket rocket."

Peyton squeezed her eyes shut and shook her head. How had she let things get this far? "I'll position the carry-on bag in front of my nonexistent parts. Problem solved."

"C'mon," Zoey pleaded. *"Get it out of the box and hold it up. I'll walk you through the rest."*

Peyton found her assigned seat in first class and set her carry-on in the space beneath her feet. The flight didn't appear to be full. With any luck, she'd have this row all to herself. She set her jacket on the seat beside her and kept her gaze fixed on the tarmac outside her window as the other passengers settled in.

A flight attendant made her way down the aisle, introducing herself with a smile and a warm welcome to everyone in first class. When she reached Peyton, she kept to her script. "Welcome aboard, Mr. Bacca. I'm Natasha. Please let me know if there's anything you need while we're"—her gaze dropped to Peyton's lap—"in the air."

Peyton followed the attendant's startled gaze to the crotch of her jeans, mortified to find that Twinkie the Dinkie was now standing at full attention. She grabbed for her jacket and draped it over her lap as Natasha averted her gaze and hurried down the aisle.

Peyton mentally chastised herself for not checking that Twinkie was properly adjusted prior to taking her seat. A rookie mistake. Hiding her enormous erection under the jacket was a clear admission of guilt and, in hindsight, probably not the best idea. The carefully staged jacket now made it look like she was masturbating. Would they kick her off the plane for having a boner? She tried wiggling around in her seat to adjust herself, lifted the jacket to take a quick peek, and found Twinkie looking like the soldier he was.

Peyton pushed with all her might against the woody in her pants. It didn't budge. Felt like it was made of steel. Twinkie wasn't going down without a fight.

*Oh. My. God.* She intuitively knew that Zoey was somehow responsible for the hard-on currently taking place in her pants. Her cheeks burned with embarrassment. She wasn't sure which was worse—the colossal stiffy in her lap or the fact that she was such an easy target for Zoey.

She kept the jacket in place and buckled her seat belt as the plane started down the runway. For now, there was nothing she could do. She'd just have to sit tight and be sure to keep both hands above the jacket at all times, in plain sight.

Peyton decided, then and there, that she'd save Delta Force the trouble and kill Zoey herself when she found her.

❖

Zoey took a deep breath as she watched the man beside her. Sacha's mannerisms reminded her so much of Sterling's. She suddenly found herself wondering about the nature of their relationship. She stepped around to the rear of the SUV and sat on the tailgate. Both dogs leaped up, turned in the small cargo space, and lay down beside her. She began to stroke their bellies.

Sacha followed and set his hands on his hips. "What the hell are you doing?"

"Reinforcing my relationship with Ruger and Rem so they never try to eat me again." She met his harsh gaze, undaunted. "Besides, I think better when I snuggle."

"No thinking required." He glared at his dogs. "I did that already."

"I'll take one giant ego with a side of Sacha, please," Shadow said through the earpiece. "Just who does he think he is?" Sacha had obviously struck a nerve. "Tell that artifact you already have a think tank, thank you very much, one who's younger, better looking, and thinks at, like, warp speed."

"Sterling told me about you," Zoey said.

"I gathered that." Sacha raised an eyebrow. "You are *here*, after all."

"He was in love with you." How could she not have seen that before now? It had never occurred to her that Sterling was gay. All the pieces came together quite suddenly—the stories that Sterling had shared with her over the years, the wistful look in his eyes when he'd told them. And then there were the letters. They arrived on the first of every month, disguised as a bill for a nonexistent account. For many months, she'd wondered why Boston Gas sent two bills every month—one on the first and one on the fifteenth—until she'd held one up to the light and seen the neat handwritten script inside. She hadn't been able to make out much at the time and, out of respect for Sterling's personal life, had decided not to pry further. It was one of the few times in her life that she'd felt compelled to respect someone's boundaries.

Zoey felt her mind spinning. She did her best to keep her poker face intact.

"Bullshit. Sterling told you nothing."

There it was—an admission of sorts. Not only was Sterling gay, but he was *in love*. Had he really denied himself the pleasure of companionship all these years?

Sacha sighed and stared off into the distance. "We started visiting again after we retired."

"And by visiting, you mean—"

"Dating." He nodded. "Imagine that. Dating at our age." He met her gaze with a dry laugh. "But it was more than that. We committed ourselves to one another decades ago. I was set to move there next month." Tears coursed down the wrinkles on his cheeks. "After all this time, we would finally be together."

The fact that Sterling had loved this man—and been loved by him—

brought her a profound sense of comfort and peace. Zoey searched for something to say, but words eluded her because none existed for such an occasion. She set a hand over Sacha's arm and squeezed, realizing, too late, that she'd just committed the worst sin of all—an arm hug. Peyton was rubbing off on her.

Sacha set a strong, calloused hand over hers and squeezed back. "Glad we finally met. Sorry about...well...them." He gestured to the dogs.

She shrugged. "Meeting your partner's kid for the first time can be daunting."

"For the record, I didn't know it was you."

"Was he ever going to tell me?" she asked, hurt by the fact that Sterling had withheld something so important.

Sacha nodded. "He planned on hiding me wrapped in a big red bow when we broke the news. Said it was the best gift he could give you because you hated that he was alone."

Zoey laughed through her tears. He was right. She'd never shared that with Sterling, but he knew her better than anyone.

Sterling had a keen eye for spotting the inherent goodness and talent in others. He'd chosen to spend the rest of his life with Sacha. She had no doubt that the man sitting beside her possessed just as much integrity as her mentor had.

"What's done is done. We can grieve later." Sacha dried his eyes with the back of one sleeve and glanced over. "I'll find out where the US is making and storing the vaccines that they're planning to sell to the rest of the world."

"And do what, exactly?" she asked, wondering what he had up his sleeve.

"Hijack them. Your government wouldn't dare release Bird of Prey if they didn't stand to make a profit."

Shadow's suddenly upbeat voice sounded in her earpiece. "Like our Robin Hood plan but on a grander scale."

Zoey knew better than to underestimate the vast resources of the United States government. "They'll quadruple their manufacturing facilities, streamline the manufacturing process, and have their warehouse shelves restocked within weeks."

"Not if we hack into their database and alter the vaccine's formula," Sacha countered.

"We can alter it just enough to make it ineffective," Shadow announced, readily climbing aboard.

She stood from the tailgate and began pacing as she considered Sacha's plan. Hijacking a small portion of the vaccine supply to inoculate their own people was one thing. Hijacking the entire vaccine supply for the rest of the world was a whole different ballgame. She and Shadow had never even considered that course of action because they lacked the manpower for such a complex operation. Zoey met his gaze defiantly. "First of all, let's get something straight—they're *not* my government. Not anymore."

"Understandable," Sacha said, nodding. "I'd feel the same if I were in your shoes. Happy to put in a word for you with MI6 when this is over. I'm quite sure they'd welcome you with open arms."

"Our first job offer of many," Shadow whispered. "And so it begins."

She narrowed her eyes. "Finding volunteers with enough tactical training to hijack the entire Bird of Prey vaccine supply is a tall order. Assembling that kind of manpower would require time, time we don't have right now. Our window of opportunity here is finite."

"Let me worry about that," he said with a wink. "In the meantime, you just keep sharing that formula with as many country leaders as possible."

"This could work, Z. If Sacha can do what he says, we might actually be able to pull this off."

Zoey struggled to wrap her mind around the magnitude of Sacha's plan. If there was anyone qualified to lead such a complex and dangerous operation, it was him.

"The cool old white guy arrives in the nick of time to save the human race," Shadow went on. "Next time around, the least we can do is make sure our hero is, you know, more diverse. Even if he is gay."

Sacha grinned. "She called me cool."

"He can hear me?" Shadow asked in a slightly panicked voice. "How the hell can he hear me, Z?"

Sacha pointed to his ear. "You're not the only one who knows how to play with cool gadgets."

"But these earbuds are *unhackable*," Shadow said in a tone of disbelief that Zoey was unaccustomed to hearing.

Sacha crossed his arms. "Not to me."

Zoey's protégé grew suddenly quiet.

"Cat got your tongue?" Sacha sighed. "I expected more from the younger, better-looking version of me who thinks at, like, warp speed."

Zoey decided enough was enough. She couldn't, in all good conscience, let Sacha dig himself in so deep that there was no hope of escape. "Careful," she warned. "Shadow's more dangerous than these dogs. Trust me, you want her to like you."

"I already do," Shadow chimed in. "Just finished reviewing his file at MI6. His career spanned half a century. Sacha's missions are legend."

His smirk faded. "That's classified."

"Not to me," Shadow replied with an audible smirk of her own.

Zoey shook her head as she met Sacha's awestruck gaze. "She'll always be a step ahead. I've accepted it." She reached over and patted Sacha's arm. "In time, you will, too."

## CHAPTER TWENTY-EIGHT

Peyton wheeled her suitcase behind her as she trekked through Charles de Gaulle Airport in Paris. *Now what?* Zoey had allegedly made a pit stop here, but she still had no idea what Zoey's agenda was or where to even begin looking for her.

She stepped through the automatic doors and had just reached the sidewalk when Zoey's voice jolted her from her thoughts. The earbud Zoey had given her yesterday was so comfortable and small that she'd almost forgotten it was there.

"Welcome to the City of Love. Your chariot awaits, madame."

Peyton glanced at the long line of taxis outside the terminal. She was about to ask which one when she spotted a driver holding a *Star Wars* sign above his head. "Where's he taking me?"

"To your hotel."

"What happens after that?" Peyton asked, annoyed at being strung along, inch by agonizing inch.

"One step at a time, mon amour."

"Don't call me that. I'm not in the mood for your games, Zoey."

"Then…mon amie."

"I'm not your friend, either. A friend wouldn't have slipped me a Viagra without my consent." She shifted her carry-on bag and glanced down at the straining crotch of her jeans.

"Not my lover, not my friend. How about my bitchy acquaintance?"

Better. Peyton had to stifle a laugh. "Lower the tentpole or our affiliation ends here."

"Can I get a quick glimpse first?"

She unzipped her carry-on, withdrew the stuffed bear, and dangled it over a nearby trash can.

There was a brief silence as Peyton felt the seat of her pants instantly relax its viselike grip around her pelvis, buttocks, and thighs. Finally. All she wanted now was to get to her hotel, rip off the disguise—namely, this suffocating chest wrap and itchy beard—and reclaim her body. She'd take stilettos over a boner any day of the week.

"Better?" Zoey asked.

"Much." She left her suitcase with the driver and climbed inside the taxi.

"I've reserved a room for you at the Bourg Tibourg in the Marais district."

Peyton watched as the driver popped the trunk and loaded her suitcase inside. "I'm familiar with it," she said, tucking the bear under one arm as she fastened her seat belt. Zoey was obviously calling the shots here. If there was any hope of apprehending this rogue agent—*her* rogue agent, she reminded herself—she had to find a way to turn this around and get the upper hand. But she had nothing whatsoever to go on. Peyton closed her eyes, took a deep breath, and resigned herself to the fact that she was being forced to relinquish all control. Every last bit of it. All she could do was play along until an opportunity presented itself. She'd just have to be vigilant, stay in the moment, and make sure she was ready to pounce when that opportunity came. Problem was, no part of that plan catered to her strengths.

She realized then that she was in a cat-and-mouse chase with Zoey. Except Peyton was the mouse when she wanted to be the cat. She had to face the truth: Zoey would *never* be the mouse. The question was, would Peyton ever get a chance to be the cat?

"There's another surprise waiting for you in your hotel room," Zoey said, sounding rather chipper.

"Wonderful." She shook her head and sighed. "Can't wait."

❖

Peyton stepped out of the shower, wrapped her wet hair in a towel, and slipped into the plush burgundy-and-gold hotel bathrobe. She leaned against the doorframe and gazed at the emerald-green Fleur du

Mal dress on the bed. The sleek, form-fitting fabric had a halter-strap neckline and a midlength hem with a sultry side-slit ruffle to show off some thigh. Zoey had even included a pair of Jimmy Choo black high heels with an ankle-strap and a glittery Jimmy Choo clutch.

Zoey had obviously spent a small fortune on the designer ensemble, but why? Peyton knew how careful Zoey was with money. It wasn't like her to spend it on something so frivolous. She reread the handwritten note that had been tucked inside the shoebox. *Will you dance with me, mon amour?* There was an address for the 3W Kafé scrawled at the bottom, along with a time: *9 p.m. tonight.*

Peyton had become well-acquainted with the Marais district during her missions abroad over the years, but she wasn't familiar with the 3W Kafé. Her breath caught in her throat when she looked it up online and realized it was a popular lesbian nightclub.

She checked the clock on the nightstand: 7:38 p.m. Her heart picked up speed at the thought of having physical contact with Zoey once again. Wearing pajamas without a bra and watching a movie together after she'd spent the day crying was one thing. Getting all dressed up for a night of dancing at a lesbian nightclub was so... provocative. So intimate.

Peyton took a breath to steady her galloping heart. Why was Zoey doing this? What did she have to gain? Perhaps she was going to turn herself in and let Peyton return her to headquarters.

She shook her head. *Fat chance that'll ever happen.* Once a cat, always a cat.

❖

Zoey seated herself at the bar and sipped her water. If Peyton couldn't drink alcohol, then neither would she. She wanted to make sure she was totally sober for their first date. "You're sure about the dress?" she whispered to Shadow on the comm.

"Thirty-six," came Shadow's reply.

She frowned. "Come again?"

"That's how many people salivated as you walked past on your way to the bar tonight."

A tiny button had been sewn into the back of her dress. It housed a wireless video camera, allowing Shadow to see everything behind her in real time—a necessary precaution against Delta Force. This took watching her back to a whole new level.

Zoey gazed down at herself. Everything about her chosen attire was intentional. She had no doubt Peyton would figure it out. She thought back to their conversation in her apartment when Peyton had zeroed in on the symbolism behind her chosen decor. Peyton's profiling skills were incredible.

She pressed her hands together in her lap. "Oh my God."

"What's wrong?" Shadow asked.

"My hands are clammy." Many people experienced clammy hands when they felt nervous, but this had never happened to her. Ever. Not even when she was in the middle of a high-stakes mission.

"Good."

"Good?" Zoey repeated.

"It means you really want her. Since you always get what you want, I, for one, welcome clammy hands. After you tell her about your mission and bring her over to the dark side, it'll mean one less person is chasing after you, which is one less person I need to keep tabs on."

But Zoey had no plans to share the details of her mission with Peyton. She'd already decided that it was just too risky. The less Peyton knew, the better. The last thing she wanted was for Peyton to have a target on her back because of her. As far as she could tell, Delta Force had been tracking Peyton only because they thought she might lead them to Zoey. If they found out Peyton knew about the government's agenda with Bird of Prey, they'd likely come after her with lethal force. Zoey was doing everything in her power to keep Peyton close so she could offer her protection if the need arose.

She'd even give her life, if it came to that.

Peyton stepped inside the 3W Kafé. The bar was eerily dark and quiet. She'd started to wonder if she was in the right place when Zoey stepped out from the shadows across the room, her face and silhouette illuminated by a nearby flickering lantern. It seemed they were the only two there. Their eyes locked as she walked over.

Zoey leaned in for the double-cheek peck that many Europeans customarily practiced. "You look radiant."

So did Zoey. Her off-the-shoulder black dress had a sweetheart neckline, revealing just enough cleavage to lure someone in for a closer look. The dress hugged Zoey's body in all the places that mattered, enhancing her natural curves. It released its gentle grip just above her knees and then seamlessly morphed into a short strip of fabric that swayed freely with every step.

Peyton's gaze returned to the sweetheart neckline. Shaped like the top half of a heart, the message was clear—Zoey's heart was open to Peyton. She glanced down. Zoey's shoes, on the other hand, were bold, edgy. Silver cone spikes adorned the thin straps of her Italian-crafted heels. Their message was even clearer—a part of Zoey would always be wild. She was the horse that must be allowed to break from the herd and run free.

Peyton set her clutch on the bar top. "Are we the only two here?" she asked as she raised her arms for a quick pat down.

Zoey stepped closer. "There's a DJ downstairs." She kept her gaze on Peyton's as she felt her way along Peyton's back, hips, and stomach, checking for a weapon.

She drew in a quick breath and felt her heart pick up speed. Zoey's touch filled her stomach with butterflies. They stood facing one another, mere inches apart. Zoey smelled divine. Victoria's Secret Heavenly, if she wasn't mistaken. She looked over as a woman in jeans and a tank top with full sleeve tattoos locked the entrance.

"That's the owner," Zoey explained, taking a step back, their moment broken. "I rented 3W for the night."

Peyton didn't need to ask why. She would've done the same if their roles were reversed. With Delta Force after her, Zoey needed to keep tabs on the people around her at all times, which would be impossible to do in a crowded, noisy nightclub. She stole a glance at Zoey's bottle of water. Zoey was definitely playing it safe, which wasn't like her at all. Either she was genuinely concerned about Delta Force, or she had something else up her sleeve.

Zoey followed her gaze. "If you can't drink, then neither will I. Misery loves company, right?" She winked. "Come on."

Zoey took her by the hand and led her to a quaint dance floor in the basement, where a hooded DJ acknowledged them with a nod. White pillar candles lined the dance room wall, serving as their only source of light. A bistro set with an elegant floral-print tablecloth awaited them in one corner. There was a small black gift box, a dozen red roses, and a bag of Lays potato chips with a big red bow in the center of the table. A silver wine bucket with a pedestal base stood off to one side, filled with ice and a bottle of sparking water.

Zoey gestured to the chips. "In case you work up an appetite tonight."

Peyton shook her head and smiled. Their trip to Niger, where she'd met her potato-chip family, felt like a lifetime ago. "What's in the box?"

"Another snack. Open it."

Peyton lifted the lid to find a Yoda-shaped chocolate bar inside. "Thank you," she said, touched by the gesture. "Am I expected to share?" She frowned. "Because Yoda isn't big enough for the two of us."

Zoey stepped very close. "Only if you want to," she whispered. She led Peyton to the middle of the dance floor, slipped out of her heels, and waited as Peyton did the same. She nodded to the DJ.

"Wait." Peyton stepped back and held her hand up to the DJ. "Who leads?"

"Me," Zoey said matter-of-factly.

"But...can't we take turns?"

Zoey closed the gap between them and pressed her body against Peyton's. "Not tonight." She set one hand over the small of Peyton's back and clasped her other hand, palm to palm. "Relax. I've got you."

A beautiful, haunting melody sounded through the speakers. Peyton assumed it was an instrumental piece until a soothing, seductive voice seamlessly slipped in, caressing the music's raw edges. "What's this called?" she whispered, trying to focus on the song instead of the palpable chemistry between them.

"Dancing."

"No, this piece." Peyton rolled her eyes. "What is it?"

"'Midnight Moon' by Eydís Evensen," Zoey whispered back.

Peyton listened closely to the lyrics. Their message was clear. Zoey was inviting her inside her private, coveted world.

The music wafted over them in gentle waves, punctuating the moment with melancholy, longing, and a raw sincerity that was out of character for Zoey. For once, Zoey was being serious, and it made Peyton nervous. Her feelings for Zoey were growing.

Instrumental compositions played, one after another, each more beautiful than the one before it. Zoey whispered the significance of each selection in her ear. Some had ties to Peyton. Others had ties to Zoey's past. Her explanations were brief, honest, and raw with emotion. "This is 'Inspiration' by Florian Christl. It's about my time with Ella," she said, her voice cracking with emotion, "before she earned her angel wings."

Her reason behind "Passions of All Kinds" by Luke Howard made Peyton laugh. "This is how we sounded together when we first met," she said at the start of the piece. "As we got to know one another, our music grew more harmonious."

The forethought that went into Zoey's musical choices was deeply moving. Each melody reverberated through the dance floor and into her body. They slow-danced to every note. Zoey led with a grace and confidence that Peyton found both captivating and comforting.

This was not at all what she'd expected. When she'd read Zoey's note, she thought they'd be dancing under strobe lights in a nightclub, sweating the night away in a sea of gyrating bodies. At the time, the idea of dancing with Zoey in that kind of atmosphere had felt much too intimate. But this—she drew in a breath as she felt Zoey's heart beating against her own—*this* was a level of intimacy she never could've imagined. Zoey, it seemed, was just as deep and sentimental as she was comedic. She was, by far, the most complex, mesmerizing woman Peyton had ever met.

"This is what heaven will sound like when your baby is born," Zoey whispered, as "A Little Chaos" by Peter Gregson played.

Peyton listened intently. Trepidation, pain, joy, hope, sacrifice, and exhilaration slowly converged in a climactic instrumental celebration that brought her to tears. It was the most magnificent musical composition she'd ever heard. Zoey had saved the best for last.

When the music ended, they slid into their heels and gathered their belongings in silence. Zoey took her hand and accompanied her for the short walk back to her hotel. They rode the elevator to the fifth floor, as quiet as two swans who'd just finished an exhausting courtship ritual. Neither of them made an attempt at conversation. Peyton realized there was no need for words. So much had been said on the dance floor.

She withdrew the key card from her clutch, disengaged the lock, and pushed the door ajar. She hesitated before meeting Zoey's gaze. "Would you like to come inside?"

"Depends."

"On what?" she asked.

"Do you promise not to take me into custody?"

Peyton sighed. "You know I can't promise that."

Zoey set the chocolate Yoda, bag of chips, and bouquet of roses on the floor. "Thank you," she said, backing away down the corridor, "for a truly magical night."

She watched, conflicted, as Zoey disappeared around the corner. Every part of her body wanted Zoey to stay.

## CHAPTER TWENTY-NINE

Zoey pushed open the door to the stairs but remained on the fifth-floor landing. She waited several minutes to make sure Peyton hadn't followed and then reentered the corridor to retrace her steps. Her handler was a creature of habit. By now, she'd be in the bathroom brushing her teeth and getting ready for bed. Zoey withdrew the key card from her bra, unlocked Peyton's door, and slipped quietly inside.

As expected, the bathroom door was closed, and the faucet was running. She found the combination safe that was built into the hotel wall and opened it on her second try—Peyton's CIA badge number, an easy guess. She confiscated the Glock, handcuffs, and badge, knowing she'd never be able to relax if they remained in Peyton's reach. She intended to let her guard down fully tonight and wanted Peyton to be able to do the same.

She slipped out of Peyton's room and into her own—she'd already rented the room next door—and deposited the weapon, cuffs, and badge inside her safe. She brushed her teeth, changed into the dark red silk pajamas that she'd kept from her sleepover at Peyton's, and returned to knock on the hotel room door.

Peyton answered, donning her long-lost Feejays and a gray *Star Wars* T-shirt. No bra. "Are those *mine?*" she asked, indignant.

"Yep." She gestured at Peyton's fashionable attire. "And I see you're putting my Feejays to good use."

"They were lonely." Peyton crossed her arms, leaned against the doorframe, and turned an accusatory gaze on Zoey. "My gun, badge, and handcuffs are missing."

That didn't take long. "I have them," she admitted.

"Give them back." Peyton uncrossed her arms and held out her hand. "Now."

"I will. But not tonight. Ask me again."

"To return my property?" Peyton said, incredulous.

"If I want to come inside."

Peyton's demeanor softened as she considered the dilemma before her. "What if I want both?"

"You can only have one. Me...or the gun, cuffs, and badge."

Peyton hesitated but only briefly. "Would you like to come inside?"

"How nice of you to ask. As a matter of fact, I would."

Peyton rolled her eyes and held the door ajar, closing and locking it behind her.

Peyton shut the door and set the latch lock. She took a deep breath to steady her nerves and then turned to face Zoey. Hadn't she promised herself she wouldn't let things get this far? She couldn't lie to herself any longer. This wasn't about doing whatever it took to rein in her rogue agent. She was falling for Zoey. Hard. If she went through with this tonight, how would she ever trust herself to be professional again?

Zoey read her in an instant, as astute and intuitive as ever. "There's a new zombie movie on Netflix," she said, obviously trying to ease the tension. "Should we call room service and order some popcorn?"

Peyton shook her head. "Why can't you just tell me about your mission?"

"Because it'll put you and your baby in danger."

There it was, Zoey's protective nature rearing its head yet again. "I'm your handler. You're supposed to be able to tell me anything."

"True." Zoey stepped closer, her dark, knowing gaze filled with concern. "And I do feel like I can tell you anything. But I can't tell you this. Not yet."

"Then, when?"

"When it's safe."

"*My* mission is clear—secure your capture and return you safely to headquarters. Whatever does or doesn't happen between us tonight won't change what I'm sworn to do."

"Since it won't make a difference, I vote for *does*."

She stared at Zoey, confused. "What?"

"You said *whatever does or doesn't happen between us.* I'm officially casting my vote for something to happen." Zoey slipped her hands underneath Peyton's shirt and caressed her stomach. "Truce?" She ran her thumbs over Peyton's nipples. "Just for tonight," she whispered, closing the distance between them. Zoey kissed her, gently, seductively, giving her the chance to change her mind and back out.

But there was no backing out now. Not for Peyton. She'd never wanted anyone more. She could hardly stand the anticipation. If Zoey's tongue felt this good inside her mouth, she could only imagine how good it would feel on her body.

Zoey caressed her breast with one hand and reached down with the other, stroking her core through the fabric of the Feejays. Peyton felt herself instantly grow wet with desire. She pulled Zoey closer and ran her hands along Zoey's back and buttocks as their tongues danced.

Zoey led her to the bed. They undressed one another and stood, naked for the first time together. Zoey's body was just as beautiful as she'd imagined. Her skin tone was darker than Peyton's. Her nipples and areolas were darker, too. Peyton skimmed the tips of her fingers along Zoey's neck, collarbone, and shoulders, down her arms and hips, across her stomach, over her breasts. Her nipples hardened.

Zoey pressed her breasts into Peyton's and kissed her, more forcefully this time, reminding Peyton that she had needs, too. She pushed Peyton down on the bed, thrust her pelvis between Peyton's legs, and began grinding against her in slow motion as they kissed.

Peyton was going to explode if she had to wait one more second for Zoey to take her. "I need you...inside me," she begged, breaking free from their kiss. She was drawing short, rapid breaths now.

Zoey ground against her one last time, pressed her cheek against Peyton's, and whispered seductively, "Can I taste you?"

"God, yes."

Zoey made her way down her body, kissing, licking, sucking, nipping. She wandered slowly over her breasts, stomach, hips...along the inside of each thigh...inching her way ever closer to where Peyton needed her most. She writhed beneath Zoey's lips and tongue, begging for release as she spread her legs wider. Finally, Zoey's tongue caressed her clit, eliciting a moan of pleasure.

Peyton was throbbing now. Just when she thought she couldn't take it anymore, Zoey reached for her hands, entwined their fingers, and settled between her legs. She took turns licking her lips, her clit. The sensation of Zoey's tongue at her core was exquisite. She was on the edge now. Zoey released one of her hands and slid her fingers inside, thrusting deeply, slowly. Peyton rocked her hips back and forth to match her new lover's rhythm. Zoey kept licking her clit in all the right ways. She couldn't hold back any longer. She held Zoey's hand, arching her back as she climaxed in waves so intense that she was left gasping for air.

Zoey moved up Peyton's body, gently thrusting her fingers in and out, giving Peyton all the time she needed to ride out the waves of pleasure. She was still so wet. Peyton writhed beneath her and greeted her with a long, seductive kiss. "Lift up," Peyton whispered when she finally caught her breath.

Before she knew it, Peyton was underneath her, returning the favor with a hunger and ferocity that took her by surprise. Zoey braced herself against the headboard as she straddled Peyton, unable to do anything but open herself up to her lover's lips and tongue.

Peyton held nothing back as she kissed and licked at the center of her, finally pushing her fingers inside. Zoey heard the telltale sounds of her own wetness as she allowed Peyton to penetrate her fully. She rode Peyton's fingers, rubbed her clit against Peyton's tongue, and cried out in pleasure as the orgasm tore through her body.

Peyton woke up naked under the covers in the hotel bed. Her mind flashed to Zoey riding her fingers and throwing her head back in ecstasy. Being inside Zoey and feeling her orgasm was even more amazing than she'd imagined. Last night had barely whetted her appetite. She needed to feel Zoey inside her again. She reached across the bed, intent on waking Zoey with a long, seductive caress, but she was already gone. The sheets were still warm. She scooted over and nuzzled into Zoey's pillow. It still smelled like her.

Peyton sat up in the darkness and pulled the sheets over her breasts. The reality of what she'd done with Zoey hit her hard. What in the world had she been thinking? She'd lost control, plain and simple. Her body had betrayed her. She'd traded in her responsibilities as a federal agent for sexual gratification.

Her libido was definitely in overdrive. Was it her surging pregnancy hormones or Zoey that made her feel so, well, *horny*? She squeezed her eyes shut. It didn't matter. Now that she'd had a taste of Zoey—literally, she reminded herself—she knew she wanted more.

But she had to face the truth and admit that it wasn't just physical. Was she falling in love with Zoey? Their sexual and emotional chemistry was like an intoxicating vapor that made it difficult to think. This could only end in one of two ways—Zoey evaded capture indefinitely, or Peyton eventually caught up with her and returned her to the CIA. Neither scenario boded well for their future.

What would a future with Zoey even look like? Being on the lam with a baby in tow? Visiting Zoey in federal prison? Peyton covered her eyes in the dark to try to stop herself from heading down the rabbit hole of worst-case scenarios. Even as she pushed with all her might, the truth refused to budge. A future with Zoey was simply out of the question. No matter how much she wanted it.

❖

Zoey finished the meeting with her Brazilian contact and retreated to her hotel for a well-deserved nap. Traveling through five continents in just four days was a record for her. *Jet-lagged* didn't even begin to cover the bone-deep exhaustion she was experiencing. She could only imagine what Peyton was going through right now in her current state of pregnancy.

Pushing Peyton to keep up with her set Zoey on edge. Peyton was past the first trimester, but she was still early in her pregnancy and, therefore, vulnerable. Zoey was torn between doing what was best for Peyton and the baby and pushing forward for the greater good. It was an endless struggle of conscience, to which there was no good, easy, or right answer.

She reached out to Shadow. "Where's Mere on the map?" she asked, yawning.

"Left South Africa a few hours ago. She's on her way to Mexico now."

"Wait," Zoey said, halting in front of her hotel room door. "I thought I was taking Mexico."

"You were, but she made better time." Shadow paused. "Mere didn't have any layovers."

"And by *layovers*, you mean Peyton," Zoey said, shaking her head at Shadow's clever use of the word. She thought back to her date with Peyton in France. Even if the human race was on the verge of extinction, it had been time well-spent. She regretted nothing. "Is Brazil my last stop?" she asked, feeling hopeful that they'd complete the mission ahead of schedule.

"Last stop," Shadow confirmed.

"And what's the latest on Sacha?"

"That man takes workaholic to a whole new level. I'm starting to wonder if he has an identical twin. He never sleeps, and he's always at the top of his game. How's that possible?"

Zoey knew what was behind his superhuman endurance. Sacha was trying to get his leg of the mission over with as quickly as possible—hijack the US government's Bird of Prey vaccine supply—so he could devote his resources to finding the men responsible for Sterling's murder. "Did you send him the audio file of Sterling…" The sudden lump in her throat made it difficult to finish. Her current state of physical and mental exhaustion made her grief bob precipitously close to the surface.

"I didn't want to," Shadow explained. "Didn't think it was something he—or *anyone*—should ever have to hear, but he wouldn't take no for an answer."

Her heart went out to Sacha. "It's okay. You gave him what he needed." If she knew Sacha—and from all of Sterling's stories over the years, she felt she did—then one thing was certain: the men who tortured and murdered Sterling were about to come face-to-face with their worst nightmare.

❖

Peyton decided there wasn't a word in any language that could even come close to describing how frustrated she felt. She hadn't spoken with Zoey since their night together in Paris. She'd been receiving perfunctory texts with travel information on the cell phone Zoey gave her in Canada. She wasn't even convinced the texts were from Zoey. They were all business, lacking Zoey's devilish wit and charm. She suspected the texts had been drafted by whoever had just sent her an encrypted email with the details of Zoey's mission. It was the same no-nonsense writing style.

A part of her felt hurt, resentful, and angry that Zoey hadn't reached out to her at all. She understood the radio silence for what it was: regret. Zoey obviously wished they hadn't slept together.

For the last four days, all she'd done was follow Zoey from country to country, like a well-trained greyhound chasing the mechanical rabbit around the racetrack. Around and around she went. She was exhausted and at her wit's end. And it was clear that Zoey was closing in on the finish line.

Zoey had given her a bag of coins from ten different countries at the very beginning of their journey, but they'd only visited five countries—Canada, France, China, Egypt, and now Brazil—skipping five others that would have made sense for Zoey to visit en route. There were several plausible explanations that could account for the itinerary change, but intuition told her that someone was now helping with Zoey's mission. She believed Zoey and this mystery agent were essentially leapfrogging countries. That would be a question for another day, though. Peyton thought back to her interaction with Shadow at Zoey's apartment building. She knew Shadow must be involved on some level, as well.

Whatever the case, time was ticking. There was a very real possibility that Zoey would disappear once she finished her mission, never to be seen or heard from again. If Peyton was going to make a move, she had to do it now. She sat in her rental car and studied the entrance of Hospital Israelita in São Paulo, Brazil. What she was about to do to Zoey was cruel, but she was out of options.

## CHAPTER THIRTY

G riffin stepped out of the shower, covered himself with a towel, and grabbed his vibrating cell off the vanity. "Bick."

"Team Cobra reporting—"

"I know who this is, Commander," he said, impatient. "What do you have for me?"

"We've pinpointed North's location. She's been tracking the target. We're rallying now. ETA is forty-four minutes."

"Good." It was about damn time. "Where?"

"São Paulo, Brazil, sir."

"São Paulo," he repeated. What the hell was Agent Blackwood doing out there? "Use whatever force is necessary to gain North's cooperation. Once you acquire the target, get rid of North. But we need the target alive." He intended to find out who Agent Blackwood had seen and exactly what she'd been up to for the last five days. "I repeat, we need the target *alive.*"

"Copy that, sir."

Griffin ended the call. Once he squeezed every last drop of information out of Blackwood, he'd keep his word to Sterling and give her to Polluck—or Commander Slice and Dice, as Sterling had aptly nicknamed him.

It was a small price to pay, and Polluck had more than earned the reward.

❖

Zoey opened her eyes, momentarily disoriented. Shadow had woken her up after just two hours of sleep. She was hungry, tired, *and* sexually frustrated. She glanced at the empty space on the hotel bed. She wanted Peyton there beside her in the worst way. "Where am I again?" she asked on the heels of a yawn.

"São Paulo, Brazil," Shadow replied through the comm.

"Right." It was coming back to her now. "What's up?"

"Peyton knows."

"Knows what?"

"About the virus, the vaccine, our evil government's plan to sell the vaccine, your presumed attempt to thwart said plan, etcetera, etcetera."

"How?" she asked, suddenly feeling wide awake.

"How?"

"That's what I asked. How?" She sat up, interpreting Shadow's pause as an admission of guilt.

"Peyton checked her email and downloaded the encrypted file I sent."

"You sent her a file without telling me?"

"You've been keeping Peyton on the outskirts of this mission because you're afraid of putting her in danger. I sent that file to her because we really need Peyton's help."

There was something else. She could smell it. "What aren't you telling me?"

"The DOD hacked her email account, found my file, and attached a tracker. When she downloaded it, they were able to ping her location. I'm sorry. If I could undo this, I would."

Zoey ended their call. She needed to warn Peyton.

Peyton now had a target on her back.

❖

Peyton sat in the hospital bed, racked with guilt and feeling like a bald-faced liar. She was stealing time from other patients who were genuinely in need of medical care. She'd walked into the emergency room with a fabricated story about waking up in the middle of the night with a general sense of malaise and doom. The nurse had already taken her vitals, given her a private room in the maternity ward, and scheduled an ultrasound.

She was banking on the presumption that someone from Zoey's team was monitoring her conversations via the earbud. She figured it was only a matter of time before they alerted Zoey to her medical emergency. If Zoey truly cared about her, she'd make an appearance at the hospital to find out if she and the baby were okay.

As if on cue, Zoey poked her head inside the doorway to her room.

"That was fast," Peyton said, glancing at the clock. Just eight minutes had passed since she'd shared her fake ailment with the nurse.

"What was fast?" Zoey stepped inside and closed the door.

"You. Getting here."

"I didn't show up because of your fake emergency."

Peyton was caught off guard and at a loss for words.

"I know what you look like when you've been crying," Zoey went on. "We've been down this road, remember? Puffy eyes, stuffy nose, general aura of misery and despair." She stepped closer and waved her hand around Peyton's head. "No evidence of that here."

Peyton slid her handcuffs out from under the pillow and slapped them on Zoey's wrists like a striking cobra.

"How long have you been practicing that?" Zoey asked without even looking down.

"Since Canada," she admitted happily.

"There. You caught me." Zoey held her wrists up. "Happy?"

"Very." Peyton shut her eyes and took a deep, cleansing breath.

"I'll give you another few seconds to savor this moment. Go ahead, savor away."

"I am." Peyton couldn't help but smirk.

Seconds ticked by in silence. "Done?"

Peyton opened her eyes. "I think so."

"Good." Zoey slipped out of the handcuffs as deftly as if she was doing a well-rehearsed magic trick.

Peyton felt her mouth drop open as she stared down in wonder.

"I rigged your cuffs when I borrowed them in Paris."

"Stole."

"*Borrowed*," Zoey insisted. "We can argue about this later. Right now, we need to get you out of here."

There were undercurrents of panic in Zoey's usually calm voice, something Peyton had never heard before. Peyton studied her. She was tense. "What happened?"

"You," Zoey said, obviously agitated. "You happened."

"You can't do that."

"Do what?"

"Be mad at me when you're the one who seduced me, got what you wanted or didn't—either way, I don't care—and then *ghosted* me."

"You obviously do care, or you wouldn't be so mad." Zoey grabbed her by the arm and started walking to the door.

"Do *not* touch me." Peyton yanked her arm away.

"You're really going to pick a fight now?" Zoey cracked the door open and peeked into the corridor. "Delta Force is breathing down our necks, thanks to your compulsive need to check your email."

"Which I wouldn't have had to do if you'd just confided in me," she said, crossing her arms.

Zoey glanced over her shoulder at Peyton. "What I don't understand is why you lured me here now that you know the full story."

She shrugged. "I wanted to offer my assistance."

"And you knew I wouldn't accept your offer because—"

"I'm pregnant. Exactly."

"You really believe that's the only reason?" Zoey shut the door the rest of the way, stepped over, and reached for her hand.

Peyton backed away. She'd promised herself she wouldn't fall into Zoey's trap a second time. "What happened between us shouldn't have happened. I'd do anything to take it back. But your cause is just, and it's something I want to be a part of. It's not your job to protect me. I can take care of myself."

They locked gazes. Neither wavered. The few feet of distance between them felt like a chasm.

A familiar voice sounded through Peyton's earpiece. She'd suspected Shadow was involved. Now she knew for sure.

"You two are either kissing or staring each other down," Shadow said, her voice like silk. "Which is it?"

"Staring," they said in unison.

"It might interest you both to know that Delta Force has all the hospital exits covered."

"How does she know that?" Peyton asked.

"She knows everything. Just go with it."

"They're starting a floor-by-floor sweep of the hospital as we speak," Shadow went on. "What floor are you on?"

"Sixth," Peyton answered. "Maternity. How much time do we have until Delta Force finds us?"

"I'm looking at a map of the hospital right now. By my calculations, you have about three minutes."

"Nearest supply closet?" Zoey asked.

"Left from the room. Four doors down on your right."

Zoey turned to Peyton, her gaze razor-sharp. "Stay here," she ordered, and then she fled from the room.

Zoey grabbed what she needed from the supply closet and sprinted back to Peyton's room. She handed Peyton a johnny. "Put this on," she said, already stripping off her own clothes to change into blue scrubs.

"Why?"

"I'm about to deliver your baby." She stuffed some towels inside a pillowcase and molded it into a ball. "Here, put this under your johnny."

"Why can't I be the doctor?"

Zoey threw her clothes into the laundry bin. "My idea, so I get to be the doctor." She pulled a surgical cap over her head, covered her face with a blue mask, and slipped into some latex gloves. "Besides, this'll be good practice for us."

"You mean, for *me*." Peyton shed her clothes, shrugged into the johnny, and stuffed the pillowcase inside. "You are *not* delivering my baby."

"Panties need to come off, too," Zoey urged.

"No way. I am not letting you look at my…"

"I already saw it." She watched as Peyton blushed. "Like, up close, so what's the big deal?"

Shadow piped up, "Sort it out, lovebirds. Three soldiers are nearing the sixth-floor landing."

"Damn you," Peyton spat, sliding her underwear down her legs.

Zoey handed her a surgical mask. "Put this on, so they don't see your face."

"Women in labor don't wear masks."

"If they ask, we'll say you have the flu. Can't risk passing that to a newborn."

Peyton put on her mask and watched as Zoey snapped the stirrups in place. "Take a seat, Ms. North."

Peyton sat on the hospital bed, pulled the johnny down over her knees, and looked around the room. "Where's the blanket?"

"Didn't think to get one. Now, lie back, spread your legs, and rest your feet in the stirrups."

"They're at your door in seven...six...five...four...three..." Shadow supplied.

Peyton lay back on the bed, set her heels in the stirrups, and parted her knees. Zoey placed one hand over Peyton's towel-filled belly and positioned a gloved hand as if to initiate an examination as a soldier in black riot gear barged into the room. Peyton leaned forward and pretended to push with all her might as she howled in response to the feigned agony of childbirth. Her timing was perfect. She looked— and sounded—the part. The Delta Force soldier stopped in his tracks, turned, and promptly exited the room, slamming the door behind him.

Zoey doubted he'd come back for a second look. She peeled off the gloves.

Shadow instructed, "Hold your positions—well, not literally, of course—until Delta Force finishes their sweep. Sounds like you were pretty convincing, so I doubt they'll double back. I'll keep watch and alert you if they decide to make a second run."

Peyton brought her knees together, hopped down from the bed, and retrieved her panties.

"Copy that," Zoey replied. She turned her back to Peyton to give her some privacy. Better late than never.

Griffin sipped his bourbon, stared out at the courtyard through the window of his study, and eagerly awaited an update. He was glad to be home for this momentous occasion. If all went well, he'd be interrogating Sterling's daughter by nightfall.

The sound of a man clearing his throat made him turn. There, standing in the doorway of his study, was a stranger—tall, broad-shouldered, thick white hair, his face hardened with wrinkles and rage.

"How'd you get in here?" he asked, stepping forward to press the panic button under his desk.

The stranger pulled out a gun from the small of his back and flourished it as he talked. "Go ahead. Push it. Nobody's coming."

Griffin's thoughts went to his wife. He wondered if she was okay. "My wife—"

"Spared. She's running an errand. Like you even care." The stranger shook his head. "If you loved her, you wouldn't cheat on her. You really think she doesn't know?"

Griffin shrugged. Maybe she did. As long as she kept her mouth shut, he didn't care one way or the other.

"You're vile, and you disgust me."

Everyone was entitled to their opinion. "What do you want?"

"I dropped by to thank you for your generous donation."

"And what donation was that?" Griffin asked, growing more annoyed by the minute.

"The World Health Organization is distributing your vaccines all over the world as we speak. You won't be able to make more because a younger version of me hacked into your database and altered the vaccine's formula." He flicked his wrist to check his watch. "Details of the Administration's plans to profit from the deaths of millions—if not billions—of lives is set to air tonight on the eleven o'clock news. Eastern Standard Time, of course. Might want to set your DVR. I'd hate for you to miss it."

# CHAPTER THIRTY-ONE

Zoey waited with Peyton in silence. Since Peyton was sitting in the only chair, and she wasn't a fan of the hard metal stool, she'd opted for the bed. It was actually pretty comfortable. She folded her hands across her stomach and stared at the ceiling.

The reason for Peyton's anger was obvious—she resented that Zoey had gone silent after they'd slept together. Making love to Peyton and then leaving her bed the very same night had required a level of willpower that was frighteningly close to exceeding her limit. It was one of the hardest things she'd ever done.

But to complete her leg of the mission—and, by default, keep Peyton safe—she'd needed to avoid further contact with Peyton. Their best hope, their *only* way out of this, demanded that she invest all her skills as an agent into the mission. The world couldn't afford for her to be distracted. For the past four days, she'd devoted herself entirely to traveling undercover, meeting with her contacts, and overseeing Shadow's work with Sacha and Meredith Pokale. The greater good often called for personal sacrifice. The sacrificial lamb in this case just happened to be Peyton.

Maybe there was something to Sterling's logic, after all. If she had followed his advice, Peyton wouldn't have gotten hurt. Hell, if she'd kept her handler at a respectable distance from the beginning like she should have, Peyton wouldn't even be here right now, in Delta Force's crosshairs. She and her baby would be safe and sound at her Beacon Street condo in Boston.

Zoey shook her head, upset with herself for being so shortsighted and selfish. *God. What've I done?*

Shadow jolted her from her thoughts. "Delta Force is making a second sweep. Checking IDs now. All exits are still covered."

"How much time?" she asked, sitting up.

Shadow hesitated. "Eight minutes, give or take."

She met Peyton's gaze across the room.

"I'm studying the hospital's blueprints now," Shadow went on. "There are no viable escape routes."

Peyton stood from her chair. "There has to be something—"

"There isn't," Zoey insisted, cutting her off. "If there was, Shadow would've found it by now." So escape was off the table. That left hiding in plain sight. "Can you send me one official national identity document?"

"I'll send it to the sixth-floor nurses' station printer. Is this for you or Peyton?"

"Peyton. Give her glasses and a hijab."

Several minutes ticked by in silence, the tension palpable. "Done," Shadow finally said. "Printing now."

Zoey replaced her surgical mask, sprinted to the nurses' station, and grabbed the document as it came sliding out. She plucked a pair of scissors from a nearby desk, cut the document to size, and slipped it inside a clear pouch intended for hospital IDs. If her plan worked, Peyton wouldn't need the identification card. But she wanted her to have it, just in case. "What floor are they on?" she whispered.

"Third and moving fast," came Shadow's reply.

She poked her head inside a room a few doors down from Peyton's and stepped over to a small suitcase in the corner. When she'd first stepped off the elevator earlier, a Muslim woman with glasses was being wheeled away for an emergency C-section. She only hoped the woman had packed an extra hijab. She unzipped the suitcase and rifled through the woman's belongings. Bingo. One pale blue hijab. The woman's glasses had been removed before surgery and returned to the bedside table. She grabbed those, as well.

Zoey jogged back to Peyton's room, handed her the hijab and glasses, and tucked the fake ID under the pillow. "You're now Eliana Ribeiro. Get back in bed and sit tight."

Peyton complied without protest.

"Remembered the blanket this time," she said, draping it over Peyton's legs. She fluffed the towels around Peyton's midsection until they were uniformly even and round, stepping back a few times to inspect her work. "There. You look like you're about to pop."

"Where's your ID?" Peyton asked.

"I don't need one."

"Why not?"

Zoey ignored the question. "I owe you an apology. I shouldn't have taken advantage of you the other night. I seduced you to distract you and further my mission. That was wrong, and I'm sorry." Parting ways here would be much easier on Peyton if she believed Zoey didn't have feelings for her. Turning herself in to Delta Force would create a distraction and give Peyton a chance to escape. It wasn't guaranteed, but she was pretty sure they'd leave Peyton alone if they acquired their true target. This was Peyton's best shot at survival.

"What are you doing?" Shadow asked, cuing in on Zoey's lie and probably figuring out what she was about to do.

Zoey withdrew her earbud, tossed it in a nearby trash can, and walked out of the room.

❖

Peyton's mind was spinning. She'd watched as Zoey's orbicularis oculi tensed. It was Zoey's only tell—at least, that she'd been able to find—which meant Zoey was lying. Her brain was still processing the reasoning behind the lie when Zoey removed her earpiece and left the room.

"She just took her earbud out, didn't she?" Shadow asked.

"She did." Zoey always had something up her sleeve. But something told Peyton this time was different. She climbed out of bed, slipped out of the johnny, and got dressed.

"Sounds like you're moving. What're you doing?" Shadow asked.

"I'm turning myself in to save her."

"Shit. You two really are impossible. Give me a minute to think."

But they were out of time and out of options. Peyton exited the room, ran to the nearest stairwell, and hurried down the stairs.

A Delta Force soldier already had Zoey pinned against the wall. Peyton withdrew her Glock and fired a shot, hitting him behind the knee. He went down hard. She came up behind him and knocked him out cold with the butt of her gun.

Zoey spun around. Her hands were now cuffed behind her back. "What the hell are you doing?"

"Saving you."

"No," Zoey said, staring down at the unconscious soldier. "I was saving *you.*"

She pushed the earpiece back inside Zoey's ear. "Just because I'm pregnant doesn't mean I'm more important." Peyton fished around in the soldier's pockets and withdrew the key to Zoey's handcuffs. "As much as it pains me to do this..." She unlocked the cuffs.

"Now what?" Zoey asked, rubbing her wrists.

"We wait for Shadow to come up with a plan."

"Can I at least get a kiss before we die?"

"No time for that," Shadow interrupted. "Sacha's on the line. Patching him through now."

❖

Sacha's voice sounded through Zoey's earpiece. "Can you hear me?"

"Sure can," she replied. "If you happen to be in Brazil, we could use some backup. Peyton went all Rambo on me."

"I can do better than that. I'm here with a mutual friend," Sacha said, his tone patronizing. "Anything you'd like to say to—"

"Bick the Dick?" she asked, amazed at Sacha's torpedo-like pace. He was making her look bad. "Tell him to call off the dogs."

"Agent Blackwood is politely requesting that you tell Delta Force to stand the hell down." There was a brief silence. She heard a muted voice in the background. "You want something in return?" Sacha asked, his tone rife with loathing. "How about I let you live instead of cutting you up into little pieces and feeding you to my dogs?"

Zoey peeked over the stairwell landing as booted footsteps sounded below. Four Delta Force soldiers were coming up fast. She and Peyton hugged the wall. "Any chance we can speed this along?" she whispered.

"He's on the phone with the commander now," came Sacha's response. There was another brief silence. "Operation Black has been aborted. Can you confirm that?" he asked, presumably to Zoey.

She glanced at Peyton. "Only one way to find out." She held up her hands and jogged down the stairs. Peyton followed closely behind her. As they approached, the four soldiers stepped aside to let them pass.

She and Peyton kept moving without so much as a backward glance. "Confirmed," she said as they exited the building. They jogged across the parking lot, climbed in Peyton's rental car, and regarded one another as a gunshot sounded on the other end of the earpiece. "For Sterling," Sacha said in a trembling voice.

Zoey froze, stunned. "You said you were going to let him live."

"I lied."

She thought back to what Peyton had told her when she'd shared the news of Sterling's death. *Agent Thirteen prepped him, but it was Bick who delivered the kill shot.* "And Agent Thirteen?" she asked.

"John Polluck was his name."

"Was?" Zoey repeated.

"Was," Sacha confirmed. "Think about MI6, Blackwood. The nosy doctor, mini me, and Rambo can come, too. Let me know what you decide."

The ensuing silence told her that Sacha had disconnected the call.

Peyton reached over and held her hand as she cried. More than anything, she longed to celebrate this victory with Sterling. She squeezed Peyton's hand, grateful for her reassuring touch.

❖

Zoey followed Peyton into her hotel room. They ordered room service, ate a quick dinner, and took turns showering. It was nine o'clock by the time Zoey emerged from the bathroom, feeling refreshed and donning her American-flag Feejays with a *Star Wars* T-shirt.

Peyton looked up from the bed with a frown. "Is that...*mine*?"

"Nope. Bought my own," she said proudly.

Peyton pushed the covers aside to reveal a brand-new pair of Feejays—pale gray with tiny red hearts. "Me, too," she said with a smile. "But, honestly, I'm not sure why we bothered." She stood, slid out of her Feejays, and kicked them to the floor.

"Rule number one"—Zoey picked up the Feejays, folded them neatly, and set them on a nearby chair—"never disrespect the Feejays."

"I'll try to remember that." Peyton slid her shirt over her head, tossed it aside, and lay back on the bed, naked. "What's rule number two?"

"Feejays must be worn with a *Star Wars* shirt at all times from this point forward."

Peyton nodded. "Seems fair."

She stood in place at the foot of the bed as she gazed at Peyton's body. A sight for sore eyes, she was stunning from every angle. Her washboard stomach still wasn't showing any signs of the life growing within. Zoey knew that was bound to change. Watching Peyton's body undergo those changes would be an amazing journey and incredibly sexy, in its own way.

She undressed and lowered her body over Peyton's as they kissed. The tenderness with which their tongues danced quickly turned more feverish and urgent. Peyton reached up to stroke her breasts. She broke away from their kiss and whispered teasingly in Zoey's ear, "Who knew I'd enjoy breasts so much when I have two of my own?"

Zoey took her cue, inched forward, and brought her breasts to Peyton's mouth. She kissed, licked, and sucked on them hungrily. The sensation of Peyton's tongue on her nipples was exquisite. It shot straight to the center of her.

She felt herself breathing more rapidly, her core wet with anticipation. Peyton rolled her over, straddled her, and guided Zoey's fingers inside. Already soaked, Peyton readily accepted her, rocking her hips back and forth as she made wordless sounds of pleasure.

Zoey's core throbbed. She felt herself dripping onto the bedsheets below. Watching her fingers sliding in and out of Peyton—and seeing the pleasure it brought her—made her feel like she was about to implode. Peyton mercifully ended the torture and reached down. She glided her fingers over Zoey's clit and between her folds as she continued to ride her. Zoey spread her legs wider, uttering her own groans of pleasure as Peyton sank her fingers deep inside.

She pushed her fingers slowly in and out of Peyton as her lover returned the favor and matched her rhythm. Unable to hold back, they soon quickened their pace, deepening their reach with every thrust. She felt Peyton tighten around her fingers.

"Come with me," Peyton begged, breathless. She met Zoey's gaze and ground wildly against her, her lips parted in ecstasy.

Zoey reached up, set her hand on Peyton's cheek, and held her gaze as they climaxed in unison.

"I love you," Peyton whispered.

"I love you more," Zoey whispered back.

# EPILOGUE

Peyton watched as Zoey paced back and forth in the exam room. She was thirty weeks along now and finally showing. "Sit down. You're making me nervous."

"This is my first ultrasound. I'm excited." Zoey shrugged. "It's either this or singing."

"I've heard you sing. Keep pacing."

Zoey frowned and opened her mouth to say something but was interrupted by a knock at the door.

An ultrasound technician stepped inside the room. He applied gel to the ultrasound wand and guided it over Peyton's uterus as Zoey held her hand. "There she is," the tech said, directing them to the computer screen image. "Look"—he pointed to the baby's mouth—"she's already sucking her thumb."

Peyton couldn't take her eyes from the monitor. The new life growing inside her was endlessly fascinating. They all watched as the baby shifted position. Peyton felt the movement within.

The technician set the wand aside and wiped the gel from Peyton's stomach. "I have everything I need. The OB will be in shortly to discuss your results."

"Results?" Zoey asked, squeezing Peyton's hand a little too hard. "Is something wrong?"

"Just a formality. Your baby looks healthy," he assured her before exiting the room.

"He said *your baby* when he was looking at me," Zoey said with a grin. "Doesn't seem fair when you're the one doing all the work."

Peyton pulled her shirt down to cover her stomach. "I've thought of a name, but I'm not sure how you'll feel about it." She sat up and met Zoey's gaze. "Ella Calliope North." It would honor Zoey's sister, as well as her best friend, Callie. She'd already decided to keep Ben's last name because Ben would always be a part of her.

Zoey's eyes welled up as she stared at Peyton, quiet and seemingly dumbfounded.

"I'm sorry," Peyton stammered. "We can put our heads together and come up with something else if—"

"It's almost perfect."

"Almost?" Peyton repeated, curious.

"Nearly there." Zoey reached inside her coat pocket, withdrew a small velvet box, and opened it to reveal a diamond engagement ring.

Now it was Peyton's turn to cry.

"I like Ella Calliope North-Blackwood better," Zoey said as she leaned over to kiss Peyton's belly.

# About the Author

Michelle is an author of lesbian romantic thrillers, a long-distance runner with no sense of direction, and a nunchaku-wielding sidekick to a pair of superhero sons.

For more information, please visit: www.bymichellelarkin.com.

# Books Available From Bold Strokes Books

**The Business of Pleasure** by Ronica Black. Editor in chief Valerie Raffield is quickly becoming smitten by Lennox, the graphic artist she's hired to work remotely. But when Lennox doesn't show for their first face-to-face meeting, Valerie's heart and her business may be in jeopardy. (978-1-63679-134-0)

**Cold Blood** by Genevieve McCluer. Maybe together, Kalila and Dorenia have a chance of taking down the vampires who have eluded them all these years. And maybe, in each other, they can find a love worth living for. (978-1-63679-195-1)

**Greener Pastures** by Aurora Rey. When city girl and CPA Audrey Adams finds herself tending her aunt's farm, will Rowan Marshall—the charming cider maker next door—turn out to be her saving grace or the bane of her existence? (978-1-63679-116-6)

**Grounded** by Amanda Radley. For a second chance, Olivia and Emily will need to accept their mistakes, learn to communicate properly, and with a little help from five-year-old Henry, fall madly in love all over again. Sequel to Flight SQA016. (978-1-63679-241-5)

**The Hummingbird Sanctuary** by Erin Zak. The Hummingbird Sanctuary, Colorado's hottest resort destination: Come for the mountains, stay for the charm, and enjoy the drama as Olive, Eleanor, and Harriet figure out the meaning of true friendship. (978-1-63679-163-0)

**Journey's End** by Amanda Radley. In this heartwarming conclusion to the Flight series, Olivia and Emily must finally decide what they want, what they need, and how to follow the dreams of their hearts. (978-1-63679-233-0)

**Secret Agent** by Michelle Larkin. CIA agent Peyton North embarks on a global chase to apprehend rogue agent Zoey Blackwood, but her commitment to the mission is tested as the sparks between them ignite and their sizzling attraction approaches a point of no return. (978-1-63555-753-4)

**Something Between Us** by Krystina Rivers. A decade after her heart was broken under Don't Ask, Don't Tell, Kirby runs into her first love and has to decide if what's still between them is enough to heal her broken heart. (978-1-63679-135-7)

**Sugar Girl** by Emma L McGeown. Having traded in traditional romance for the perks of Sugar Dating, Ciara Reilly not only enjoys the no-strings-attached arrangement, she's also a hit with her clients. That is, until she meets the beautiful entrepreneur Charlie Keller, who makes her want to go sugar-free. (978-1-63679-156-2)

**With a Twist** by Georgia Beers. Starting over isn't easy for Amelia Martini. When the irritatingly cheerful Kirby Dupress comes into her life, will Amelia be brave enough to go after the love she really wants? (978-1-63555-987-3)

**The Witch Queen's Mate** by Jennifer Karter. Barra and Silvi must overcome their ingrained hatred and prejudice to use Barra's magic and save both their peoples from not just slavery, but destruction. (978-1-63679-202-6)

**Business of the Heart** by Claire Forsythe. When a hopeless romantic meets a tough-as-nails cynic, they'll need to overcome the wounds of the past to discover that their hearts are the most important business of all. (978-1-63679-167-8)

**Dying for You** by Jenny Frame. Can Victorija Dred keep an age-old vow and fight the need to take blood from Daisy Macdougall? (978-1-63679-073-2)

**Exclusive** by Melissa Brayden. Skylar Ruiz lands the TV reporting job of a lifetime, but is she willing to sacrifice it all for the love of her longtime crush, anchorwoman Carolyn McNamara? (978-1-63679-112-8)

**Her Duchess to Desire** by Jane Walsh. An up-and-coming interior designer seeks to create a happily ever after with an intriguing duchess, proving that love never goes out of fashion. (978-1-63679-065-7)

**Take Her Down** by Lauren Emily Whalen. Stakes are cutthroat, scheming is creative, and loyalty is ever-changing in this queer, female-driven YA retelling of Shakespeare's Julius Caesar. (978-1-63679-089-3)